We Fought for Ardnish

ANGUS MACDONALD

BIRLINN

First published in 2018 by
Birlinn Limited
West Newington House
10 Newington Road
Edinburgh
EH9 1QS

www.birlinn.co.uk

ISBN: 978 1 78027 505 5

British Library Cataloguing-in-Publication Data
A catalogue record for this book is
available from the British Library

Typeset by Hewer Text UK Ltd, Edinburgh
Printed and bound by Clays Ltd, Elcograf S.p.A

To my wonderful siblings: Peeps, Mairi,
Jane and Charlotte, who have been so
supportive of my writing endeavours

Author's Note

We Fought for Ardnish is the sequel to *Ardnish Was Home*. In it we follow the life of Donald Angus Gillies, from the Ardnish peninsula in the West Highlands, as he joins the Lovat Scouts and then the Special Operation Executive (SOE). My grandfather, Andrew MacDonald, commanded the Lovat Scouts during the Second World War, as his father did in the First World War. Both men feature as contemporaries and friends of Donald Angus and his father in these books. I also bring in Cape Breton in Canada as the home of Donald Angus's fellow SOE agent Françoise, where many Highlanders emigrated to – including my cousins – in the nineteenth century. Combining the hard rural way of life in the 1940s with the most fascinating military links of the Scottish west coast at that time has been a delight to write about.

I would like to thank Alison Rae at Birlinn, Erica Munro and Jo-Anne MacDonald for their editing. Also Pierre Dupraz, Hugh Cheape and Lynn Philip Hodgson, as well as many others who helped me with my research.

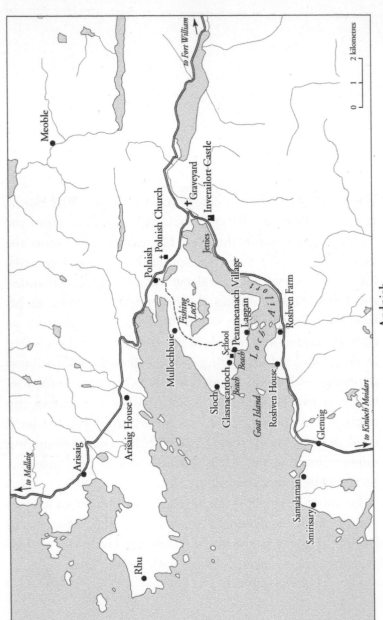

Ardnish

Prologue

I knew my father had died in a terrible accident – the knowledge had always been buried deep within me – but I had never really discussed it with my mother. She would break down in tears when he was mentioned, and even as a boy, I had no wish to distress her.

But one winter's night, as the icy Atlantic blast rattled the windowpanes of our croft, the story finally emerged. I must have been eight or nine at the time.

We were lying together on the box bed gazing into the peat fire. I could feel the warmth of her body beside me and somehow I knew that she was ready. She was the first to speak.

'Well, Donald Angus, I think it's time I told you about when I first arrived at Ardnish. I was so upset after what had happened to your father, I couldn't take anything in on the train journey. There was so much beauty all around that I knew he had loved so dearly. He would have pointed out every hill and hamlet and told me a story of each of them. He had the brightest, twinkling eyes and a constant smile, and I could imagine him there on the train with me chattering away.

'When your uncle Owen and I finally reached Lochailort, we were told to go down to the inn and that the landlady would see us straight. I was six months' pregnant with you and not very nimble to say the least. We had these heavy suitcases and your father's bagpipes. The landlady said the walk would be too much, so Mrs Cameron Head lent us a couple of men and a boat. The landlady was keen to find out all about us and finally she asked me the question I had been dreading: where was your father?

'I burst into tears and everything just poured out. I remember she put her arm around me and told me they'd been wondering whether something was wrong. Your grand-parents, Mairi and your uncle Angus had all been there to meet the train a few days before, when we were meant to arrive. It was a long row up the loch in a biting cold wind and I was so nervous about meeting the family. Anyway, I managed to hold myself together as the boatmen helped me over the side when we arrived – it was Archie and Calum from Inverailort, you know them. Owen and the dog were over the bow into the sea and he passed our bags to Grandfather.

'Your grandmother knew something was wrong. I could tell from her expression. She looked at me so keenly; her eyes seemed to penetrate my soul. She asked where your father was, and I knew she was willing me to say he'd be here tomorrow but of course . . .'

Mother fell silent for a moment. I could feel my heart pounding under the blanket.

'My legs gave way and I dropped to the sand, crying all over again. Then I turned to your grandmother and told her that her son was dead. It was the hardest thing I've ever had to do in my life.'

'But how did it happen?' I asked, longing for, yet dread-ing, the truth. I could scarcely breathe.

'He was knocked over by a tram,' my mother whispered, 'in Glasgow. His eyesight was so poor from his injury and he was rushing, and it was just . . . a horrible accident. We were on our way to Ardnish, the war was over, I was expecting you, and I thought we were the luckiest couple in the world, and then . . .'

'Oh, Mother . . .' I began, but I didn't have the words to comfort her.

'It was all over in seconds,' she said, a tear falling from her face onto my hand. 'Such a waste.'

'He was our hero,' I announced proudly, tears pricking my eyes for this man I had never known.

Mother looked at me and nodded, managing a half-smile. 'Your grandmother fell to the ground and held me so tightly. I remember my whole body shaking with grief. I was weeping and weeping, clawing at the sand. Others from the village came running down to see what the commotion was. They helped me up the beach to the house, sat me in the sun outside the door and brought me a cup of sweet tea with a drop of whisky in it. Your grandfather said it would help me relax.

'It wasn't until the next day that I told your grandparents everything about the accident. It's the only time I've seen Donald John angry. He was shouting with rage about the unfairness of it all. "My boy survived being captured and tortured in the hell of Gallipoli!" he was yelling. I remember his face red with fury and the injustice of it all.'

I pulled the quilt up to my neck to get more comfortable. The rain was still hammering against the windows and the light from the kerosene lamp was flickering in the draught.

'The first few days at Ardnish, I was made to feel so welcome by the whole community. I felt straight away as though I was part of this extended family. People brought shawls, a blanket for the bed, a dress that might fit me, piles of food, venison stew, scones, but, most of all, they gave me their time and their care. The Gaelic was difficult at first, of course. Your father had taught me a few words during our long journey from Gallipoli to Malta, and everyone kindly tried to speak English, but they couldn't help lapsing into Gaelic. It took me a good year to become fluent.'

I desperately wanted to hear more about my father. 'What happened next?' I couldn't bring myself to say more but Mother seemed to understand.

'Father Angus, your uncle, went to Lochailort to make arrangements for the funeral. He collected the body from the train and took it to the church. I'm afraid I can barely remember the funeral.'

I could sense my mother's grief overwhelming her and cast around for an easier question. 'And then ... I was born?'

This made her smile. 'There hadn't been a baby born here since your father, and that was over twenty years before, so your arrival caused great excitement.'

'He never saw me.'

It was some time before she spoke. 'No, but you look just like him. The same lovely red hair and freckles, a nose that turns up a bit and a beautiful smile.' She fought back tears. 'He was the kindest man you could ever meet. He cared for everyone, whether it was the stubborn old donkey that carried him on our journey, or looking after me when

I was so sick. He couldn't do enough to help. He got that from your grandfather.'

'I wish I'd known him,' I whispered.

'I do, too. But now it's time for sleep, dearest boy,' she said.

'But, Mother . . .' I didn't want our talk ever to end.

'School tomorrow,' she insisted. 'Say your prayers, and sleep tight.'

*

So that was that. My father, Donald Peter Gillies, known as DP to everyone, had been a soldier in the Lovat Scouts in Gallipoli and was appointed personal piper to the commanding officer, Colonel Willie MacDonald, my godfather. DP had been sent on a mission with Sandy, his great childhood friend from the village, to shoot a senior Turkish officer. The mission was accomplished, but both men were captured and tortured, and poor Sandy had died. My father was rescued by his regiment but was in a bad way, with a bullet in his shoulder and a serious eye injury which meant the remainder of his short life was endured with very poor sight.

After the mission in Gallipoli with Sandy, my father had been brought to the medical station on the beach where my mother was working as a nurse. She cared for him day and night and listened to his tales about his childhood in Ardnish. One day it became clear that the regiment was going to have to leave them behind as my father was unable to travel, and so they found themselves cut off behind enemy lines. These tales of how the pair, alongside my mother's great friend and fellow nurse Prissie, made their way back to safety enthralled me.

I understood why my father's death had been so painful. My parents had endured unimaginable dangers, fallen in love, married, and wanted nothing more than to get to Ardnish where they could begin peaceful married life in my father's beloved Peanmeanach village. Instead, my mother journeyed here alone, a stranger, and gave birth to me in the place my father loved above all others. It was almost too much to bear.

Ardnish was an ageing community, apart from my mother, her close friend Mairi and me. The next youngest was my grandmother Morag, an old woman though strong as an ox. It was difficult to get the essential things done: repairing the thatch on the roofs, clearing drains so the vast field behind the village didn't revert to a bog, managing the horse and plough, cutting the peat, chopping firewood. The chores were endless.

Peanmeanach sits a hundred yards back from the crescent-shaped shore. The smooth machair, full of flowers in the spring, was perfect for playing on, and a sparkling burn, ideal for damming, flowed down to the salt waters of Loch Ailort. Beyond, the high hills of An Stac and Roshven loomed over the village. If you looked to the west you would see Goat Island in the foreground and beyond that, the small isles of Muck, Eigg and Rum. Yet, despite this idyllic setting, there was often fireside talk, especially on a bad winter's night, about whether we should all just move to Arisaig and leave Peanmeanach to crumble. But although their heads knew the sense of the idea, their hearts told them otherwise. My mother and grandparents would be the last to leave. They knew my father had loved the place more than anything and would only have left in a coffin. Maybe Peanmeanach was their memorial to him.

The Ardnish peninsula was the best playground that any boy could wish for, and the adults were always on hand to help me make a catapult, dam a burn, or tie a fishing fly. Aged eight, I was allowed to ride over to Slioch on one of the smaller Highland ponies to help the Bochan stack wood or clean his house. It was school three days a week, and chores you wouldn't believe, carrying water to housebound old Eilidh, and cutting wood and peat for her and our grandparents. In the evenings I would fall into bed, dead tired from all the exertion.

Aunt Mairi was like a second mother to me. She would tell me of the mischief her son Sandy and DP had got up to. 'When they were your age, Donald Angus, they were the scourge of the village, always in trouble. They made a den in the cave at Slioch and stayed for two nights without letting on what they were off to do. Everyone was hunting high and low, fearing they were drowned. Another time they hid from the teacher, poor man. Your father got a good skelping that day from your grandfather, that's for sure.'

'Grandfather hit him?' I was astonished.

'He had a leather two-tonged strap called a tawse that the boys would get walloped with. "Six of the best" he would cry as the boys pulled down their breeks. He will still have it somewhere. I'm telling you, Donald Angus, he must be getting soft in his old age that you haven't felt it.'

I resolved never to ask Grandfather about this for fear of rekindling his enthusiasm for skelping.

I was the pet of the village, made welcome in every house. A jam-covered scone or other tasty treat would always be found for me with a whispered 'Don't tell your mother'. Daffie, Mum's old collie, was never far from me, and half of every scone or bannock I got was his. When I was a baby, Daffie would creep into my cot and sleep beside me, taking up three-quarters of the space. Mother said I would cry incessantly if she shooed him out. Daffie and I shared a bed until he died.

Uncle Owen was my mother's wee brother, but also my best friend in those early years despite our ten-year age gap. He had had a rocky start in life, brought up in Wales by a mother who cared little for his welfare and too young to escape, as my mother had been able to do.

On the way back from Malta to Ardnish, my parents had spent a few days with Mother's mother in the Valleys. They realised Owen wasn't flourishing so they took him north with them. Never had a young lad been happier in the Highlands, utterly content in his own company. It had been the making of him. People found him a wee bit shy at first and it soon became clear that he was not one for school. Our teacher would be beside himself with frustration as Owen couldn't recite the times table or Latin tenses, despite hours of repetition. But give him a saddle to mend or a tree to cut down and he would work all hours until it was done, and done perfectly. 'Stick to things you're good at and avoid what you struggle with. You can't make a square peg fit a round hole,' Grandfather would say. 'Learn a trade, laddie, and it'll feed you.'

And learn a trade he did. He'd always been good with horses and now worked for a blacksmith in Mallaig. He helped to make the beautiful gates at Inverailort Castle, and if the car at Arisaig House broke down, everyone knew that our Owen would stand the best chance of getting it going again.

Grandfather had pushed him gently away from Ardnish, not long after he left school. I remember the night well. Grandfather, Owen and I were sitting at the table. We had just finished our supper.

It was a difficult conversation, not only because Owen had declared that he never wanted to leave, but, aged eighteen, he was the only fit and strong man left on the peninsula. Every man's job was given to him, and he worked hard and willingly. Grandfather knew that sending him away would only accelerate the slow death of Peanmeanach.

Grandmother and Mother sat by the fire, pretending to be concentrating on their darning, but in reality listening to every word.

'Owen,' Grandfather began, 'God knows you are important to us, but you must do what is right for yourself. You need to get a trade and see a bit of life away from here. You can always come back in a few years, maybe with a wife of your own, having saved a bit of money.'

You could have heard a pin drop.

The women stayed silent; I think they knew the truth in my grandfather's words. I opened my mouth to make a suggestion, but my mother snapped, 'Don't!' in such a sharp tone that I realised the gravity of the moment and buttoned my lip.

Grandfather nursed his glass of whisky and puffed on his pipe. 'Go and work with Angie MacLellan in Arisaig,' he said. 'He's getting on a bit, and working with horses and machinery is a young man's job. He might not think he needs a hand, but he does. He'll pay you a pittance to start with, but within a year you'll be making good money.'

And so it was arranged. Not long after, he and Owen headed off to Arisaig. It was an arduous journey for Grandfather. He had fought with the Lovat Scots in the Boer War and lost a leg. His wooden leg was awkward to manoeuvre. They journeyed with two ponies, as Grandfather had a lengthy shopping list of provisions for the winter.

Owen's trial with MacLellan was a success, and everyone at Peanmeanach had mixed emotions when we learned that he was being taken on permanently. But such was the way of the Highlands. Because there is little money to be earned, the young are forced to seek employment elsewhere, and as likely as not they meet a girl or a boy and stay where the work is – often in Glasgow.

Owen had been away for a year now, although he would come and stay with us for a night whenever his work brought him close by. Mother loved his visits. She drank in the news of Arisaig and Mallaig as if they were the bright city lights of Glasgow. Last time he came we heard that Iain Mackinnon from Canna had died of influenza, that Aggy Macrae at Tarbert was having a baby and no one knew who the father was, and she wasn't telling, and his boss had a broken toe from one of the plough horses at Traigh standing on his foot. Mother remarked that the only thing that had happened at Ardnish was that the grass had grown a wee bit longer, and sighed.

I loved learning, languages in particular, although with one-to-one tuition I was always likely to thrive. The teacher, Mr Campbell, and I became firm friends. Even when I was a young lad, the older folk would sometimes defer to me when it came to questions of the world, the galaxy or, for instance, how electricity worked. I loved the attention. 'He'll be off to the university before we know it,' Aunt Effie would pronounce gloomily, 'and that'll be the last we'll see of him.'

Grandfather had been involved in the building of the big house at Roshven and had become friendly with the owners, the Blackburns. Often, when their son Peter, his wife Pauline, and Peter's cousin Margaret (who had been my aunt Sheena's best friend when they were growing up) were visiting, they would row across from Roshven on the other side of the loch to picnic on the beach and we would join them. Peter's mother, Jemima, had been a renowned artist and lover of nature and was a great ally of Grandmother's. Margaret was always keen to hear how Sheena was getting on in Canada.

The talk was always friendly and wide-ranging. 'Well,' said Grandfather, during one such picnic, 'the people are leaving, whatever way you look at it. Colonel Willie told me that over in Glen Roy, a company of men, that's about a hundred soldiers, was raised to fight in the Napoleonic war, and now you'd be lucky to find a dozen.'

Peter nodded his agreement. 'My father could get twenty men to help build a pier, and now we struggle to get four to get the hay in.' This led to a conversation about whether the Clearances might ultimately have been a good thing for the people; after all, their life here could be desperate and places like Australia and Canada offered so much opportunity. Everyone had a strong view on the emigrations, citing examples of the persecutions in Sutherland and evictions on Knoydart versus reports of the children of locals who had gone to Australia or South Carolina and become doctors and engineers. Peter mentioned Joseph McCoy, a drover's son who now lived in Kansas and had moved two million cattle in two years, becoming known as 'The Real McCoy'.

'It's not the land of plenty over there,' Grandmother pointed out quietly. 'I've got a recent letter from Sheena, with Cape Breton press cuttings, too, about the coal mining. Donald Angus, run back and get them, will you? They're on the sideboard.'

I did as I was told, glad to escape the conversation which I found dreary compared with the stone-skimming and fishing I might have been doing instead.

'It's in Gaelic,' Grandmother began, 'so I'll translate it. It's dated only last month. Here goes . . .

My dear Mother and Father,

I enclose a cutting from a newspaper here. I know people in the Highlands sometimes think of Cape Breton as the Promised Land, but these articles show what the children and grandchildren of your friends from the Rough Bounds are suffering.

Thousands of miners in Sydney are working, part-time at most on an hourly rate, the lowest in Canada. They get coal from the company, the British Empire Steel and Coal Company, as well as water and electricity. The only shops allowed are the company-owned Pluck Me stores. Children are dying on their four cent meals. The company wants the hourly rate to be cut, hours to be reduced and credit withdrawn from their shops. The boss has said the company will hold out, the miners 'can't stand the gaff'. So, of course, the miners are determined to stay on strike. The unions have stopped the water pumping from the shafts, and people say the mines will never re-open. Coal, electricity and water have been cut off by the company now, including at the hospital. The company has its own police force, hired from away, and they are being brutal. Last week 3,000 men marched on a company power station and fought with company police and hired men. Men were shot and killed. The miners locked up the company men in the town jail, company stores have been raided and then burned.

There is a stand-off now. Money is being raised from people in Boston and many other places to help stave off destitution for the miners. There is a lot of pressure for the government to get involved, and there is no doubt they will after this. The problem has been going on for some years now.

I will write again next week, rushing now to catch the post. Hoping this finds you in good heart,

Your loving daughter
Sheena

Chapter 1

Courmayeur, the Italian Alps, March 1943

Françoise and I stared into the darkness. We were leaning against the wall of a filthy cattle shed, our hands bound tightly. We could hear Italian voices outside. They were discussing what they should do with us, waiting for an officer to arrive and make a decision.

We'd been there all night. We had told them we were a French married couple trying to get away from Vichy France. Françoise wore a wedding ring. She explained that we were hiding from the authorities so that I wouldn't get drafted into the STO – the *Service du Travail Obligatoire* – and sent to a German labour camp. As long as they believed this we might stand a chance of being released, or at worst held with other deserters, perhaps with an opportunity to escape. But if they made the connection that we were SOE – Special Operation Executive – operatives and had been responsible for a month's worth of attacks and destruction all along the Alps we would almost certainly be tortured and killed.

Exhausted, we had been captured while taking shelter in a hut during heavy snow. It was our misfortune that an

Alpini patrol had chosen to do the same. They were armed, and we were not. It was clear that the presence of French people in Italy concerned them greatly, so we were locked up in the cattle shed that adjoined the hut.

Françoise wore dark-brown trousers, a heavy overcoat and headscarf. I was dressed in slightly worse-for-wear woollens and corduroy trousers, along with stout boots, and had been instructed not to shave or have my hair cut for some time beforehand. They searched us thoroughly; we had backpacks with a couple of blankets and scraps of food but nothing to arouse suspicion that we were anything other than we claimed. My French Army ID card stated that I was Xavier Cret, born September 1915 in nearby Les Contamines and serving in the 21st Bataillon de Chasseurs Alpin d'Antibes. I was confident that it would appear authentic, nonetheless I had been filled with anxiety when they turned it over and over, scrutinising every detail while Françoise explained that I was a deserter from the Vichy army and that we had been hiding out in shepherds' huts for months.

I don't know how much of her French they understood – or whether they believed her. I was terrified that they would expect me to speak, as my French was still fairly basic despite my intensive language training before the mission.

We huddled close together for warmth. We hadn't slept a moment throughout the long night, and had tried to keep our spirits up by exchanging childhood stories; mine in the West Highlands of Scotland and hers in Paris. Although she had then moved with her family to Canada, she still spoke with a Parisian accent. She talked of her misery at being plucked from her cosmopolitan life and how, at first, she had hated the loneliness and boredom of rural Canadian life, but that she had grown accustomed to it and ultimately grew to love it.

'These places take hold of you, don't they?' I said wistfully, my mind full of my own Highland home. Françoise nodded, and we were quiet for a while, deep in thought.

I had been in the Alps for a month, having been parachuted into Les Contamines with a ton of explosives, Morse transmitters, guns, ropes, ice axes and clothing, enough to equip a dozen men for a month or two. I met up with four Resistance fighters as planned, who helped me to sort and repack the kit. Then, laden with rucksacks, we made our way over the mountains to Courmayeur.

My mission had been outlined a week before the drop-off. The Italian troops in the Alps were not carrying out their job effectively and we knew the Resistance movement could create real disruption, given support and arms. The families of Courmayeur in Italy and Chamonix in France had intermarried for centuries and the Italian Alpini had been relaxed in their role as the occupying force of the French side of the Alps. It was rumoured that the Italians were going to be replaced by German soldiers and, if so, things would be much more difficult. I had been given several tasks. The first was to arrange the destruction of the intricate lace of metal chains, cables and ladders bolted onto the otherwise impassable cliffs, nine thousand feet above sea level, known as the *via ferrata*, or iron road. The *via ferrata* allowed the Alpini to move back and forth across the mountaintops with ease and therefore had to be destroyed. Then, I had to block two mountain passes to Switzerland from Italy and France.

I met first with the Italian Resistance leader, an extremely capable and brave man named Luigi, and after briefing him, felt confident that he could be entrusted with the task of dismantling the *via ferrata*, allowing me to move on to help the Resistance around Chamonix block the route through to Switzerland.

Françoise told me that she had been parachuted in a week before. She had been met by one of Luigi's men down in the valley, but when I tentatively asked what the purpose of her trip was she had become tight-lipped. 'All in good time, Angus,' she said, disarming me with her smile. All I knew about her was that I had to take her back to my friend Claude, the leader of the partisans on the other side of the Alps at Les Contamines, in France.

I accepted her response, but it troubled me. Weren't we supposed to be allies? I had been open with her about my role; it was unsettling that she had chosen not to divulge any details of hers with me, despite the bond we had struck up through the freezing hours of darkness.

Fierce winds and snowstorms had been pounding the mountains for days, and we guessed that it might be several days until conditions let up and we might be taken to an officer.

We knew that we could untie the ropes pretty easily, but decided against doing so until the right time presented itself. Huddling under the two blankets one of the men had given to us, we joked about the intimacy to try to stave off embarrassment, but we were grateful for each other's warmth as we shivered. As the day wore on we would jog on the spot and do exercises to keep ourselves occupied, always hoping that the Italians might bring us a hot drink or some of their own meagre rations. We knew they wouldn't have much even for themselves.

We talked constantly of escape. 'If they came in during the morning, just two of them,' I mused, 'I could wish them a polite "good morning" in Italian, to disarm them, and then we could take one each. They'd have their hands full with breakfast.' I practised it softly: '*Buongiorno, buongiorno.*'

'What if there are three of them?' asked Françoise.

'Then I'll grab the one with the gun and we'll see how it goes from there.'

That evening, Françoise lay with her head resting on my shoulder. Entwined under the blankets, I felt her now familiar warmth against me, enjoying the sensation of her slow breathing, her body rising and falling. I could hear the Italian voices through the wall; there must have been be six or seven of them, and from their high-spirited chatter I suspected they had drink with them. We had been captive for over twenty-four hours now, and in the building for twice that. Surely the storm would blow over soon?

'Why did you join the SOE?' I asked.

'You tell me first, Donald Angus. I'm sleepy.'

'It was my boss in the army who suggested it. He reckoned that our regiment, the Lovat Scouts, would be stationed in the Faroes for a couple of years, and that with my experience I should join the SOE – I would be perfect for it. What's more, they were based only five miles from my home, and he knew how much that would appeal to me. The larger houses in the area had all been requisitioned and were the centres for all sorts of specialised training: sniping, demolition, unarmed combat. Exciting stuff.'

I was sure Françoise had fallen asleep, but then I felt her stirring.

'So, when you switched from the Lovat Scouts into the SOE, you trained in the Highlands?'

'Yes and no. I was at what is called the Irregular Warfare School at Inverailort Castle, first as a student then later as an instructor. I had spent some time at Brickendonbury Manor in the middle of England, where specialised weapons were developed. Then, just after the SOE was formed, I was transferred to Arisaig House to be one of their first instructors. I was delighted to be posted so close to home, let me tell you.'

'I can imagine.'

'There was a rumour before I came out here that I'd be sent abroad to help the SOE get going in America and Singapore – rather like with your Camp X in Ontario.'

'You've done your homework,' Françoise whispered.

'I'm a sabotage expert, really. You wouldn't believe the explosives and armaments that are being designed these days and we need to show the agents how to get the best from them. There's a senior SOE man, Brigadier Gubbins, who looks after me. His son, Michael, was at Arisaig House as a trainer at the same time as me, and we've become good friends.'

Françoise had fallen asleep. We were entwined like lovers and I couldn't help but think how attractive she was. I wondered what on earth had persuaded her to sign up to the SOE. If agents were captured they were invariably executed. A woman like her could have had any job in Canada. Not knowing the true nature of her mission gnawed at me. In my two years in the SOE, it seemed that the few female agents were always given the most dreadful tasks, often involving intimacy with senior Germans.

My right arm grew stiff, but I didn't want to disturb her. With hay beneath us and blankets tucked under our chins, we had become quite comfortable as the wind rattled against the door. I could sense heavy snow piling up outside. I dozed off, feeling strangely content.

The next thing I was aware of was the sound of the wooden door latch. We were both instantly wide awake. Two men came in. I caught the aroma of acorn coffee. I fingered the 'L' pill sewn into the collar of my jacket – standard issue potassium cyanide since the compromising of a Dutch operation a few months ago, after which our agents had been mercilessly tortured.

One of the men untied our ropes as the other kept his gun pointed at us. We rubbed our aching wrists and clapped our hands to warm them. They spoke to us in Italian, cautiously but friendly enough. Françoise replied in French. The soldiers watched as we ate the stale bread and drank the bitter coffee. They looked to be around eighteen years old, and I suspected they were overawed by Françoise with her dark hair, big smile and pretty features.

After we had finished eating they retied our ropes. Françoise cried out, gesturing that hers were too tight. The soldiers understood and loosened them a little.

'*Grazie, grazie!*' She beamed at them and the men made to leave, pleased with themselves at having made a friend. But Françoise was not their friend. Within a minute, she had both our ropes undone, had grabbed a plank and hidden behind the door.

Françoise stood at the door and called out, '*Mi scusi, mi scusi!*' Her tone was light and appealing, and our young guards obligingly returned. Françoise walloped one behind the head with the plank and I broke the neck of the other with a sickening crunch.

Françoise and I stared at one another; she was wide-eyed with shock. I took a pistol from one and a rifle from the other, and, listening for sounds of alarm from the rest of the patrol through the wall, we strapped on our snow-shoes, gathered all of their snowshoes from under the eaves, and struck out into the heavy snow. We knew our tracks would be covered in minutes, and without the proper footwear, our pursuers would struggle.

My mind was racing as we battled through the snow. My God, there would be hell to pay for the remaining four, especially if senior officers managed to make a connection between us and the recent Resistance successes, something they were bound to do given the efficacy of our escape.

Once we had made some headway we stopped for a breather, jettisoned their snowshoes in a snow hole beside a pine tree, and pressed on for our rendezvous with Claude and his men.

Françoise hadn't said a word. 'Are you all right?' I panted.

'That's the first man I've killed,' she replied.

'Me too.'

'Really?' Surprise was evident in her voice. 'I was told you were battle-hardened.'

There's more to battle than hand-to-hand killing, I thought, though I said nothing.

We had a long way to go. The route was obvious, though, despite the poor visibility. The tree line was on our right and on our left, the plateau with its summer pastures, four thousand feet above the villages in the valley. We were making for a pass that would finally take us over to France and down to the village of Les Contamines. The snow provided vital cover for us but made for exhausting going. I knew that unless we bumped into another patrol we would be fine, but the snow was so deep it was heavy going. I knew that Françoise was no slouch but my admiration for her grew stronger and stronger as the day went on; she battled on without a word of complaint about the cold or hunger, or even fatigue.

I had hoped to take an easier route, but after encountering the patrol, I suspected the mountains would be crawling with the enemy. We would have to take the difficult route I'd been told about, over a ridge. It would be steep and possibly icy, but if I managed to navigate the way to the correct spot, there would be a fixed rope to help us.

After many hours we reached the bottom of a gulley, and stared up through the falling snow. My spirits soared. This must be it!

'Here we are, Françoise, just as I was told. Look! Three distinctive pine trees together on a rocky ledge on the left – that must be them. It's about a two-hour climb to the top but we're running out of daylight. There should be a building somewhere around here where we can spend the night and tackle the climb first thing tomorrow.'

We scanned the area for the hut, snow dumping all around us in the twilight. At last Françoise called out, 'Over here, I've found it!'

'Thank goodness! I thought we'd be spending the night in a snow hole,' I called back, rushing over to where she stood.

'I must have been standing on the roof,' she exclaimed. 'See, there's the chimney.'

We cleared the snow away from the door, using our snowshoes as shovels. Soon we were wrapped in our blankets in front of a roaring fire with our outer clothes hanging up to dry. We optimistically searched for food but there was nothing to be found. We'd had a hard day on only the bitter coffee and bread provided by our unfortunate guards that morning. The blizzard raged outside, but in the warmth, with Françoise beside me, I felt I could relax. The building was well hidden by the woods and thick snow, and the smoke wouldn't be seen in the dark.

As we lay on the hard bed wrapped up in blankets, my tummy rumbled, sending Françoise into fits of giggles.

'I was thinking of chicken casserole,' I admitted. 'Claude's wife Marie makes the best one I've ever tasted. Fingers crossed there will be some waiting for us in Les Contamines tomorrow.'

The fire illuminated her face, only a few inches from mine. I realised I was looking too intently at her and averted my gaze.

'Your turn,' I said. 'How did you come to join the SOE?'

'Well, as you know, my family is French, but we've lived in Canada for ten years. We still have other family members back in France ...' Her words trailed away, and she took a moment to compose herself. 'They suffered terribly at the hands of the Nazis. All the rumours that we hear are horrifying ... Anyway, that's what made me want to do something, to join the war effort and fight. A woman at the recruitment office put me forward as an agent. Apparently they needed native French speakers.'

'Where in Canada do you live?' I asked.

'Oh, a tiny place, you won't have heard of it. Chéticamp, in Nova Scotia on the east coast.'

'My aunt Sheena lives in Nova Scotia, near Mabou on Cape Breton Island!' I exclaimed. 'My goodness, I'm surprised there are French speakers there; I've only ever heard of Highlanders settling in that part of the world.'

Her eyes lit up. 'Mabou is only fifty miles from us, I know it well. You must tell me about her. I might even know her, though the French and English-speaking communities tend to keep to themselves, I'm afraid.'

I was astonished. I had known another agent was joining me, but not that she would be female or Canadian. And now here we were, two people from different continents, finding this shared connection.

'I would love to go there some day,' I said.

'You must. Visit your aunt, Angus, it's lovely. Mabou is right on the sea; it has the most beautiful trees. In the fall they glow golden and red and you walk on a carpet of beautiful leaves. Go to Lake Ainslie, too. The Mull River flows into the estuary there. Fantastic fishing. Do you fish?'

I nodded.

'Chéticamp is about the same size town as Mabou but French. They speak Gaelic in Mabou, though. We have our own school and hospital ... you would think the two places were a thousand miles apart. The young from both villages speak mostly English these days; it's becoming the common language. It's lovely and hot in the summer and cold as death in the winter.'

Her face was radiant, animated by the discussion and the flickering light from the fire.

'Aunt Sheena came over just before the war,' I said, 'to see her family and to meet me and my mother. She stayed for two months. She works as a teacher at the school in Mabou. My grandmother Morag and I promised Sheena we'd go out after the war. I'll come and find you in Chéticamp.'

'You must,' she said, nodding enthusiastically.

We lay quietly, enjoying the warmth and companionship and soon dozed off. But I woke, shivering, in the middle of the night and got up to fetch more logs. There was no sound from outside. I opened the door. Behind me, I could hear Françoise waking up.

'It's stopped snowing,' I said. 'I can see stars. Another couple of hours and we'll need to move.'

I stoked the fire then went outside and filled a saucepan with snow which I placed on the embers to melt. 'We must drink a couple of pints of water before we get going.'

'A couple of *pints*?' Françoise looked aghast.

'We don't want to get dehydrated today. We have a lot of ground to cover.'

'I hardly slept,' she groaned. 'The farmer must bring a mattress up with him when he uses this place; this bed is rock-hard.'

I handed her the water can and she began to drink. 'Françoise, we have a little time before we set off. Can you tell me something about Camp X?'

She smiled. 'Well, what have you heard?'

'Only that it's our training centre in Canada. Some of the training officers we had went over there. I knew Mad Major Fairbairn and Hamish Pelham-Burn.'

'Fairbairn is extraordinary,' said Françoise. 'He invented the amazing knife we use, didn't he? He must be well into his fifties and yet he can throw the fittest twenty-year-old agent on his back in a second, with a knife to his throat.'

'True enough ... but I'm more interested in you,' I prompted.

She laughed. 'Well, I applied to join the Canadian Women's Army Corps, and when I arrived at the recruitment centre in Halifax there was a leaflet explaining all the various units and what they did, but I saw that all the interesting stuff was for men. I resigned myself to sitting behind a desk for the rest of the war. So, my expectations were low when I was taken in for interview by a very impressive lady, a major. I decided I had nothing to lose in telling her I wanted a real challenge, to be outdoors, that I was good at sports, was reasonably intelligent and of course bilingual.'

'Quite right.'

'Anyway, she asked me to give her some time. She said she had an idea and could I come back two days later. So I did. I was given a train ticket to Toronto and instructed to go for an interview at number 25 King Street, which was a bank, and then on to Whitby to undergo more interviews and some tests. I had no idea what I was in for, but it turned out to be a three-day initiation course with eight men.'

'What did you have to do?'

She shrugged. 'Where to start? We had to run for five miles carrying a pack, swim in Lake Ontario – breaking the ice on the surface before we got in, stand in front of armoured glass and get shot at with a Tommy gun to test our reaction, then they got us very drunk to see if we were loose-tongued. We weren't allowed any sleep one night and then we had hostile interviews the next day, in French, to see how we reacted. Only three of us got through to the next stage.'

'Well done. Sounds similar to what we had to go through. Tough going, isn't it?'

'It certainly is, but my goodness, when the course started at Camp X there were no weak links. I was the only woman there and I wasn't given any leeway, apart from a lighter pack. We had no idea what we were training for.'

'Was your course run by Canadians?'

'No, it was largely run by the British Security Co-ordination, but the students were French speakers – Poles, Czechs, Romanians and so on – all recruited with the intention that they would go back into their own countries to train the resistance.'

'So you went straight into training?'

She seemed surprised. 'Not straight away. I had the test first.'

'Oh?' I leaned closer.

'I was called in to see Colonel Brooker, the Commanding Officer.' Straightening her back, she mimicked a posh English accent: '"Right, Villeneuve, we have a problem. We need a dangerous enemy agent eliminated, and we think a woman will be most effective. It would appear that you are the only one we can call on. His real name is Hans Bauer, but he's in room seventeen at the Royal York under the name of Graham Hamilton."'

'They wanted you to do *what*?' I asked, astonished.

'I know! I felt I'd only just started my training. But he took out a revolver, loaded it and gave it to me. "Report

back to me straight away. Mac here will be your driver." I
was pretty shaken, I can tell you.'

I stared at her, horrified. 'So what happened?'

'Well, it was about midnight when Mac dropped me at
the front door of the hotel. I told the woman at the reception I was Mr Hamilton's wife and needed an extra key as
I was surprising him on his birthday. She gave it to me.'

'Just like that?'

'Just like that. She obviously couldn't see my knees trembling under my coat. So I walked as confidently as I could
to the door of room seventeen and just flung open the door.
He was sitting bolt upright in bed. I raised the gun, fired,
and missed, so I fired twice more – and missed again.'

'Wait . . .' I began. Something wasn't right.

'Exactly,' she laughed. 'Of course, then I realised they
were blanks. My colleagues were killing themselves with
laughter when I got back to the car, but they seemed to be
very impressed with me.'

Françoise continued: 'One of their concerns was that
female agents wouldn't be able to kill in cold blood.
Fairbairn was convinced that at the crucial moment we
would be reluctant and become the victim instead. His
view was that our maternal instincts would kick in and we
would be more likely to injure the person, which would
then backfire. "Kill or be killed," he would repeat, over and
over.'

'What an initiation,' I said, impressed. 'So what did
Fairbairn teach you? Same as he taught the troops in
Scotland, I'm guessing?'

'I imagine so. He did say something about how this test
for female agents never failed. Did you read his book,

All-In Fighting? I was shocked I must say, me a quiet girl from the backwater. We weren't taught mouth slitting, eye gouging or garrotting at school. Mind you, the tips from his books on self-defence for women came in useful, especially "The Cinema Hold, a Defence for Wandering Hands".' She grinned cheekily.

'But anyhow, the course. It was five weeks' long. We had to run up and down dunes with sixty-pound packs and rifles for fitness training. There was fieldcraft, map reading, silent killing, interrogation, lots of wireless work, and obviously parachuting, otherwise I wouldn't have been floating down a few days ago. Oh, and climbing – I enjoyed that side of it. We went to the Blue Mountains at Collingwood for three days, and it was wonderful. I'm light and fairly strong; it seems I can pretty well go up anything.'

I nodded. 'I was impressed watching you in the couloir.'

She smiled. 'Oh, were you indeed?'

I could feel myself blushing.

'There was lots of boat work on Lake Ontario, too. I loved the canoeing. Why there isn't more done in Cape Breton I've no idea. Then we did weapons training and a whole week of demolition work. There isn't much I can't blow up, you know.'

'Sounds like Fairbairn,' I murmured. 'Intensive.'

'Exactly. No time off at all, and long days and nights. But anyhow, that's my story – then I got posted to F section because they wanted French-speaking women agents.'

'Did they say anything about reprisals? That's something that causes me the biggest difficulty.'

'Reprisals? Oh yes, it was your Scottish instructor, Captain Pelham-Burn, who covered that sort of thing. He gave us some horrific examples. He said it was best to know in advance. Not far from here, in Annecy, an SOE agent led a team of French Resistance fighters who blew up an arms factory. The next morning, Gestapo troopers burst into houses, dragged out whole families and hanged ten men in the town centre in front of their wives and children.' She shuddered. 'No wonder so few French are prepared to get involved, even to turn informers. Imagine, Angus, if one of the Resistance men were to tell his wife about an attack planned on Germans in a certain village and she were to tell a friend. Mightn't that friend be tempted to tell the Germans, to save her village from destruction?'

'That's why I struggle with it,' I admitted. 'Some choice.'

'But we had something you wouldn't have had,' Françoise went on. 'Just down the road was Bowmanville, which was an internment camp for German officers. Believe it or not, sometimes a German officer would be sent along to inter-rogate us. There was an underground room set up with all the torture paraphernalia, and we were given electric shocks and stripped naked to demoralise us. We were told we had to hold out for forty-eight hours whatever happened, in order to allow our Resistance circuit to move away.'

'Nothing if not thorough,' I murmured, shaking my head. 'I remember, at Arisaig, men who had been tortured, but managed to escape, came to talk to us. We would all listen with our mouths hanging open.'

'The whole point is that I know what might happen to me and I'm prepared for it.'

We sat in silence for a while. I supposed we were both thinking of other agents – friends – who had been captured and tortured.

Then Françoise yawned. 'I'm famished,' she moaned. 'Take my mind off my stomach, Angus, and tell me a story about Fairbairn. He's such an intriguing man.'

I handed the water can back to her, urged her to drink more and stoked the fire.

'I first met him at Inverailort Castle. He was standing at the top of the stairs at the big house with his friend Eric Sykes. They were both wearing casual army fatigues and looked for all the world like harmless elderly men, ready to greet our arrival. About twelve of us students were lined up at the bottom. All of a sudden, Fairbairn seemed to lose his footing. He clutched at Sykes and the pair of them came crashing down the entire length of the staircase, head over heels. We couldn't believe our eyes. But in a moment they were up on their feet, and each had a student on his back with a knife at his throat. Fairbairn told us he had learned his trade in Shanghai, training the police to break up the gangs. God, he was hard.'

'That's what I've heard.' Françoise nodded.

'It was January when I arrived at Inverailort. On the second day we had to swim almost a mile across Loch Eilt, then climb up to the top of An Stac, a craggy mountain almost three thousand feet high, then run back down into a Nissen hut and assemble our pistols from pieces, in the dark. I remember shaking with cold and exhaustion. If we didn't do it within the allotted time we had to do it the next day and then the next. If we failed on the third attempt, we were sent back to our regiments in disgrace.'

'Our tales are similar,' Françoise remarked. 'He really did have a method, didn't he? Tell me, where is Inverailort?'

I smiled at the way she pronounced 'Inverailort'. 'If I start telling you about the West Highlands I may not stop,' I confessed. 'The place is so close to my heart.'

Françoise stood up and looked out of the window. 'Still no sunrise.' Then she walked back to the fireplace, sat close beside me and linked her arm through mine. 'Go on, tell me about your home. We have a long, hard day ahead of us so give me something nice to think about.'

I relished the chance to tell her all about my beloved Ardnish.

'Very well. Just shut your eyes and try to picture my home in your mind. Can you hear the murmur of the waves as they wash back and forth, the mewing of the kittiwakes? And there's the call of the corncrake from the big field behind the house. You're sitting on the bench at the front door, looking south towards the sun and across Loch Ailort. To your left are another ten houses in a crescent, replicating the curve of the beach. Two of those houses are occupied, with smoke curling out of their chimneys. The others are in various stages of collapse, their heather thatch and wooden struts jutting up with sheep taking shelter inside. Beyond is a steep knoll that you need to go over to get to Laggan farm, and at the end of the bay, a steep, smooth rock face dropping down to the water. Turn your head to the west and you'll see a burn where you can hear the water tumbling on its way down to the sea. Beyond that, and out of sight, is Glasnacardoch and the school that I went to until it closed ten years ago.

'The village is called Peanmeanach – that means Pennyland in English.'

'You have a gift, Angus,' Françoise murmured. 'I'm enjoying this.'

I was elated by her words. 'Well, my father used to say Ardnish is "the place where God was born". Although it's remote, with cold, hard winters, it's a beautiful area – one where few visitors come, yet people don't ever want to leave.

'Our district is known as the Rough Bounds, because it's so hard to get to over such wild countryside. The mountains rise, rough and grey, straight up from the shore. Loch Ailort is five miles long and a mile across, narrower in places. And part of the military training centre is at Roshven House, owned by friends of my family and which my grandfather helped to build. I could swim across the loch to it. At the top of the loch is Inverailort Castle; I can walk or row there in three hours. And just behind the peninsula, to the north, is Arisaig House. So you see, Ardnish is right in the centre of the SOE patch.'

'How funny that you ended up training right across from your childhood home,' said Françoise.

'You'd love it, Françoise. The sea sparkles in the sun like you've never seen before, and the bed of flowers on the machair is so remarkable – yellow, pink, white, blue – it seems sacrilegious to walk on it. When I was tiny I used to lie on my mother's lap while she made daisy chains for me to wear. We would bathe in the burn, tingling and refreshing in August, harsh and painful in the winter. That river was the life blood of the village for cooking, drinking, washing clothes. After bathing I would roll myself dry in the grass and my mother would worry about my getting stung by bees.

'My mother Louise and my grandparents live there with a friend, Mairi. My mother is Welsh; she was a nurse at Gallipoli in the Great War and she met my father when he was a patient. He had been wounded on a mission and she nursed him back to health. They fell in love, married, and she was pregnant with me when my father was killed in an accident as they made their way home to Ardnish at the end of the war.'

'How tragic,' Françoise whispered.

'My mother's dream was to marry a farmer and live in the country. I suppose she did both, but her life hasn't exactly turned out as she might have hoped. She has a widow's pension and she makes a little money collecting whelks and making tweed, but it's hard. Now that I'm earning, I send her money whenever I can. She has pined for my father ever since he died. Do you know, when she is out and about by herself and thinks no one is near, she talks out loud to him? "DP, do you think there are any wooden pegs I could fix this roof with?", or "Will the lamb prices be better this year?" I feel so sorry for her.'

I felt Françoise give my arm a comforting squeeze, but I couldn't trust myself to look at her.

'Peanmeanach is the last of the four communities on Ardnish peninsula where people still live,' I said softly, 'and when my grandparents die then I'm sure my mother will leave. The only place where a man can make a living is Laggan, my farm. I ran it for a few years until the war broke out and now my grandmother is farming it on her own.'

'Is it close to your mother?' Françoise asked.

'It is, and it's a grand piece of land. I have eighteen Highland cattle, and five hundred Blackface sheep.'

I glanced at her to see if she thought I was boasting, but she smiled warmly. 'My mother is a fantastic shepherdess,' I went on. 'She's always had great dogs, and although she's slowing up a bit now, I think she'll be good for another few years. She has a girl come to stay in the summer and they manage things between them.'

'I think it's lovely you have your own farm,' Françoise said. 'I can tell how fond you are of the place.' She smiled, then pulled away and reached for her boots. 'We should go.'

Chapter 2

There wasn't a cloud in the sky, and Françoise looked apprehensive. We would be visible. But we had no choice. The Italians would be looking for us and we had to step out. There was nothing in the hut we could use to carry water, so I made sure we gulped down as much as we could before setting off and tried to ignore the increasing hunger pangs. If we didn't get food before long, we'd really start to weaken.

It was a gorgeous morning. The sun was just beginning to touch the peaks, crowning them in a deep orange glow, as we began a half-hour walk across the plateau before the ascent up the gulley. The snow would have been up to our waists if we hadn't had our snow shoes.

As we walked side by side we conversed quietly.

'I expect you're Catholic, being French?' I asked.

'Of course,' she replied.

'Where I come from, Lochaber and the southern Hebrides are almost entirely Catholic. John Knox, the Presbyterian, just didn't make it to our part of Scotland; the terrain was too much of a challenge for him, I think! And my uncle is a priest.'

'Is that Father Angus?' Françoise asked.

'Yes. He's my father's older brother; he'll be about fifty-seven now. He comes to stay every year and sometimes brings my grandfather's great friend the Archbishop with him. He's very keen on fishing. My mother became a convert, too. She used to go to Mass regularly with my grandparents at our beautiful wee church, Our Lady of the Braes, and one day she just decided that she wanted to be baptised a Catholic. Uncle Angus was coming up to stay, my grandparents were delighted, and so they decided to make a big party of it. I suspect a part of it was that Mother knew how pleased my father would have been. Mind you, she always insisted that her mother was religious, too. Anyhow, they had a gathering in the hotel in Arisaig, where many of their friends live now, after Mass at St Mary's. Religion was always a big part of my upbringing. My grandparents have great faith.'

'I can sense that,' Françoise said.

We laboured on through the deep snow, tipping over frequently and having to help each other up. As the ground steepened, we walked in silence; but my brain was hyperactive and eventually I summoned the courage to ask the question which had been troubling me from the outset.

'You don't have to answer this, but why exactly are you here? There's something I don't know, isn't there? I mean, I've done this job for a month by myself and all of a sudden I'm supposed to need a female, fluent French-speaker, and an SOE agent at that?'

She hesitated, colouring slightly. 'You're right, Angus, I have a separate mission. But I'm afraid I can't tell you what it is. If you were captured, my mission would be compromised and, frankly, it's too important.'

I forced a smile. 'Fair enough, lass.' But of course, I wasn't satisfied with her response.

We plodded on. I turned things over and over in my mind. I suspected the worst and knew Françoise wasn't there to learn from, or to support, me. There was an ulterior motive – some big job on. Would it involve me and my network, or was she going to go it alone? I felt myself growing increasingly preoccupied with possibilities and it was all I could do to stop myself from pressing her further.

Instead, I turned my mind to home and how things might be going there. Were they having a wet winter? Was my grandmother coping with the farm? I prayed we had enough hay cut for the cows over the winter; the big field was getting full of reeds as the drains clogged up and it desperately needed some lime on it to cut the acidity of the peat. But getting workers in, with the men away at war, was almost impossible.

I thought of St Kilda. Ten years before, the islands' people had asked the government to arrange an evacuation – for the same reason as we may one day have to leave Peanmeanach. The young could not make a living and were forced to head to the cities or join the armed forces, leaving the old to fend for themselves. On St Kilda you needed at least four strong men to pull the boat onshore after a fishing trip or an expedition to harvest fulmars. When that could not happen, their income went. People were prepared to handle terrible weather, personal tragedies or hunger, but there finally came a time when the familiarity of their homeland and the beauty of their surroundings was not enough.

I feared Ardnish was at that stage now. Everyone was old. My grandfather, now in his eighties, was badly incapacitated with his one leg. Mairi Ferguson and grandmother must be approaching Grandfather's age, too. I'd heard that my father used to bemoan the likely end of our community thirty years ago. Well, it had survived one more generation at least, but if I were to die in this war, the rest of them would be away within the year.

We had a hard, two-hour climb up the near-vertical couloir in the sunshine, taking it in turns to lead, kicking deep into the soft snow, our snowshoes secured on our backs. We looked constantly over our shoulders, conscious that we might have an Alpini patrol in pursuit. If that were the case, we would stand out – black dots against the white snow – visible for miles around. So we made haste and soon, dripping in sweat despite the cold, we reached the top, ten thousand feet up, gasping in the thin air.

My fair skin put me at a disadvantage in these conditions. With the back of my neck exposed to the sun and the glare bouncing off the snow onto my face, I was getting dreadfully burned despite my efforts to keep my collar up. We were desperate for water now. But up on the ridge we had the consolation of a breathtaking view of Mont Blanc, Aiguille du Midi and a hundred other peaks. We sat in the sunshine, recovering and admiring the view of France in front of us.

'I've never seen anything like this,' marvelled Françoise. 'It's magnificent. I hear the Canadian Rockies are similar, but I've never been there either.'

I was growing uneasy. 'We need to keep going, otherwise we'll freeze to death. It'll be dark before we get down off the glacier. There's supposed to be a descent rope some-where around here. You look over there and I'll search this way.'

A minute later she cried out, 'It's here, Angus, but it's not good.'

I rushed to her. There was a rope, sure enough, but only a short length, tied around a rock. The descent rope was nowhere to be found. The Alpini must have cut it to stop the Free French using the route.

'We can try to make it down anyway, can't we?' said Françoise. 'I mean, we can hardly go back with a lot of angry Italians on our tail.'

She was right, of course. We had no option. Nervously, we began to head down, placing each foot with extreme care. It was my most difficult ever descent. Rocky at first, with stone crumbling under our feet, it felt like my boots were on marbles, rolling under the leather. Our gloves, soaking as we began, soon froze solid as, with our faces against the hillside, we kicked our boots into much harder snow, ice in places. How I longed for the crampons and ice axes we had in training in Scotland.

I knew I was climbing beyond my ability here. Weak with hunger and without a rope, one mistake would mean a vertical fall of over three hundred feet and certain death. My whole body was trembling and the muscles across my shoulders were rigid. I had to force myself to relax. The sweat caused by the sun during the early morning climb had switched to the cold sweat of fear. It had been fifty-six hours since we had eaten the morsels of bread the day before. But Françoise seemed to be doing well. Her slight frame was deceptively strong and agile, well suited to this type of challenge. It was I who was struggling to keep up with her, I realised.

'Your steps are too far apart for me,' she had said. 'Let me lead.'

I knew that she could sense I was the weaker climber and was simply being mindful of my feelings. I felt a surge of gratitude as I followed her gingerly downwards.

It was afternoon by the time we reached the bottom of the cliff. We still had a good four hours of difficult walking ahead of us until we reached Claude's house and, hopefully, a good meal. My whole body was cramped and shaking uncontrollably. I wanted to hug Françoise in my exhilaration at our managing the descent, but I thought better of it.

She was busying herself strapping on her snowshoes. 'Quick,' she urged, 'we need to head off and into that warm sunshine.'

We set off across the glacier, building up a good pace, keeping a good distance apart in case of crevasses, and soon settled into a rhythm. I couldn't help glancing covertly in her direction from time to time.

I'd had very little to do with girls. I was twenty-six years old and my life had been sheltered, to say the least. I had been the only child at school for most of my time there and then the opportunity of farming Laggan had come up and I'd gone straight into that. I'd never even kissed a girl. Grandmother often sent me off to ceilidhs in Mallaig with my uncle Owen and to weddings of people I'd never heard of in Fort William. 'You need to get away and meet people,' she would plead. I'd go to please her, and I would try my best to have a good time, but secretly I dreaded these

events. Françoise was attractive, but she oozed sophistica-
tion and professionalism, and I confess I felt a little
overwhelmed.

She could tell that I was tiring now; she had to wait for
me from time to time but she did so with tact, chatting to
me to take my mind off the effort.

'My father is a doctor,' she told me, 'and my mother is
headmistress of the local school. They were both born in
France and moved to Canada to work. France was in a bad
way after the Depression and Canada was keen to get
professional French-speaking immigrants. The money was
good and my parents were just married and wanted to try
something new together for a few years. The years after the
Crash weren't great for them, of course, but they were a lot
worse for others. At least with my father being a doctor, he
could get work. We had a nice house and two decent
incomes, so my sister and I had a comfortable upbringing.
There aren't many in Chéticamp who could claim that.'

I nodded. 'There are few in the Highlands of Scotland
who have good work like your parents. That's why there
has been such a move to Glasgow or abroad. At school,
Gaelic was forbidden – everything was taught in English. I
think because there was an expectation we'd need it when
we moved away.'

'That's a shame,' Françoise said.

'Yes, but it didn't seem so at the time. You know, as a
boy, I had a pony of my own. She was called Barra, after
the island. She was a Highland garron; they're bred to
carry deer carcasses down from the hill. She was built like
a tank, and so slow.'

I chuckled as I recalled an incident.

'Why are you laughing, Angus?'

'Something that happened just after I stopped school. One day I had to go to Lochailort for coal. Barra could carry two hundredweight with no problem, but I had to drag her along the track, she was so stubborn. At the end of our path, when you get to the Fort William to Mallaig road, there's a big clearing. A group of Irish travellers had set up a camp of six wagons, with a large tarpaulin stretched over poles and a fire underneath.

'There was a pretty girl there, about my age. Her name was Maureen and she had beautiful long black hair. I was always looking for an opportunity to stop and talk to her. Whenever I arrived, their dogs would bark like mad and nip my ankles. I'd have to carry my own collie, she was so frightened.

'That day, Maureen shouted at them to go away and lie down, and off they went. She was wonderful with animals. She was trying to get a young piebald mare to stand still while she got a cart on her. She needed it to fetch the whelks the others had collected down at Loch na Uamh. She told me that this mare was a nightmare, wouldn't work for her at all, and bucked and fidgeted the whole time. So I lent her Barra, who reversed between the shafts and off they plodded, while I took the mare to see if she would carry my coal bags. We planned to meet back at Maureen's camp in a couple of hours. The mare was just fine with me as I rode her to the station, and stood steady as I stitched the coal sacks together over her back in pairs so that they hung well. And when we set off we moved at twice the speed. I wondered if Maureen would do a swap.

'She said, "Well, handsome Donald Angus, I'll give you my perfect Jester for your slowcoach Barra, but only if you give me a guinea as well."

'She always called me handsome, but we both knew that if I made the slightest move, her menfolk would give me a thrashing. They stick with their own, the travellers.'

'Did you want to make a pass at her?' Françoise asked.

I ducked the question and carried on with the story. 'I reminded her that Barra could pull twice the weight of the little mare, so I offered to give her a lamb in the spring instead of a guinea. Maureen was intrigued, saying, "Well, handsome, don't the creatures on God's earth not belong to us all anyway?" And then she gave me this knowing wink . . .

'And so, yes, the deal was done. I headed off back to the village with Jester, the coal and a big smile on my face. I couldn't wait to see my grandfather's face.

'Right enough, everyone came out to look. Grandmother ran her hand down the pony's legs and doubted whether I'd get a bargain from people like that. Grandfather felt the same. He thought Jester would bog herself, maybe get pneumonia in the winter rains. But I could tell my mother was quite proud of me.

'I told Grandfather that Jester's ancestors had been on the west coast since the railway was built forty years before and that she would be fine in bad weather. I'd need to teach her to plough, but she was definitely promising. And as it turned out, she was.'

Françoise and I kept up a brisk pace, crunching over the icy glacier, but she would always end up a few yards ahead. Then she would wait for me to catch up, and for a while we would step out side by side.

As the shadows lengthened we needed to find the path through the woods down into the valley. We were at the face of the glacier, where the enormous seracs tumbled down and you could hear the ominous groans and creaks of shifting ice. We had to make haste, but choosing a safe route down the face of a glacier was tricky; rushing it would have been suicide.

I had been in similar situations before. 'Be careful,' I cautioned. 'It might be three hundred feet deep in there and there'd be no way out.'

'Ever the optimist,' Françoise observed wryly.

'I'm serious,' I retorted sharply. 'Claude told me one of his men fell into a crevasse not long ago, and there was already someone in there – dead. And they had a rope to pull their man out; we don't.'

Both of us were silent as we inched our way to safety – a stumble either way would be lethal. It was only a hundred feet down the face of the glacier, but it took us a good hour, and night was falling.

We made it, and found to our relief that we had only a few hundred easy yards to the wood. We talked as we walked, Françoise in French. 'You need to speak like a native, Angus. Practise, practise,' she urged.

She talked about going to university, St Francis Xavier, how her sister Simone was at McGill in Montreal, and how their parents would spend hours doing homework with them.

I was silenced. Françoise was educated and wealthy. Me and my farming would be of little interest to her. I could have gone to university – everyone said so – but the tie of Ardnish had been too strong.

Françoise chattered on, but I had stopped listening. Had I taken the right path in life? If everyone else left Peanmeanach, would I stay at Laggan by myself, with no wife? I'd be talked about at the auction mart or in the Fort William shops as that mad Gillies fellow, the recluse. What girl would be happy to be so cut off these days? How would our children go to school? I was worrying myself into despondence, but tiredness and hunger always made me miserable.

'It was a man from near Ardnish who made McGill what it is,' I said impulsively, in an attempt to appear sophisticated.

'Really?' Françoise sounded sceptical.

'Honestly. A hundred years ago, John MacDonald of Glenaladale emigrated to Prince Edward Island. His grandson William was based in Montreal. He was knighted and became the richest man in Canada. I think McGill had been all about agriculture before he became involved, but he introduced science, mathematics, engineering, that sort of thing. Have you heard of MacDonald tobacco?'

Françoise nodded.

'Well, that was his company.'

'Oh, you're such a knowledgeable man, Angus Gillies,' she teased. Somehow I felt quite the opposite when she said this.

'Actually, my name is Donald Angus Gillies. At home it's usually Donald Angus but the army dropped the Donald bit.' I smiled. 'My father was Donald Peter, my grandfather Donald John – we aren't very imaginative with names in the Highlands. You can call me Angus, or even Angie, as my grandmother sometimes does, if you want. It's Donald with everything in my parts. There are even girls called Donaldina.' I felt a bit embarrassed saying all this, certain that Françoise would think us parochial.

'I did have a field name but one day I blurted out my real name by mistake, so now I'm Angus to everyone.'

Françoise laughed, delighted at my admission. 'Well, we French aren't much better; every family has a Jean-something, a Jean-Pierre or Jean-Charles. So, you see, Donald Angus, I do understand.'

We'd been going hard for over ten hours and were running on empty, as the army lorry drivers would say, but when we finally caught sight of the kerosene lights through the windows of Claude's farmhouse we whooped with joy.

Chapter 3

We received a warm welcome and then devoured a mountain of chicken stew, washed down with jugs of wine. The room was dark, and my eyes stung from the fug of smoke from cigarettes and the crackling log fire. I struggled to stay awake as Claude and his wife Marie chatted to Françoise in French, talking too fast for me to understand much. I had sent a Morse message to report that we had arrived safely. The Germans had recently adopted direction-finding vehicles to identify the locations of radio transmitters so I kept it as brief as possible.

Claude was keen to talk about his group and the plan but I had hit a brick wall. 'Tomorrow, my friend, please, tomorrow,' I begged him before collapsing on an armchair under a heap of blankets.

I slept soundly, awoke refreshed, and the next morning got straight down to work. We had been joined by four men from Claude's team who were sitting around the kitchen table sipping strong black coffee. 'Thank God for the American coffee,' Claude declared. 'It's their biggest contribution to the war!'

I had already told the others that the first mission was to close the pass from Sallanches up to Chamonix. We had a week. Claude and I had worked on this plan already and his team had plenty of additional information to share. I would then retrace my steps over the mountain to carry out my next mission, which was to close the Great St Bernard Pass so that the Italians couldn't use it to bring tanks and supply vehicles into Switzerland in the spring. The War Office was convinced that an invasion of Switzerland was imminent: the Germans saw it as a hiding place not only for those attacking Hitler's armies but also for Jews and the wealth of the immensely rich – gold that could be used to shore up their rapidly emptying coffers.

With his round, unshaven face, bronzed by half a century of sun and brandy, and black beret, not to mention the Gauloise that dangled permanently from his mouth, Claude was a veritable vision of Frenchness. His rough, swarthy appearance belied his dry sense of humour and fierce intellect. I liked him from the moment I met him. When he said something, people listened. He was the perfect leader of a Maquis team.

During a lull in our planning I found myself thinking about my friend Michael Gubbins, who had been their SOE contact before me. He'd been at Claude and Marie's home twice, weapons training with the men and planning sabotage operations.

Michael and I had been in Lochailort together and met in the inn there before I left for France, so he could give me a final informal briefing over a pint. We were always happy to get together, and he made me laugh like no one else. Tears would often pour down my face as he told me some ridiculous story or other. He was also, of course, an impressive soldier.

He told me Claude was a clever man, much respected, but that he was too old and unfit now to get actively involved. His sidekick, Charles, was capable but quiet. He had been in the Chasseurs Alpins – an elite infantry unit who were used to the mountains and all their challenges and had a knowledge of guns and military discipline. Claude's men were rather scruffy, untrained mountain types – 'Rather like you, Angus,' he'd teased me. He told me that when he had gone to France the first time, a year before, there had been only eight Maquis, spread across a wide area, but now many more men were joining. Although these raw recruits had no training or any idea how best to go about their role, every one of them was 'up for a scrap – just like you Scots'.

Michael had taken some of them down to the valley where they'd blown up a small power station and a railway track. Suddenly, they became like boys with new toys. It was all Michael could do to stop them blowing up everything they came across. Getting them to turn up on time, with the right equipment, and to listen to instructions had been a challenge, because if they had a sickly child, or a cow that needed milking, that always took priority. But he assured me that they were good men, and loyal. He ended his briefing by raising his glass to me – '*Sláinte*' – and wishing me all the luck in the world.

After our arrival at Les Contamines, the snow fell for two solid days. There must have been three feet of it outside as Françoise and I sat chatting over morning coffee and hunks of delicious fresh bread, warm from the oven. Claude and Marie were out in the yard attending to the livestock, and his men were still asleep. We'd spent the last

two days in intensive discussion about strategy, and everyone was exhausted.

It felt good to be alone with Françoise for a while.

'So, you've always known where your family comes
from?' she asked.

'Just about. I could tell you the story if you like?'

'Go on then,' she replied.

'Very well, and then I want you to tell me about your
mission.'

She rolled her eyes. 'You know I can't do that, Angus. It's
safer for everyone. I can't compromise the mission – it's too
important.'

She was right, of course, though I longed to know what
she was up to. But Françoise was a woman who would not
yield on anything.

I held my hands up in surrender, and began my story.
'Well, the men in my family are the hereditary bagpipers
for the MacDonalds of Clanranald and were there in 1715
when the chief burned down Castle Tioram to stop the
English capturing it . . .'

'I'm lost already!' Françoise exclaimed. 'Clanranald?
What chief?'

'The chief, centuries ago, was seen as the father of the
clan, of the extended family. He would provide protection
and a livelihood for his people, and in return they would
work and fight for him. Clanranald was our chief. My
great-great-grandfather Ronald was born in the 1770s, not
many years after Bonnie Prince Charlie landed at Loch na
Uamh, to the back of Ardnish. His father had gone with his
bagpipes to meet the prince and had travelled with him to
Kinloch Moidart, then up Loch Shiel to Glenfinnan, where

he stood at the front of the boat and piped as it was rowed up the loch to meet the Camerons and the MacDonalds, who had mustered to try to defeat the Hanoverians and drive them from Scotland.

'Ronald was known as "the bard", which means poet or storyteller, and he wrote two books that are held in university collections in Edinburgh. He was well known throughout the whole country and used to travel the Highlands giving renditions, as they're now called. He loved the *craic*.'

I noticed her blank expression. 'He loved a good story.'

'Ah.'

'Once a professor came to visit us, looking for a copy of these books. In fact, we had one of each, which my grandmother had given us, with stern words never to part with them. I remember my grandfather saying to this professor that he was welcome to read the books but he would have to do so in the house. That's how precious they were to us. They were kept on a shelf beside the issue of the *Oban Times* that described my grandmother's rescue of the people of St Kilda – but that's a story for another time! You should see them, Françoise – well thumbed from handling over the years and discoloured from the damp. Ronald's first is a book of songs about the people and way of life around Arisaig, and the second is a collection of poems along the same theme – both in Gaelic.'

'Did he make a living from his writing?' Françoise asked.

'He was a fisherman first, and after that a drover, taking cattle across country to the auctions in Stirling. I remember a family friend who had spent her youth in the West Highlands saying, "There, every man is a hunter, a fisher and a steersman, there is a musician in every house and a poet in every hamlet." Ronald MacDonald was all of these. When I was little my grandfather would tell me droving tales. On one of the last big cattle droves, there was almost a thousand head of cattle gathered together at Corriechoillie by Spean Bridge, southeast of Ardnish. They were then driven over the hills to the auction house of Falkirk which lay a hundred miles south. "You should have seen the sight of it," Grandfather said. "Cattle stretched out mile after mile along the glen as the beasts wound their way to the auction, then from there to the pastures of the south and eventually to the tables of those who could afford to eat beef." According to him, the last of the great drovers was a man called John Cameron. He was known, as people in the Highlands often are, by the name of his property, Corriechoillie. He was a crofter in Brae Roy and he used to drive the laird's cattle for him, and for others, too, on occasion. Over the years he would expand further and further afield, sending men off to places such as Skye and Badenoch to collect cattle. When he died he could rest the animals on his own land from Glenelg to the Stirling auctions. A truly self-made man.'

'Such beautiful names.' Françoise smiled.

'But a hard life. My great-great-grandfather worked for Corriechoillie for many years. Wrapped up in his plaid while blizzards blew around him, often spending a week on the drove in hard rain, soaked through day and night. He was said to dunk his plaid in the burn as it was warmer when wet.'

'I don't believe you!'

'It doesn't seem to make sense now but my grandfather assured me it was commonplace a hundred years ago.

Drovers often died when the weather got desperately bad. Grandfather had a story about a big avalanche of wet snow on the track through to the head of Loch Treig. There had been heavy snow for two days at the start of the week and the drove had been delayed. They had left the south of Skye two weeks before, swum the beasts across the narrows at Glenelg and had been gathering animals as they went along. The beasts had to be at Stirling within the month or they would miss the sale, and if that happened they would have to stay down, at great expense, until the next auction. After lunch one day the weather cleared and it grew unexpectedly warm for the time of the year. The snow turned to slush and Corriechoillie decided to get the cattle moving as quickly as possible up through the pass of Lairig Leacach, always a slow haul. But just before dark, with only a couple of miles to go before they were through and safely on the flat area towards Rannoch Moor, there was a sudden whoosh and the whole hillside of two-foot-thick snow came tumbling onto the pass. There were at least forty beasts trapped under it and Ewan Kennedy, a man from Loch Lochy. Everyone rushed to help, but what with the dark and all those injured cattle thrashing about, he was long dead when he was found.'

'What did they do?'

'The drove was called off and they left the beasts at the lochside for a few days under the eye of a couple of youngsters while they carried Ewan's body back to his widow. Corriechoillie was a kind gentleman and we heard he settled a sum on Mrs Kennedy to see her by despite its being Ewan's first time on the drove.'

'What about Ronald?' Françoise asked.

'He had been there at the time. My grandfather believes it must have been during these days of the droving that he became the poet and bard. I can imagine it; with a good fire, a long night, a bottle of whisky and plenty of time to practise. Of course, with the good schooling we have now it's difficult to remember that he couldn't read and write as a child. He would have been helping with milking or thatching as soon as he could walk. It wasn't until my grandfather's days that children got any education. It's so hard to believe – my grandmother is such a bookworm. But Ronald was thirty before he learned to read and write. He and Corriechoillie were taught together by Father John, the priest in Roybridge. He never learned English, though. He used to say, "What need would I have of it? The cows and my dogs speak the Gaelic in any case."'

While I was relating these stories I once more realised how self-conscious I was becoming. Françoise was from an educated family and I was painfully aware of my shortcomings.

'You know,' she said, sensing my discomfort, 'there is a difference between being intelligent and having common sense and being educated. It's far better being the former. The way I see it, you wouldn't have been promoted from a private to a sergeant in four years if you didn't have intelligence. And your ability to pick up French is impressive.'

'I hadn't thought of it like that,' I replied. 'Thanks.'

'You come from an interesting family,' she said with a smile. 'You're right to be proud of it. Writers and musicians, soldiers and farmers. Do you play the bagpipes yourself?'

I smiled; it was my favourite subject. 'I couldn't not,' I joked. 'Grandfather taught me mainly. He still plays the chanter every day, but he complains that he can't remember the tunes and that his fingers are stiff. I'm told my father was a gifted player, too. It was one of the first things my mother learned about him – that he was a renowned piper. I was a piper in the Lovat Scouts in the Faroe Islands before joining the SOE.'

'My goodness, Angus, what a fascinating man you are!'

Claude came in, rubbing his hands. He seemed agitated. 'Angus, my cow is not feeding her calf. Could you come and have a look?'

'Of course.' I stood up, jolted back to the present. 'Don't forget you have a wireless call at five tonight,' I reminded Françoise. 'Maybe you'll get your instructions for your mission.' The thought filled me with foreboding.

Later, Françoise was on the transmitter for just two minutes. She came back into the room with an announcement: 'I'm off the day after next if the roads are clear. Claude, I'll need four people for two days – it would be helpful if two were women. Can you help? They'll need to stay here overnight, and we'll head in the morning before dawn. I can brief everyone fully tomorrow night.'

'It should be possible,' Claude replied. Later, Claude, Marie, Françoise and I sat in front of the fire after another delicious supper of braised rabbit and root vegetables, with a bottle of brandy doing the rounds.

'Our friend Michael is a good friend of yours, too, isn't he?' Marie asked me.

'He is indeed. We trained together at Arisaig and we know each other's families. He's on a mission now, not sure where. His father is our boss.' I indicated Françoise.

'Really? Who?' asked Françoise, surprised.

'Brigadier Gubbins,' I replied.

Françoise nodded. 'Oh yes. I've heard of him.'

'So what made you join the army, Angus?' Claude asked.

I took a sip of my brandy, and in my less than perfect French began. 'My father and the generations before him had no choice except to join the army; it was their only means of earning a living. But I had no plans to take the King's shilling once I knew I would have the tenancy of a three-thousand-acre farm that would support me and my family well. I was only seventeen when I got it.

'When I first found out that war looked likely, I was at the auction mart at our local town, Fort William, selling some sheep with my grandparents. We were at the bar, which was where everyone met to celebrate good lamb prices or commiserate on bad ones. My grandfather's old ally, my godfather Colonel Willie MacDonald was there, too. Now Colonel Willie has always been very good to me and it was he who stood surety for the lease of my farm.

'Anyway, he told my grandfather that they were recruiting again, that we should make sure it would be the Lovat Scouts and not the Camerons. "My goodness," Grandfather said, "you had my signature for the Boer War, and now you're wanting me again? Me with only one leg and over my seventies?"'

Everyone laughed as I mimicked my grandfather's voice. 'Of course Willie roared with laughter and said, "Away with yourself! It's young Donald Angus I'll be having." My grandmother protested that farming would be vital for food production and I ought to be exempt from conscription, but this was brushed off. In truth I didn't wish to argue with the colonel. I was keen to get out and see the world. Ardnish is a quiet place for a young man, and I was content knowing that I would have the rest of my life ahead of me there.

'The colonel told us I'd be with his son, Andrew. He was at Mons doing cavalry training and would join the regiment shortly. He said we could look after each other, just like my grandfather had done for him in South Africa.'

'Your poor mother,' Marie said.

'Indeed. The journey back to Ardnish was tense as I knew my mother would be very upset. There were tears at dinner, and I remember my grandmother wailing to my grandfather that war had taken his son, his leg and the best years of his life, and now it was taking me. I tried to reassure her, but it was a sad evening . . . very sad.'

Françoise must have heard the catch in my voice because her hand rested on my shoulder briefly while I collected myself.

'We got on to discussing how the farm would be run, then Grandfather took charge. He reminded my grandmother that in wartime farming was always done by the women and that she could run the farm blindfolded, and that my dog worked better for her than it did for me! He suggested that they ask John Mackellaig's daughter from Glenfinnan, or Islay Mackenzie from Morar, to help out during the busiest times; the girls would be glad of the money.'

Françoise spoke up. 'It's old men who start wars, and then the boys get drawn into the excitement, but it's the women who are left with little children, loneliness and a struggle to make ends meet.' She was flushed and animated; Marie nodded in agreement.

There was an awkward silence, which I eventually broke. 'I suggested that my grandparents should sell the cattle at the end of the summer and concentrate on the sheep as they're far less work. But they loved our Highland cattle – who wouldn't? They're so beautiful to look at, with their three-foot-long horns, shaggy red hair and fringes over their eyes, and they're so well suited to the terrain – immune to the rain and able to find grazing on the roughest ground. But they're wild beasts and hard work, so it made sense to let them go, unfortunately. It's tough for my family. They're now living in a protected zone, with training exercises going on all around, lots of shooting and explosives and strange goings-on at night. They need a pass even to go to Fort William.'

'So you joined the Lovat Scouts?' Claude prompted.

'Yes, I joined the regiment in Leicestershire in April 1940. We all went through full cavalry training with horses, just in time to see the horses taken away from us as the War Office finally recognised that cavalry charges against machine guns and tanks were utterly ineffective.'

'Thank goodness,' said Françoise. 'I've read some terrible things about the suffering of horses in battle.'

'The Lovat Scouts are made up of stalkers and ghillies and other Highland men, with the lairds as the officers; we're a good-humoured lot, of about seven hundred. We have a vital role as spotters and snipers, greatly respected. Anyhow, immediately after I joined, the Germans invaded Norway and we were convinced that was where we would be sent. But to everyone's surprise we were sent to Glasgow to the docks and put on ships bound for the Faroe Islands, near Iceland. It was a baptism of fire for me. Endless patrols, guard duties, fitness and arms practice interspersed with occasional shooting at German planes that would strafe the towns. I threw my heart into everything and was made a corporal within months.'

'I'm not surprised,' said Claude.

'Oh, I must tell you this story. Many of the soldiers only had the Gaelic, scarcely a word of English. The correct challenge by a sentry was "Halt", followed by "Who goes there?" One Hebridean soldier, hearing footsteps approach, shouted "Halt" as he had learned, but then there was a long pause, followed by "Who am I?" The sergeant major was heard to bellow, "I don't know, but I'll damned soon find out!"'

It was good to hear my companions' laughter. Outside, the weather had taken a turn for the worse. Marie brewed fresh coffee, and I went on with my story.

'I was sent back to the mainland twice on courses. My grandfather's friend Colonel Willie's son was in the same company and he made sure that all the opportunities for advancement came my way. It was about eighteen months ago that he sent for me and told me of an opportunity that might appeal to me. He explained that the War Office had put together a separate unit, all very hush-hush, to infiltrate German territories, help the Resistance, that sort of thing. They were looking for the fittest, bravest and most intelligent soldiers, and to my surprise, they thought I would be up for it.

'Of course, I jumped at the chance. I was flattered and excited. You see, many of us in the Lovat Scouts had resented being sent to the Faroe Islands. We saw ourselves as a leading reconnaissance unit and wanted to be in the thick of it, rather than defending a distant little island. I definitely agreed with that thinking. I was told that Lord Lovat was running the new team, and that was enough for me.

'Before the month was out, the team of six had been assembled and briefed, and we were on our way to Stodham Park where we were put through an assessment. Two of us were then sent on to the training course at Inverailort and Roshven, which was right across the loch from home.'

'That must have been wonderful,' Françoise said. 'To be posted home, even if only for a while.'

'The crash course in French was the biggest challenge for me, I confess. Fourteen hours a day and so many technical terms. We learned things like how to hold a time-pencil in one hand, set the delay for ten minutes, thirty minutes, twelve or twenty-four hours, and how copper chloride corrodes the iron thread, which holds a striker held under pressure by a spring . . . It went on and on and we knew that accuracy was vital. Just imagine if the detonation went off on the railway depot in ten minutes when you were still in the compound – rather than half a day distant as you thought you had planned . . .'

'It sounds as though you were happy, though, despite the challenges,' Marie said.

'Oh yes. The early years of the war were pretty pleasant actually. I even danced with the Queen.'

'Tell us more!' Françoise implored.

'It was after training at Inverailort and before I got my orders. I had three weeks to spare so I went back to the

Scouts, who were guarding the Queen at Balmoral. I was a sergeant by then, so I was asked to lead the grouse-beating line for King George and his family. It was exhausting, but we had tremendous weather and the heather was in full bloom.'

'Did the Queen shoot?' asked Marie.

'No! But we were asked to attend the annual Ghillies' Ball, which was held in a beautiful room in Balmoral, covered in stags' antlers. Her Majesty danced the Dashing White Sergeant with two of us sergeants. She found that most amusing: "Two dashing white sergeants!" she said.'

'What is a ghillie?' Claude asked.

'Ghillie means boy, and the guide on a salmon river or a pony boy is called a ghillie. Oh, and I must tell you this: the King, who has a terrible stammer, said to me, "Wh-wh-what's your name?" I replied, "Gillies, your Majesty." To which he said, "I asked your name, m-m-man, not what you do!"'

I had my audience spellbound by this time. The fire was crackling and our faces were glowing from the brandy.

'The morning after the ball, I was asked if I could take some men across to help shoot some deer. The army was very short of rations and it was a task perfectly suited to the Scouts. We had to take half a dozen men, plus twenty ponies, from Balmoral to Newtonmore for a week, and I hand-picked my men with care.

'We took lodgings for a night at Cluanie House, normally where the Macpherson chief lived, and were to be joined by Ewan Ormiston, an old army friend of my father's and five of his men, all Lovat Scouts who had served in the Great War and whose sons were serving now. Ormiston and I were old friends, so I telephoned in advance to find out who was with him. After he told me, I said we should maybe get the fathers and sons together as a surprise. Ormiston thought this a great plan. He told me he had Archie Mackenzie from Gairloch, Tommy Addison from Rannoch, Hector MacQuarrie from Gaick, Ewan Matheson from Tulloch and big Jock the Fish from Ullapool. It was an easy task for me to get their sons released from the battalion for this job.

'Well, when we turned up at the Balavil Hotel and walked into the bar, you should have seen how pleased the fathers and sons were to see each other! It brings a tear to my eyes just telling you all about it.'

'What a wonderful thing to do,' Marie smiled. 'I wish I'd seen their faces!'

'It was marvellous, I must say. After some drinks in the bar, including the appearance of some illicit whisky, we had our dinner – venison, of course. Ewan told me he had a contract to supply eight thousand head of deer each year for army rations and so, allowing for some severe weather and avoiding the calving season, he had to shoot thirty-two beasts a day. He had three teams out a day somewhere or other, with trucks to transport the carcasses and men to get them ready for butchering. Then the carcasses would be shipped off to Dewhurst's, the butchers in Edinburgh where they would be prepared for bully beef and canned or whatever. As well as army rations, the best cuts were sold to the public for a fair price, as fortunately venison wasn't rationed, unlike other meat. Our deer were for ration packs, he assured me.

'For the next few days we saw the Highlands at their best. Cheerful father-and-son stalking teams setting off with half a dozen ponies led by local women. The men were in army fatigues or tweed, Tam o'Shanters or deer-stalkers on their heads, dragging ropes and telescopes over one shoulder and a rifle over the other. I was proud of them; as fine a group of men couldn't be found in the whole of Scotland.

'The heather was deep and glorious, and the sun shone every minute of the week. The men worked hard, often covering twenty miles in a day as deer were far scarcer than they had been before the war. At the end of the week, we had our two hundred beasts. They were prepared in a Nissen hut which had been converted into a larder behind Ewan's butcher shop in Newtonmore, then loaded onto a goods train carriage. Everyone involved was delighted.'

I began to suspect that this story was less interesting to my audience than it would be to fellow Highlanders, but it was a great pleasure for me to recount. It was comforting, calling up images of home and of dear friends.

'I should stop talking,' I volunteered. 'I'll have you all asleep.'

'Not at all,' Françoise said.

'This place . . . Inverailort,' Claude said, stumbling over the pronunciation. 'I am curious about it. Was it built as a training centre?'

'Goodness, no. Inverailort is a castle near my home. In fact, all three of the big houses around Ardnish were requisitioned for military training – Inverailort, Roshven and Arisaig. It happened all over the country. Apparently, the army just pitched up and took possession of Inverailort when the owner, Mrs Cameron-Head, was in London. The house contents were sent in trucks to Fort William, but one truck spilled and much was broken, to her fury. She has passed away since, poor thing.

'The Blackburns at Roshven were moved out to a house on the estate and Miss Astley Nicholson of Arisaig went to live with her sister.'

'Must have been quite a change for everyone,' said Françoise.

'Inverailort is the sabotage school now, known as "the big house" by the men. I teach them about explosives and the best way to infiltrate airbases, how to set explosives on planes and escape before they go off. Sometimes they explode when the planes are in the air. We have agents from many countries on the course: Poles, Czechs and French, too. I show the men – and some women as well now – how to disable a power station with just a rucksack of Nobel 808 that can be moulded around a structure. That's the stuff in the containers that was parachuted in here last week. Plastic explosive.

'Roshven House is five miles west of Inverailort and is now a commando training camp used for sea training. I spent a week there, training with mini submarines, canoes, practising beach landings. And all so close to home.'

Ardnish. I could picture it so clearly in my mind as I continued.

'I was given a week's leave from training at Inverailort and so of course I decided to spend it with my family at Peanmeanach, to take them by surprise. They thought I was still in the Faroes. It was a lovely day when I set off for home, baking hot, so I stripped to my underwear and swam across Loch Ailort from Roshven. My mother told me later she thought she saw something in the water, so she got my grandfather's old telescope and, well, suffice it to say that by the time I stepped onto the sand I was surrounded. My grandfather was up outside the house with his pipes, playing the "Pibroch of Donald Dhu" as a jig. It was a magical moment, one I'll always treasure.'

'Does your family get caught up in the war, like we do?' Marie asked.

'Well, we don't get bombed or anything, but Grandmother was telling me of the hirl and birl around Ardnish when I was home last. They were forewarned, but it was still quite unsettling, especially the first time. Apparently Peanmeanach is part of a challenge for the soldiers from Inverailort. They have to seize the village, and their enemies are the various locals – you know, the Home Guard?

'She told me that at two o'clock in the morning in the early days of the war, there was a knock on the door. It was John Alex Fraser, a retired butcher from Morar. He said, "I'm just warning you there'll be a bit of a battle on for the next wee while." So, they sat in the living room with their tea, and boats come onto the beach, flares going up, machine guns firing, explosives, men shouting, and the dog barking as if the end of the world was upon them all. Anyway, an hour later, the boats were off again, John Alex put his head around the door and announced that our side had won and he was off to bed. Of course, no one could get back to sleep; the dog kept pacing around whining, the farm animals had white eyes and they couldn't settle them for days.

'The funny thing was that my aunt Mairi didn't wake until the battle was full on and she was up in her nightie, running around outside convinced that the Germans had invaded.'

Everyone was in fits of laughter.

'She thought Ardnish was where the great invasion would start!' I said. 'Later, I asked a couple of the signals instructors if they would set up a wireless aerial at Peanmeanach, so they could get the BBC. They had a link with the Roshven House mast and completed the job in no time. It was enormously popular; Aunt Mairi and the family spent hours listening to the Home Service and Forces Radio, with my mother and grandmother waltzing around at breakfast to Vera Lynn. Mother loved telling people about the wireless. We must have been the only civilians in Lochaber to get it.'

The embers of the fire were burning themselves out. I felt as though I had been talking for hours.

Françoise turned to Claude. 'Why do Italian soldiers patrol the Alps, rather than German?'

'Ah,' Claude said, 'just as France have the Chasseurs Alpins, the Italians have their own mountain troops. They are stationed just over the mountains in Courmayeur. We don't mind having them. Many are related to people living on this side of the mountain, and they don't bother us as long as we don't bother them.'

'For now,' I said. 'But the Germans see this area as a hotbed of Resistance fighters who destroy factories, train tracks and power stations while the Alpini do nothing. It must change, I'm afraid. The Germans will take control and then you will really experience the war.'

There was a long silence, which Claude eventually broke. 'You are depressing me too much, my friends, so I'm off to my bed. Someone has to get up to milk the cows at five.'

'I'll help you in the morning, Claude,' I replied. 'Goodnight.'

Marie left with Claude and I was alone with Françoise. 'It's a big day for you tomorrow,' I said quietly. 'Do you want to talk about it?'

She yawned expansively and shook her head. 'I'm too tired,' she replied. 'Thank you for your wonderful stories but it's too late for any more. Goodnight, Donald Angus.'

I kept my gaze on the dying fire as she climbed onto her mattress and pulled the covers over herself. It was only when I heard her breathing grow slow and regular that I, too, turned in. I lay there thinking about Françoise. I was falling for her. I didn't get any feeling it was reciprocated, though. As well as we got on, I sensed a distance between us, that she didn't want to become too intimate.

'Goodnight, Françoise,' I whispered.

Chapter 4

I woke early, with Françoise still on my mind. She was only two feet away; I could hear her deep regular breathing. This time tomorrow she would be gone and I still felt that I knew so little about her. She wore a wedding ring, but was she actually married? She hadn't mentioned a man, but then, I'd done all the talking. Would she really be an SOE agent if she was married?

She coughed.

I steeled myself to ask her. 'Françoise, you wear a wedding ring.'

'I do,' she replied sleepily.

'Tell me about your husband.'

She laughed. 'I'm not married! It's to throw people off the scent, so they don't think of me as someone they can make a pass at. All the female SOE agents wear them, hadn't you noticed?'

I laughed – relief, really. 'Well, it worked with me,' I replied, smiling deep within.

It was just as well she couldn't see my face; the game would have been up.

Shortly after, I heard my French friend let himself out. I got up, ready for my role as milkmaid, and was with him a minute later. Soon we were sitting with our heads pressed against the warm flanks of the placid cows, with the regular swish-swish of milk jetting into the wooden buckets. We discussed in low voices our plans for the next two days and Françoise's mission.

'I have people in mind, my friend,' Claude murmured. 'After coffee, I will go and find them.'

I nodded.

'Marie and I enjoyed your stories last night,' he said. 'So, you don't have a family of your own, Angus?'

'Just my mother. My father died in the Great War. I never met him,' I replied.

'No wife? No lover?' he tried again.

'No.'

'How did your father die?'

It was strangely comforting to recount the tale of my father's life and death again, though I kept it brief. 'My poor mother,' I concluded. 'Everything was looking so hopeful, then suddenly – no longer.'

'My God,' said Claude, crossing himself, 'what a sad story.'

After we finished the milking, Claude took away the pails and I sat in the barn. In the week I'd had at Ardnish, I'd visited my father's grave with my mother and grandparents. My uncle Owen went, too. He was a blacksmith and fisherman in Mallaig now, and as fishing was a reserved occupation he was excused National Service. We decided to travel the same route as my father's coffin would have done, hefted on eight men's shoulders; the Bodach on his gelding.

First, we stopped at Our Lady of the Braes at Polnish to say a prayer. On the day of the funeral, the Mass was said by Andrew MacDonald – now Archbishop – as our own Father Angus was still in France with the 51st Division. Polnish church gleamed white and proud on a knoll overlooking Loch Ailort. As we emerged, a train thundered past, its steam engulfing the building. Then we continued along the route to Lochailort Inn where the coffin was set down for a spell and over two hundred mourners took a dram.

The procession then continued across the bridge, over the Ailort. We sat on the very cairn where the mourners had each placed a stone to mark their attendance, and had a few moments with our own thoughts. From there, we could make out the huts and tents for the students and trainers at the Special Training School. The place was a hive of activity, assault courses were being used with gusto, field guns being fired incessantly, smoke was wafting in the still afternoon, and men were running around in uniform wherever we looked.

We rose and followed the path up to Glenshian Lodge and then to a small island in the most unexpected spot in the River Ailort – *Innis na Cuilce*, the island of reeds. Grandfather led us in prayer and then recited an old Gaelic verse which I remember to this day:

To Ailort's shore the war-worn hero homeward
*   wending*
Seeks a land where battles cease
He rests and dreams as from circ'ling hills descending
Falls a soothing balm of peace.
Instead of clashing steel and cannon's roar
He hears a west wind soughing ever more
He hears the sea birds calling

He hears a light sea-wave
Ripple along the shore.

But sounds of war in days of autumn echoing loudly
Coire a Bhuridhe's fastness thrill,
Where antlered stags bellow and crash
In combat proudly challenge clear from hill to hill,
The warrior fancies again the cannon's roar
He seems to hear the clash of steel once more,
Past battles surge around him,
Till silent, night draws down
On Ailort's peaceful shore.

My grandfather had told us that it was written over a hundred years before, to commemorate the death of Major General Alexander Cameron of Inverailort. He thought it very fitting for Donald Peter.

Owen had forged a steel crucifix, and we planted it to mark the spot where my father was buried, aged only twenty-three. It was the 17th of May, 1916. Mother cried, of course, and my grandparents clung together.

We rounded off our day by wandering up to the Lochailort Inn for a meal of freshly caught salmon, and to admire the newly arrived electricity and telephone – courtesy of the War Office. I wondered what my father would have made of it all. He would certainly have known how deeply he had been loved.

Mother was fifty now and looking well on it. She still spoke English with a Welsh accent, and even when speaking in Gaelic, she had been known to call her brother 'boyo' in the middle of a sentence. The pair of them, maddeningly, spoke Welsh when they didn't want us to know what they were saying. She, my grandmother and Mairi had become inseparable over the years, and they were always to be found together collecting shellfish, which were stored in hessian bags until the next MacBraynes boat called by, collecting crotal, a lichen used for dyeing the wool, or working the loom to make tweed. She didn't get too involved with the animals – that was Grandmother's job – though at clipping and lambing times, everyone worked side by side. Money was tight at times and the ration card didn't go very far, but she and Grandfather had war pensions which helped. It meant we could grow vegetables, own a cow, have hens, and, of course, there was a plentiful supply of fish in the lochs and the sea. Strange to think that wartime had shown those living at Ardnish to be comparatively well off, for the first time. City life was far tougher, with strict rationing and poorly paid jobs.

Despite her closeness to Morag and Mairi, I knew my mother got awfully lonely. Social by nature, she needed people around her. It took her several years to get used to the long winter nights, with no light to read by and no one to talk to. She missed my father desperately. 'He would have filled the hole in our lives,' she would say, 'the spark in our day, the love in my nights.' She had been far too young to become a widow. She often called me Donald Peter by mistake, when her mind wandered back in time to the happy days spent with my father and before then with her best friend from the Queen Alexandra Corps: Prissie.

Prissie had come to stay with us twice when I was younger. For my mother, her visits were the best of times and she would fall into a depression when she left. Prissie was great fun. She loved playing tricks on my mother – who fell for them every time – like rushing in at six in the morning, shouting, in her broad Liverpool accent, 'There are deer amongst the vegetables! Quick, get up!' She really just wanted my mother up for company. She used to get the sleeper train up from London on an army warrant, then the train to Lochailort where my mother would meet her. She would recount every conversation she had struck up with strangers in the dining car in minute detail, much to our amusement. You couldn't help but love Prissie; she was a friend to everyone.

Prissie remained in the Queen Alexandra Corps for her whole career, ending up as a senior matron in the same King Edward VII hospital where she and mother had trained. She married a dull older man from Kent called Stephen and had a daughter, Emily, who was three years younger than me and came with her to Ardnish quite soon after the Great War, although I was too young to remember. Prissie stayed with her husband, but no one knew why. 'Loyalty,' said Mother. Prissie was my godmother, and always sent me the biggest and best presents at Christmas, I remember.

The last time Prissie visited, I was about sixteen. My mother was determined to show her a good time. On her first evening we went with the grandparents over to Roshven House and had tea with the Blackburns. Grandmother enjoyed these visits as she could pore over the remarkable wildlife paintings by her friend, the renowned artist Jemima, and then regale us with tales of their time spent together.

The following night, Mother and Prissie went to the Astley Hall in Arisaig for a ceilidh where, I learned later, they danced like dervishes and chatted up anyone in trousers. I had stayed at home because we had three tiny lambs that weren't faring well and I had been told that if they lived I could have them. They returned home at dawn, full of whisky, giggling madly and clinging to each other. I heard them before I saw them and went out to meet them but, instead of going indoors to sleep off their excesses they stripped off to their underwear and went for a swim in Loch Doire a' Ghearrain, splashing each other and shrieking. I was so embarrassed I ran back home.

After that, we all went to help make hay at Roshven farm for a few days. Prissie loved it. Trousers rolled up, turning the hay and loading up the cart, all the while she would be telling the most risqué stories and teaching me some inappropriate English.

My mother kept Prissie busy during her stay. After the haymaking they weeded the vegetable garden, chatting incessantly. They rewarded each other with a trip to Fort William by train and returned with a case each full of new clothes. I remember the day ended with a fashion show after supper.

Prissie loved teaching my mother new recipes. One in particular – a *pizza*, she said – was all the rage in London. She was at pains to point out that it was made there with fresh ingredients and Italian cheese and meats but she cooked a Highland version for us, spreading cheese from the farm, chicken, egg, spinach and tomato paste onto a home-made bread base and cooking it on the range. She also bought some curry paste and rice in Fort William and made a chicken curry. Grandfather would have nothing to do with it, declaring it inedible, but the rest of us loved it.

I knew my mother confided in Prissie. I would enter the house and they would stop talking, look sheepish. Prissie felt strongly that mother should leave the peninsula. 'Your life is passing by, Louise,' she would say. 'If you were in the south you could meet someone who would love you. You could even have another baby, it's not too late.' I could tell my mother was tempted and I felt sorry for her at times. Now and then she would make a comment about the sameness of her life, or she would wistfully mention a friend of a friend who had found a house and employment in Glasgow or London, but she always stopped short of expressing a desire to leave. I think she knew Father would be pleased she had stayed, to bring me up and to help his parents.

I'd lie in bed and hear them giggling in the big bed, talking about men.

My mother and Owen and went to see their mother in Wales one day, not long before the war. The trip had been a long time coming. It was Grandfather who pushed her.

'You need to go and see Bronwyn, Louise,' he said. 'You may have drifted apart over the years but I know for sure that she'll miss you.' For some reason, she was always known as Bronwyn to us – never Mother or Grandmother.

The last time Mother had seen her was in 1916, when my parents had made a surprise visit. Bronwyn's flat in Abergavenny had been squalid and my mother was upset. Bronwyn was living with an awful man called David, and as soon as they realised that there was nothing to be done, my parents couldn't get away fast enough.

Mother and daughter had exchanged letters for a few years, with Bronwyn promising to visit but never doing so. However, recently even these had stopped. My mother didn't even know if her own mother was alive.

'I'm going to send her a telegram, and if she replies, we'll go,' promised Mother after being pressed once too often. Owen was keen, although that was as much to see their older brother Thomas as his mother. After all, he had been only fourteen when he last saw them.

The telegram was duly sent, and to everyone's surprise, a reply came back almost immediately: LOUISE DO COME STOP BRING OWEN STOP SAME PLACE STOP MAM.

So that was that. Train tickets were booked. I couldn't go, nor did I want to, using the genuine excuse of having the farm to run. I was curious to see how my other grandmother lived her life but the day-to-day necessity of my role on the farm meant that my joining them was out of the question.

It was a twelve-hour journey, but despite that, Owen stayed only two days, Mother five. They found Bronwyn frail and living on her own. David had left her not long after my parents had called in. Mother was shocked by how destitute she was. Her diet was awful and she drank and smoked far too much. I can still recall my mother's angry words: 'She does nothing to improve her lot. She won't be long for this world and it will be no surprise!'

Owen wasn't enthusiastic about his brother either, declaring that 'Thomas didn't think highly of me, so that was fine.' But I could see the pain and hurt on his face as he tried to shrug off the slight. Still a coal miner, Thomas was forty years old at the time of their visit. He had a wife he didn't seem to care much for, and four children. He wasn't interested in our life of farming or the sea, Owen and Mother quickly discovered. His life consisted of work, boozing and watching rugby matches. He would travel a hundred miles with friends to watch Abergavenny play most weekends, if he wasn't down the pit. My mother found the entire situation utterly depressing.

I was worried about Owen when he returned from Wales. My immediate family was small, and incredibly close. I couldn't imagine having a brother who didn't care about me or anyone else. But Owen, always the stoic, threw himself back into his work and avoided any talk of the visit until one night when he came to Peanmeanach.

'Thomas is a sad man. He's going the same way as our father. His body takes a hammering in the pits, his skin is never clean, he drinks too much and he's so coarse – you'll never have heard language like it. Still, it doesn't matter, because I won't be seeing him again.'

Everyone agreed that duty had been done and there was no need to visit again. Mother had returned with a photograph of her parents when they were young and she had it framed and hung in the front room. 'I want to remember the good days when I was young, Donald Angus,' she'd said. 'Later on, when your grandfather got bad with black spittle he became angry and took it out on us. He drank himself free from pain in the Miners Welfare Club until he died of it. And with him gone, your grandmother lost her confidence and let herself go.'

It seemed to me that she was being unduly kind to her parents, but I knew that she had to create what decent memories she could out of a dreadful upbringing.

*

After a breakfast of yoghurt, bread and cheese, Claude had left. Marie was busying herself in the scullery, and Françoise and I were talking.

'You're not your normal self, lass,' I said.

'No. I've got my mission on my mind.' She didn't catch my eye.

I waited for her to elaborate, but she didn't. What could I talk to her about to stop her worrying?

'I'd like to hear more about Cape Breton,' I said. 'I'm desperate to visit there myself one day. My aunt Sheena says it's just like the Highlands, apart from having no hills to speak of . . .' She didn't respond straight away so I ploughed on. 'Do you have nicknames for everyone in Chéticamp like we do at home? In Mabou Sheena told me they had Donald the Fish, a fisherman, obviously, and Ewan Dhu, because he had black hair and needed to be differentiated from Ewan Ruadh, who was a redhead. And one man was called Step and a Half because he had a short leg caused by polio and another was called Ten to Six because he permanently held his head at an angle.'

Françoise couldn't help but smile.

'Sheena says the older generation all speak Gaelic, and the younger ones can, too, but they're encouraged to speak English. And there are great fiddle players. She's taken up the fiddle herself and tells us she's quite good now. I know that most folk are fishermen or coal miners. Oh, and they're all called MacDonald.'

'All of them?' said Françoise, raising an eyebrow.

'As good as,' I replied. 'Sheena goes to Mass, as everyone else does, and works as a primary-school teacher. I don't know much about her social life, though. She doesn't seem to have a man, but she's mentioned dances at a place called Glencoe that she enjoys ... And that's all I really know. Your turn now?'

'All right. I'll start with my father. He's mad about fly fishing. When I was a child, whenever he wasn't working we would go out and cast a line on the Chéticamp River, the Middle River, or his favourite, the Margaree. It was fish or be alone in our house, so we all fished. It's still my favourite thing – and my mother and sister are keen salmon fishers, too.'

I was impressed. 'What was your biggest catch?' I could tell she relished the question.

'Oh, only a forty-three-pound salmon, caught at Portree Bridge with a fly I tied myself. I was twelve at the time.'

'*Twelve?*' I echoed.

She grinned. 'I remember it so clearly. It was a glorious September day and my mother was fishing above me. Suddenly my reel went *whizz* and I knew it was a big one. The rod was bent right over. My mother ran down with a net, and we struggled for ages before landing it in a pool further down the river. We were on vacation at the Normaway Inn – which had just opened and catered mainly for fishermen – and they cooked my fish and brought it into the restaurant for everyone to see. My mother told everyone that I'd landed it and everyone stood up and clapped.'

'I bet they did.'

'Do you fish?' she asked.

I knew this was a crucial question to get right. 'Well, I may have *landed* a few salmon in my time.' I could feel myself blushing.

'Uh-huh.'

'Well, there is a wee river, the Morar. Owen works near there as a blacksmith, and when I'm with him we're always at that river. I've taken salmon out of it every way except with a rod, I'm afraid.' I avoided her eyes. 'The river is owned by Lord Lovat and he has a ghillie, James MacVarish, whose job it is to stop people like Owen and me. Anyway, when he's away, or we think we can get away with it, we go down and string a net across the falls. On a good night we can catch twenty sea trout and half that number of salmon. Or we use a gaff, you know, a long stick with a hook that you . . .'

'I know what a gaff is,' said Françoise in a low voice.

'Sorry. Of course you do. Anyway, we would lie on our chests on the bank and gently tickle the stomach of a sea trout and then, with a flick, we'd have it on the bank. So satisfying.'

Her lip curled in distaste. 'You're the worst, Donald Angus, honestly.'

I held my hands up in surrender. 'And then Owen sells them to hotels. Lord Lovat's probably eaten his own salmon, poached, at the Morar Hotel likely as not.' I laughed anew at the thought. 'Owen got caught two years ago and went to the magistrate in Fort William. He was fined two pounds and warned that if he was caught again he would be sent to prison. He gaffed a fish again that night, he told me.'

I was enjoying teasing Françoise. 'You have hard winters in Cape Breton, don't you?' I asked breezily, changing the subject.

'You have no idea how cold. The ground is rock hard from the end of November until April. Sometimes the road has eight feet of snow along it and the walkway is like a tunnel. The water freezes in the taps, so you have to melt snow on the fire to wash with. I remember a pony was left out one night in November in minus forty degrees. And the poor thing was found the next day, frozen solid, standing up. The sea freezes as far as the eye can see and we walked across to Port Hood Island one time to see my aunt.

'They have horse races on the ice sometimes. I've only seen one, but it was spectacular. A dozen horses flying along, with studs on their shoes; the noise was deafening. At least two hundred people turned up to watch; they set up braziers to cook on and then the party continued at Port Hood Hall.'

'I can't imagine these kinds of temperatures,' I exclaimed. 'Ardnish doesn't really get cold, or that much snow, because of the Gulf Stream. So tell me, what do you do about food in winter? Heating? What about the farm animals?'

'Well, there are mines just south of us in Inverness, so there's plenty of coal and it's cheap. At home we have a stove that heats everything, including the food. The farmers make hay in the summer and all the animals live in a barn over the winter. My mother never has less than three months of supplies in the store, but vegetables are pretty scarce come the spring. We salt and freeze fish and meat and pickle vegetables. There's been electricity in Inverness for a few years now, thanks to the mine, although it only got to us last summer. Father has a telephone for work. It's a party line; three long rings gets the doctor . . .'

'Pardon?' I asked, baffled.

'A party line – we share our telephone line with other people. Madame Dubois at the exchange knows of every ailment in the area – she listens in to the calls.'

'We should recruit her,' I remarked.

'Our summers are perfect. July is the best. That's when you should visit your aunt. We have a great beach.'

'Maybe we could go fishing.'

'Only if you do it properly,' she warned.

I had a warm glow inside now.

'It must be tiresome being stuck inside for months over the winter,' I said.

'Not really,' she replied. 'Everyone is involved with hockey in some way or other, and my family loves skiing, and there's deer hunting for the men. It's never boring.'

By this time we were sitting very close together. I could almost feel her breath on my face, smell her . . . just a few inches more and I could be kissing her . . .

There was a noise at the door, and we straightened up as Marie bustled in.

Later, Françoise and Marie went for a walk and Claude did some chores in the yard. I wanted to be alone and build up a good sweat, so I set to hauling boxes of munitions from the crypt of the church and separating them into packs that could be carried in rucksacks.

That afternoon I gave a lesson in demolition to four of the Maquis. There were Jean-Philippe and Colette, who had got married just before the war started. Jean-Philippe had been sent to Germany but had recently escaped. Only two days before, the Alpini had come looking for him and he had just managed to get out of his house in time. Then there was Charles, the trusty lieutenant of Claude, and a middle-aged woman, Marie-Thérèse, a friend of Colette, whose husband had been shot in an ambush down in the valley a year before.

The Maquis were to be left with a large quantity of explosives after my departure, so I taught them three basic procedures: bringing down a single object, such as a telephone or electricity pole, onto a road; derailing a train; and putting a delayed explosive in a room or vehicle. These operations involved what were known as time-pencils with timings set by colour, for example red for thirty minutes and blue for twenty-four hours. They were also to be left with a box of incendiary devices designed to burn vehicles, houses or aircraft. My pupils were fast learners and seemed to relish their lessons. In turn, they would have the job of teaching all the other Resistance fighters in the area.

As dusk fell, we all gathered together in the kitchen.

Françoise got to her feet and began speaking rapidly in French. 'The name of this operation is Tulip and my field name is Françoise.'

I wondered if I had heard her correctly. 'Please,' I begged, 'slow down.'

She gave me a weak smile and started again, repeating that her field name was Françoise.

'Tomorrow we have a mission that is crucial to this region. We have information that Colonel Kaufmann has arrived in Nice with a dozen men to review the Alpinis' progress. He'll then visit the aluminium factory in Chedde. There appear to be plans to base an SS battalion there.

Kaufmann is notorious for his brutality, responsible for thousands of people being sent to labour camps, and his reprisals are savage. We also know that some locals have turned into collaborators through fear so we must be vigilant about who we trust. London has decided that the colonel must be eliminated and I will be leading the assassination mission.'

My heart lurched.

'Kaufmann is based at le Grand Hôtel Michollin in Sallanches and we have learned that he frequents the hot baths in a brothel in Saint-Gervais-les-Bains. A courier has informed us that our target may visit the baths tomorrow night. Claude is lending us his car to go down at five in the morning. We have organised with the madam that I will be secreted inside. Each time he visits he insists upon a new girl. Tomorrow, that will be me.'

A gasp went around the room, but Françoise continued. 'He will arrive heavily guarded – at least three vehicles.'

She continued with the detailed briefing, but my mind was racing and I could feel myself breaking into a cold sweat. Her *field name* was Françoise? I had assumed, naïvely, that it was her real name; that she trusted me. How foolish I had been. I was just one of her pawns in the great game. I could barely bring myself to think of this planned encounter with Kaufmann. It was only a few minutes ago that we had seemed to be best of friends, laughing at each other's stories. Had she juped me? Was I merely a professional colleague, a piece in a hellishly complicated jigsaw, or, and this was what I preferred to believe, was she trying to protect both of us by pushing me away? Whatever the truth was, I felt sick to my stomach.

The mood in the room was subdued. Everyone knew how dangerous the operation was, and they also knew that the woman speaking would be highly vulnerable. Kaufmann was a brute, a monster. And, were she to succeed, the inevitable reprisals would be unimaginable.

'What is our role?' Claude asked, indicating himself and me.

'You have no role, my friends. You have your own mission to focus on.' Her tone was curt and brooked no argument.

Claude shrugged. 'Well, you have Charles, my number two. He'll serve you well.'

My eyes burned into her, willing her to look at me. She refused to acknowledge my presence. She was purposely avoiding me now. Although I'd only known her for a few days, I felt protective towards her. I wanted to take her aside, talk about this plan, suggest alternative strategies, but she was utterly focused.

The briefing was over. Claude was rearranging the chairs for supper. 'We must eat, friends. It may be a long time until you get the chance again.'

At that point, Françoise left the room. We could all hear her retching outside. No one uttered a word.

I was in turmoil. I desperately wanted to hold her to me, to comfort her, but she kept her distance. Even when we all lay down to sleep on the floor, she pushed her way between the two women.

*

The next morning everyone was up early. The atmosphere was tense. Claude took charge of briefing his four compatriots and handed out weapons: a rifle and Sten gun for each of the men, a pistol for Françoise and a Mills grenade for everyone. 'Pull out the pin and drop them in the accompanying vehicles as you go past, as soon as you hear a shot or explosion from inside the building. Men, find places you can hide with a view of the entrance. When Françoise starts the action, shoot as many soldiers as you can, starting with those nearest the building. Then make your way back here and make sure I know you're back. We'll need to contact London.'

Claude embraced everyone, then shook their hands and wished them luck. Françoise had already left. I had watched her climb into the back of the truck, head up, staring into the distance. I had called her name as the vehicle moved off down the track but there was no glance backwards.

I went to the back of the farmhouse to get some privacy, listening to the truck rumbling into the night. I fell to my knees, closed my eyes and prayed.

'My dear Lord, please treasure Françoise as if she were your only child, keep her safe and return her to me. My God, today is the moment in my life more than any other that I need your help, and I beg you to protect this brave woman.'

I crossed myself.

She was gone.

Claude and I now had an agonising day and night to wait for news. We sat, wordless, in the kitchen, him smoking incessantly, looking around the empty spaces that had contained Françoise and the four Maquis. Now, it was just us. I shivered and flipped up my collar. I must have been looking miserable as Claude pulled his chair over beside mine and put an arm around my shoulder. 'We know how you feel about Françoise, my friend,' he said. 'Don't worry. She is a strong woman.'

I was surprised that my feelings had been so obvious, but I was not reassured by his words. The odds were poor. A lone female assassin and four untrained French farmers – brave though they undoubtedly were – were no match for highly trained German soldiers. I couldn't bring myself to respond.

Claude got to his feet, snapping his fingers. 'Come, Angus. We have work to do.'

Soon, he and I were absorbed over a map and drawings, discussing what needed to be done in our own sortie. We had a week to do it.

'Claude,' I asked, 'did you ever hear of Reinhard Heydrich?'

'I did, about a year ago, but never heard the full story. What do you know?'

'He was head of the secret police in Prague, brutal to the local population, known as "the man with the iron heart". Two SOE-trained agents, Kubiš and Gabčík, both trained at Arisaig, were given the mission to kill him – Operation Anthropoid.

'They were parachuted in and lived in hiding for a while. They set up an ambush on a hairpin bend where they knew his car would have to slow down. He fought back, but died a week later.

'The repercussions were swift. Thirteen thousand people were arrested, imprisoned or deported. Some time later the villages of Lidice and Ležáky were identified as having been involved and there was a massacre.'

Claude knew why I was telling him this. 'We must clear the village after Françoise's mission,' he declared.

'Yes,' I replied, 'and if she or her support team are captured then we must leave immediately. They will be tortured and likely to reveal our whereabouts. Fortunately, we haven't shared too much information.'

Claude wondered whether the villagers should be encouraged to leave right away, but we decided against it. We couldn't be certain that Kaufmann would go to the baths; the whole mission might need to be aborted.

'I think we'll have enough time afterwards,' I said.

Claude banged his hand on the table. 'I will have the place empty within hours if that's what it takes.'

At midday Claude left to meet up with some partisans who were hiding out in the valley, and I found myself alone in the empty house with a feeling of impending disaster. Françoise and her team would be finalising their positions now. She would have met the madam, seen her quarters, and hidden her weapons. She was bound to know that Kaufmann's men would check the room before he was shown upstairs. Would they be suspicious of this new girl? Was the madam trustworthy? Did she have the support she needed? How would she escape?

I paced the room. I could think of nothing else but Françoise.

Chapter 5

It was a hellish waiting game. I couldn't relax until I heard that Françoise was safe. I could hear rain drumming on the roof and went outside for a look. The snow on the ground was now slush and water was running down the track. Would this give our team some cover? I wondered.

Marie came in and desultorily cleaned the living area. I asked about her children; she told me the bare minimum. They were down in the valley now, grown up. There wasn't a living to be made up here in the mountains.

The situation was so unnatural; she knew who I was but not what I was there to do. Claude, quite rightly, had kept her out of the discussions, for her own protection. We simply had to trust one another.

Claude came back. There was no need to ask if he'd heard anything; a single shake of his head said it all. The suspense was unbearable. Dinner was a bowl of soup, our appetites diminished. It would be about now that the action would start. Sleep would be impossible.

'Can you play *le nain jaune*?' asked Claude. 'No? We'll teach you won't we, Marie?'

After the game, which none of us enjoyed, Marie retired to bed. It seemed Claude never slept; he always retired after me.

'You're a piper, Angus, aren't you? Tell me about that,' he encouraged as he poured me a brandy.

I was desperate to divert my thoughts from Françoise and so I began my story. 'My family are well-known pipers in Scotland. We and the MacCrimmons are probably the best known. The MacCrimmons were pipers for the Chief of the Macleods and we piped for the Lords of the Isles, the Clanranald chiefs.'

'Like royalty, yes?'

'Well, there was a rivalry between the two clans. The MacDonalds on the island of Eigg, which you can see from my village, had a fondness for Macleod lassies, and the time I am going to tell you about, they had taken the chief's daughter. The Macleod men sailed upon Eigg in their galleys in heavy snow, but their approach had been spotted. The MacDonalds hid in a cave behind a waterfall. The invaders couldn't find them and set sail again, but an impetuous lad came out of the hiding place and was seen, silhouetted against the snow. The Macleods turned back, landed, and followed the footprints to the cave. The MacDonalds were trapped. The Macleods stacked piles of heather and wood against the entrance and put light to it, forcing the MacDonalds to come running out, where they were put to the sword.

'The Macleods claimed later that it was only just, as we had killed many of their folk at church once, at the north end of Skye.'

Claude looked a little taken aback. 'When did this happen?'

'Let me see … it must have been about ten years ago now.' My face was grave as I spoke.

My host was shocked, before looking at my expression and seeing that I was grinning. 'No, Claude, don't worry! It was three hundred and fifty years ago!'

Claude thumped the table with his hand and wiped away tears of laughter from his face.

The story somehow forged a bond between us. We relaxed a little. 'Anyway,' I went on, 'you asked about the pipes. The *Piob Mhor*, the Great Highland bagpipes – my first love, my passion.'

'Why so?'

'Since before 1715 our family have played the pipes – and always with the same set. We have played them at Culloden, Gallipoli and a great many other battles before that. Ardnish had famous piping brothers called the Georges – George and Sandy MacDonald – who we were related to. My grandfather might well be playing those same pipes at the moment, back in the village.'

Claude said, 'We have these pipes in France, too, in Brittany.'

'Really?' I replied, rather dismissively. 'When I was a boy,' I continued, 'my grandfather would never spend less than an hour a day teaching me; he felt it vital to continue the tradition. "Fewer and fewer men are playing the pibroch," he would say. "We need to carry the torch. And I want you to compete at the Northern Meeting one day. You'll be the only one apart from the Georges in the family to do so."'

'The Northern Meeting?'

'It's the most prestigious gathering in the Scottish piping calendar. I played in Fort William at a competition and was heard by the great John MacDonald of Inverness who put me forward to compete. Apparently, few were chosen. As you can imagine, aged nineteen, and full of enthusiasm, practising for this consumed all my spare time. My grandfather knew who the judges were going to be, and the pibrochs he thought would be set were "Lament For Padraig Og" and "An Daorach Bheag". He also selected three marches, three Strathspeys and three reels for them to choose from. Grandfather's thing was pibroch, though. He used to say that if there was nobility in piping, then pibroch would be king.'

'I would like to meet this man some day,' Claude said. 'I think I would like him.'

'I know he would like you, too,' I agreed. 'So, the time came. It was early September, and Grandfather and I caught the train first to Fort William, and then on to Fort Augustus, followed by the steamer up Loch Ness to the sea lock of the Caledonian Canal. Then it was a walk to the Northern Meeting Halls, me dressed in full Clanranald piper's uniform, with a dirk, a horsehair sporran, the green kilt and gleaming buckled shoes all retrieved from their special place in an old seaman's chest under my mother's bed.

'My heart was pounding when my name was called, but I stepped up to the stage with all the courage I could muster. Well, I made a mess of the Strathspey so I missed out on the prizes there, but then, to my delight, I won the Highland Society of London gold medal for the pibroch – the top piping prize in the world.'

'Pardon?' Claude exclaimed. '*The world?*'

I nodded with as much modesty as I could muster. 'There was a full report in *The Times* of London and coverage in every Scottish newspaper as well as abroad, I'm told. My mother has a box of the press cuttings . . .'

And then there was a sudden noise outside. The door was flung open. There stood three of Claude's comrades: Colette, Marie-Thérèse and Charles, frightened and bedraggled. I looked over their shoulders into the wet night – no Françoise.

'Where are Françoise and Jean-Philippe?' Claude asked as he ushered them indoors.

'Jean-Philippe is dead – shot – and we don't know about Françoise,' replied Marie-Thérèse bluntly.

They slumped in front of the fire. Colette covered her tear-stained face with her hands.

'What do you mean, you don't know about Françoise?' I shouted at them. 'Where the hell is she?'

Claude put his hand on my shoulder. 'Steady, Angus. Let's hear what our friends have to say. And remember, Colette,' he gestured to her, 'has just seen her husband die.'

Colette began sobbing uncontrollably, bringing me to my senses.

'Please forgive me, Colette,' I said, and moved to comfort her, but Marie, who had joined us, waved me away.

'Make yourself useful and put some coffee on,' she snapped at me as she gathered Colette into her arms. I did as I was told.

'Now, Charles, what happened?' asked Claude, turning to his friend. 'Take your time but try not to miss anything out.'

'We met Marc before dawn and went to his house. Marc told us that Cynthia, the madam, was hated in the village – a possible collaborator. We explained that actually she was one of us, a plant, and London had confirmed it. We had no choice but to pray we were right.

'We decided that I would hide down by the river, and when Kaufmann's entourage arrived I would creep up to the big gates at the Parc Thermes where I'd be close to the building. When there was an explosion from Françoise's room and the Germans started leaving, Colette and Marie-Thérèse would use their grenades. And Jean-Philippe would rush from behind the building firing his Sten gun. We didn't know what would happen, we needed to be ready for anything.

'Marc and I went for a walk around the town midmorning to check exactly where everyone would be positioned. We had heard that Kaufmann would arrive well after darkness fell, maybe around nine.

'Françoise had her own rendezvous planned with the madam. Marc warned her to be cautious, that it might be a trap, but she said she trusted HQ's information.'

This sounded typical of her, I thought, confident and trusting of her people. I handed round the coffee. 'This will warm you.'

'Françoise briefed us on all possible outcomes. The first and best would obviously be if we got a clear shot of him as he arrived. Failing this, Kaufmann would enter the brothel, she would pour him champagne and flirt, he would relax and then she would shoot him and escape. If his men discovered that she was armed she would be arrested on the spot. And the final outcome . . .' Charles gazed into the fire.

'Go on,' Claude insisted, though we all knew.

'As she put it, *il me baise*. She would then shoot herself and we would kill him as he left the building.'

The mood in Claude's sitting room was grim. I was severely shaken by what I was hearing. Colette, gripping the blanket draped around her, was slumped on the floor, still being comforted by Marie. Charles said nothing.

'So we were ready. Despite Françoise's protestations, Colette went with her through the town in the afternoon, right to the door of the madam's apartment. Françoise then sent her away. She was determined to go in alone; she saw it as her risk and hers alone.

'We last saw her early evening, walking briskly up Avenue de Genève towards the baths. Her hair was pinned up and she was wearing a brown dress, nylons and high-heeled shoes ... Do you have cognac, Claude? I think I need a drink.'

'Of course.' Claude passed round glasses and the bottle. The room was thick with cigarette smoke. I was trying to envisage Françoise in a dress. She must have had it in her bag all along, knowing from the outset what she'd have to do in it.

Charles downed his cognac in one gulp. 'So,' he continued, 'I was down by the river with Marc, Françoise was in the brothel, and the others were in Marc's house down the street.'

'Were there many people around?' Claude asked, refilling his glass.

Charles shook his head. 'The town was very quiet, presumably due to the downpour. Some Italian soldiers had gone into the brothel already,' he said in disgust, 'and were with those treacherous whores. We could hear music and laughter coming from there. There were two Alpini outside, smoking.

'Eventually we heard vehicles coming up the road. Marc raced off to tell the others as they came into the village. Two motorcycles at the front, maybe five hundred yards ahead. Then another two, then two cars. They stopped outside the building. The two men smoking outside had disappeared. A group of officers got out and went into the building, but it was too dark to see who was who. The motorcyclists stayed outside. They were armed. It did not look good.'

He paused for what seemed an age, then took a gulp of his drink.

I couldn't bear the suspense.

Charles renewed his story, the words tumbling out now. 'It was a good hour, maybe more. But then there was an explosion in the baths, and the sound of a breaking window, a grenade going off. I could see that it was on the first floor where the lights were on. There was shouting. The soldiers ran inside, then one reappeared and fired a couple of shots at a shadow. I ran up to the gates, maybe fifty yards away . . .'

Claude held up his hand. 'Slowly, my friend, we need to understand what you are saying.'

'Sorry, sorry, my mind is racing. I could see Colette and Marie-Thérèse hiding around the corner of the building. Ten more minutes passed. Then I saw the door of the baths opening; the drivers had the engines running. I shot one of them through the car window, dead, I'm sure. Several German soldiers came out carrying someone feet first, covered in blood. We were pretty sure it was Kaufmann. Jean-Philippe came round the corner, all set to open fire, but then he saw Françoise . . . Two men were holding her up. Her right side was covered in blood. Jean-Philippe didn't want to shoot towards Françoise and ... I'm afraid that cost him.'

Charles looked across at Colette, who had composed herself and was listening wide-eyed, face streaked with tears. 'There was a burst of machine-gunfire and Jean-Philippe was shot in the chest. I fired two shots and saw two soldiers go down. Then I saw Marie-Thérèse and Colette running. They tossed one grenade into the car with the dead driver; the other hit the windowsill and bounced back onto the ground. They both went off, and, luckily, the women were away.'

'And then?' Claude asked.

'I shot two more Germans, but one of the motorcyclists began spraying bullets in my direction. I ran through the woods towards our rendezvous point.'

Marie-Thérèse took over the story. 'We were peering round the corner, quite far off. The officers and Françoise were squeezed into the one car that worked. We knew she was alive because we heard her cry out. She must be badly injured, though. I had to stop Colette from running to her husband as men from the brothel were pouring out onto the street by now. They turned Jean-Philippe over; he was definitely dead. I pulled Colette away and we headed off to meet Charles.'

Colette had begun trembling uncontrollably. 'I'll take her away, to her mother,' said Marie-Thérèse, 'and come back later.'

Everyone embraced and departed, leaving Claude and me.

'What will happen now, do you think?' I said. 'Reprisals?'

Claude nodded. 'Undoubtedly. They will come and they will kill people in Saint-Gervais-les-Bains.' He drew on his cigarette. 'And more locals will come to hate the Maquis. But we must not lose sight of the fact that the mission was a *success*! Oh yes, Kaufmann is dead. Your HQ will be pleased, won't it? One dead German officer and dozens of innocent people killed. A truly *successful* mission.'

Claude's anger and bitterness were plain to see. He raised his hands as if he were a priest giving a blessing and shrugged expansively. 'But your Françoise will get a medal when they find out she has been shot.' He avoided looking at me.

I took my leave of Claude, climbed up to the attic where the transmitter was hidden, and, with a heavy heart, sent my report to London. 'We will alert our local people to the agent's capture' was their immediate and unreassuring response.

The sky was brightening outside. I returned downstairs and sat exhausted in the chair; empty glasses and full ashtrays surrounded me. Claude had gone to milk his cows, refusing my offer to help. I suspected he wanted some time to himself; Jean-Philippe had been an old friend. Meanwhile, my mind was on Françoise. She would likely be at the army camp in Sallanches – if she was even still alive. My God, what would she be going through?

I was desperate to head down to Sallanches right away, but I had a sortie myself. I was going to be operating alone and there was a high risk that I, too, would end up captured or dead. Captured, interrogated, tortured and executed – it's just how it was.

Despite all that, I vowed to do whatever I could to track her down, the first chance I got. But how?

There was a soft tap at the door, and in came a man I didn't recognise.

'Hello, Angus,' he said, reaching for my hand. 'I'm Marc.'

Just then, Claude entered the room, clearly recognising the visitor. 'Well?' he demanded. 'What's happened?'

'At dawn,' Marc began, 'three Gestapo trucks came into the town and went straight to the baths, but all the women had fled. Jean-Philippe is hanging from the church tower. No one will cut him down. They broke into Cynthia's house and tore it to pieces, but she's vanished.'

'And reprisals?' Claude asked.

'None yet, but everyone is terrified. People are leaving as quickly as possible, escaping to their summer grazing, or to family elsewhere. My family has left. May I stay with you? Some people in Saint-Gervais will guess I am involved.'

'Of course, as long as you need.' Claude turned to me. 'Have you alerted London?'

I nodded. 'They know. We can only pray . . . Meanwhile we have another call tomorrow to get orders for our own operation.'

That was just what I did; I went to pray. Marie came with me. We walked up the hill to the beautiful Église Notre Dame de la Gorge. The cliffs towered over the building and a massive river full of snowmelt tumbled down beside it; the roar of the water was so loud we could hardly hear each other speak. Although it had felt warm in the spring sunshine, it was bitterly cold here in the shade.

'There is a retired priest here, an old friend of mine,' Marie said. 'We can ask if he will pray for her with us.'

The old man embraced Marie and readily agreed to her request. We sat close together in the comforting surroundings of the church, our eyes closed, listening as his prayer quietly filled our minds.

Half an hour later, we were back outside, blinking in the light. I somehow felt uplifted, reassured that Françoise may after all survive her ordeal.

*

Later, sitting in Claude's house, my mind wandered homewards and to my training at Lochailort. When I first went there it was very small; everyone felt they were part of an elite bunch. There was no bureaucracy. Lord Lovat, the Stirling brothers and others made up the curriculum as they went along, and joined in. If the students were to do a night-time patrol, falling in bogs, struggling through burns and fighting hordes of midges, then the instructors would be alongside them. MI(R), as it was known, was set up there, with the objectives of assassination, sabotage and subversion. Their agents would neither be acknowledged nor defended by their government. The selected students ranged from a baronet to ex-prisoners. One of the instructors, Johnny Ramensky, had served time for lock-picking and safe-cracking. He used to say, 'We'll have a thousand fully trained burglars by the end of the war.' I trusted the man with my life.

The innovative weapons training and levels of fitness that were pioneered at the big house were being widely introduced across the army. I reckoned that by now there must be thirty Special Training Schools across Britain using Lochailort-trained instructors.

Thanks to the influence of Brigadier Gubbins, I could choose to some degree where my postings would be. I opted first to learn about the sticky bomb at the Thatched Barn in Hertfordshire, then travelled from Loch Fyne to Knoydart, teaching what I had learned to the instructors.

Only a year before, Major Fairbairn had been sent to Canada to Special Training School 103, where Françoise had been trained. Since America entered the war they had opened an equivalent station near Washington, D.C., called Greentop Camp – last I'd heard of Fairbairn, he was off there next to teach his 'ungentlemanly warfare'.

I set about writing Françoise a letter, planning to send it to her parents. If she escaped, I was certain that's where she would eventually surface. I took care with what I wrote, aware that it might fall into the wrong hands.

Dear Françoise,

I pray you have reached home and are safely reunited with your parents. God, please may this be the case. I think of you constantly, as do Claude and Marie. It is a week since your job – can there have been any more awful? I confess to being furious with London. Everyone is desperately trying to find out where you are. If you are reading this, then you are alive. Thank you, God . . .

I sat back, sighed, and decided to be completely honest.

After breakfast on our last day I felt so close to you as we talked about our lives. Then you departed without a goodbye or backward glance. I realise that you must have been frantic with worry and preoccupied with what you knew lay ahead.

I cannot bear to think of you being in pain. So, fuelled with some of my host's brandy, I thought I would try to describe my real feelings.

From the moment that we met two weeks ago you have intrigued, challenged and amused me. You made me smile and laugh, and my heart skipped a beat when you glanced my way, or simply walked into the room. With my eyes shut I can picture your face precisely in my mind – your dark hair, the curve of your lips, always so close to a smile, your pale skin.

We barely touched, but in my imagination I hold your face and look deep into your eyes, that captivating mix of grey and green.

Of course I am uncertain whether you think of me as I do you. I can only wonder.

I will write again when I can.

May God bless you and protect you.

My fondest regards,

Angus

Chapter 6

It was midnight. I stood and faced Claude, who had summoned eight Maquis.

'My friends,' I began, 'our task is to close the route from Sallanches through to the Chamonix valley. The Germans plan to use the route through Vallorcine to Martigny in the event of an invasion of Switzerland, and this is increasingly likely, possibly this summer. Germany needs gold to fund its war efforts, and invading neutral Switzerland will at present be relatively easy for them. We must blow the cliffs just above Chedde; this should block the road for months. It will trap the Italian vehicles up in Chamonix, but, more importantly, prevent tanks and other military vehicles coming up the valley and through the pass into Switzerland. Blocking the River Arve and creating a dam would make it nearly impossible for it to be cleared. So, we'll head at first light over the mountain to Vaudagne.'

The Maquis were a motley crew, probably all STO objectors escaping the forced labour being sent to Germany by the Vichy Government. As was becoming their tradition, they all wore berets. Weapons were handed out.

'You will all stay here tonight,' ordered Claude. 'My wife will go down in the Peugeot at four o'clock to check the route is clear. Then Jean and I will go in the truck with the explosives. I'll drive. Let's hope the road is clear of snow up to Vaudagne. Obviously we can't drive through the villages down in the valley with ten men. They know me and the truck, so I should be all right, but, Charles, you will lead the rest on foot over the mountain. Take Angus with you. How long do you think it will take? Six hours, yes? We'll rendezvous at Jean-Luc's barn, you know the one.'

Charles nodded. 'Understood.'

Our team proved typical of the Resistance in that a four-thousand-foot climb, carrying a pack and rifle, and a departure before dawn were not reasons to hold back on a late night with plentiful wine. Soon the room was engulfed in a thick cloud of cigarette smoke, and a heated card game threatened to escalate into violence at any moment. I slumped in a corner, trying to doze. But I was too worried about Françoise. It had been days since her capture. I knew Claude had people in Sallanches trying to find out what had happened to her, but so far there had been no news.

I must have dropped off through sheer emotional exhaustion because I woke, stiff and sore, to the sound of the men busying dressing themselves in preparation. We stuffed hunks of bread and cheese into our pockets; it would be nightfall before we ate.

We kitted up, packed our snowshoes, and set off. For the first hour we were on a forest track so we did not need our snowshoes until we were clear of the trees and approaching the snowfields above. It was icy underfoot, though ; it wouldn't be until the sun was up properly that the snow would soften.

Charles and I talked. 'Have you heard of Jean Moulin?' he asked.

'I know the name,' I replied.

'He works directly for de Gaulle in London. Claude and I met him in Annecy last week. He wants to pull together all the Resistance forces into a single group. We are not keen.

'You see, many are Communist: the Francs-Tireurs et Partisans, the FTP. But we are not and never will be. We are l'Armée Secrète, the AS. If we were not fighting the Nazis, we would be fighting the Communists, you see? There was even a checkpoint between Les Contamines and Saint-Gervais before the war; you had to show an identity card to get through. The Saint-Gervais mayor is a hardline Communist who used to work in the factory in Chedde.'

'Tell me more,' I urged.

'We all have the same aim of blowing up railways and bridges to stop the Germans supplying their troops, but the Maquis are run by headstrong people who all want to be the boss. They want to go it alone, not be part of a co-ordinated group. Whereas for us – the AS here in this valley – we are a tight group of friends who have known each other all their lives. Far less risk of infiltration. The other Resistance groups are much larger, with many incomers, so they are more vulnerable to informers.'

'Yes, I understand. And what of the relève?'

'Well, it's the STO now, the *Service du Travail Obligatoire*, and was signed up to by the Vichy regime,' he said bitterly. 'For every Frenchman released from a prisoner of war camp, France is obliged to provide three workers in Germany. It's forced labour. The Vichy never send their own people, and if the Germans want more workers they just put a thousand more of us in prison, then let them out again in exchange for three thousand more workers. That is why so many more men are joining the Maquis now.'

Charles was growing more and more animated and angry. He was almost shouting now, and I urged him to keep his voice down. All my training had been focused on being covert to avoid ambush. In the army, scouts would be sent ahead to alert the group of danger. The rest of the soldiers would be spread out, scanning the area, guns in hand. But here it was not so. The men trudged along in their snowshoes, talking, laughing and smoking, rifles hanging loosely over their shoulders.

Finally, we reached the top and sat, dripping sweat, in the sunshine. The men were gulping water from jars and fishing in their packs for more cigarettes. We looked east towards Chamonix.

'There, you see? That is the issue,' Charles said, gesturing. 'There are a thousand people in the valley who will not get food after we blow the canyon. My sister's family lives down there. There will be reprisals. And did you know that many Jews escaped through the gorge from Chamonix to Geneva? We may be cutting off their escape route, too.'

I could see how upset he was. 'Yes, my friend, but we need to think on a larger scale – of the millions of people, not the hundreds.'

Three of the Maquis had brought skis with them and idled longer at the ridge. They would get down the hill far quicker than us. Charles and I and the other three set off in the heavy wet snow. Even with our snowshoes, we struggled.

Surprisingly, Claude didn't get to our meeting point before us. It wasn't until the early evening that he arrived; apparently the truck had started to struggle going up the hill and overheated. They kept having to stop to let the engine cool down. Several Alpini vehicles had driven past, causing some nerve-racking moments. He was more exhausted than the rest of us, who had spent eight hours climbing over the mountain. But soon the truck was hidden away in the barn, the men dispersed to stay with friends, and I was berthed in a bed of soft hay. Charles had wisely decided that I could not be explained away to the locals and should be kept out of sight.

'It is too late to do a reconnaissance tonight,' Claude said. 'I will bring you some food in the morning, and I will enjoy my casserole, my friend.' He smiled apologetically as he departed.

I was comfortable enough, but I couldn't help nervously cradling my gun. Despite not having been challenged, everyone must have seen the men in the truck grinding their way up here. I felt sure a patrol would be sent to check. And, of course, I was still fretting about Françoise.

Sleep didn't come easily that night as I went over and over the task ahead. The men arrived in dribs and drabs at the barn early the next morning, with the two long climbing ropes and baskets I had requested. We left the truck and explosives in the shed while we went to study potential sites for the planned explosion and rock fall.

I needed to find a rock fissure into which I could cram plastic explosives, on a slope to trigger a landslide. I reckoned it may take a day or two to identify the best place, transport the explosives and prepare the area.

We set up an abseil point on a tree, a thousand feet above the gorge. I was aware that we could be seen from the other side of the valley, and the sight of us of scurrying around carrying loads and lowering men with ropes would be bound to arouse curiosity. All but three of us had to stay in the barn under cover. It wasn't until late afternoon that we finally secured our place: a twenty-ton boulder sitting on a scree face of precariously balanced rocks. We examined it carefully from all angles, weighing up the options. The worst outcome would be an earth-shattering roar, shards flying everywhere and the rock remaining exactly where it was, followed by German patrols teeming over the hilltop.

As we worked we could see the enormous factory, almost directly beneath us in the valley, in Chedde. Charles had told us that it made aluminium parts for German aircraft and was probably another reason why Kaufmann had frequented the area so often. The factory was powered by the river Arve that flowed south from Chamonix. My mind was wrestling with how we could stop production by blocking the water supply and therefore their electricity, as well as cutting off the road up the valley. It was amazing how much free movement there currently was in the Alps, and still so little involvement from the Alpini. It was bound to change. And the Germans would be much more brutal.

That night I returned to my nest in the barn. Claude arrived with a bowl of cold stew, which I wolfed down. We talked while I ate. I was keen for him to get a message to a British colonel called Bettenfield, who had been in the area for a long time and was based in Chamonix. Apparently he was away, but I needed to meet him and co-ordinate plans

for the Mont Blanc area. Claude reckoned he knew someone who would arrange for the colonel to get in touch
when he returned.

After Claude had gone, I settled down to sleep, quietly
relieved not to be with my rowdy French comrades. Sleep
would come easily tonight.

Early next morning, rucksack by rucksack, the ton of
explosive was carried along a track in the forest, all beautifully packaged in War Office packaging. I'd been to the
Nobel factory in Newcastle where thousands of women
cut plastic explosive to length, added fuses and then rolled
it into shape with brown paper and a Nobel 808 label. The
place was utterly indispensable to the war effort – one
well-directed German bomb would have put back the
efforts of the SOE for a year, not to mention wiping out a
vast area of Newcastle.

Having reached our chosen explosion point, we set up a
pulley system to lower the basket down to the huge boulder and others surrounding it. I was roped up with another
man on an extremely steep face, with stones slipping away
from under our feet, bouncing over the rocks and falling
into the gorge as we gradually created a hollow under the
boulder.

I felt horribly exposed, knowing that the falling stones
and hillside covered with men could attract attention. As
the basket came down to us we would tightly pack the
explosives around the rock, and by late in the day, we were
ready to go. The detonators were in, and wire snaked three
hundred yards up the hill to the plunger. A spotter aircraft
drifted past in the twilight and circled to come in for a
closer look. We froze against the hillside. We couldn't delay

the explosion until the morning as the place would be over-run by the enemy by then.

Charles and another man volunteered to take the truck down to the gorge and leave it as a road block just below where the debris was to fall. Another man would stop traffic from the Chamonix side. The aim was to get the truck back to Les Contamines. Our men were greatly concerned about the prospect of locals getting killed, but we believed the risk was minimal at night, with no one likely to be on the road at night.

At two in the morning, with everything in place, I pushed the plunger. There was an almighty rumble and it seemed as if the whole mountain shook before the boulder bounced into the dark valley beneath us. I wondered what the people in Chedde must have thought as they lay in their beds. An Allied bombing? An earthquake?

There was much cheering and celebration, but we needed to get away fast. Claude was to lie low in Vaudagne, and the others were to make their way back to Les Contamines. As for me, my work here was complete. My next sortie was in Courmayeur, and after that I would travel back over the mountain I had crossed with Françoise.

Clasping me to him, Claude kissed me several times. 'We will pray for Françoise,' he said. 'I have a good feeling about her.'

Later, as we arrived at the path down to the village we were met by a distraught Marie. 'The Gestapo have been here, dragging people from their houses!' she cried. 'They're looking for Claude and all of you. I ran into the forest but I saw everything. We must hide.'

'Marie, I need to go to Vaudagne and find Claude. You'll be safe there,' I exclaimed. 'I need to get across the glacier.'

'Oh, and Angus, we have news about Françoise.'

My heart lurched in my chest.

'She was tortured, I'm afraid. She's alive, but seriously injured. We have a woman working at the army camp in Sallanches who took food to her. Her arm was shattered by the grenade and her feet have been badly broken. She can't walk. They'll be moving her to a prison, but we don't know which one.'

Shaken by this news, I took my leave of Marie and set off by myself, retracing my route. So, Françoise had been injured by the grenade. Because she had succeeded in killing Kaufmann, the Germans would want retribution – and information. I shuddered to think about her plight. I wondered why she hadn't killed herself – she would have had her cyanide pill and a pistol – but perhaps she hadn't had time. Would they know by now that she was a Canadian SOE agent or could she convince them she was a local? Her resolve and powers of persuasion would mean the difference between life and death.

*

My next stop was with the Resistance in Courmayeur. They had had the task of destroying the Italian network of *via ferrata*, the network of steel cables and iron rungs that allowed their troops easy movement along the steepest alps. We were to block the route over the Great Saint Bernard Pass, from Saint Rhémy-en-Bosses in Italy to Bourg-Saint-Pierre in Switzerland.

Charles had introduced me to a young guide, Jean, who was a real mountain man. Tall, fit and muscular, he had immediately inspired confidence in me. After an efficient briefing, during which he pointed out the pitfalls and likely trouble spots where the Alpini might be, we set off at a fast pace the next morning after a night sleeping rough in the forest. Jean was in the lead, and there was no sound apart from the swish of our skis and the roar of the swollen river. The skis were a blessing. I had snowshoes, too, and a white bed sheet, in which I'd cut a hole for my head, so that I wouldn't stand out so much against the snow.

It would take three days slogging up the Vallée Blanche, one to ski across the glacier to Col de Bionnassay and a third to ski down to Courmayeur.

We walked up the valley that afternoon, arriving late at a draughty mountain bothy where we rested briefly and uncomfortably in the bitter cold until three in the morning. We wasted no time getting on our way, anticipating that it would get light by half past five, and reached the Refuge du Plan Glacier by nine before laying up all day to wait for nightfall in order to traverse the glacier unseen, using the stars for light.

Jean knew where all the Alpini observation posts were located. They had good lines of sight and their soldiers were likely to be far quicker skiers than I was. We set off with only the stars and a sliver of moon to light the way. Jean had explained that by aiming for a particular mountain peak we would be on a good route, one that avoided the seracs. We roped ourselves together for safety; if one of us fell into a crevasse then the other could pull him out.

In darkness we climbed a couloir onto a ridge and Jean announced that we'd reached the Italian border. 'I'm going to abseil you down here,' he said. 'At the end of the rope you'll find yourself on a ledge. Put your skis on there, and when it's light, you'll be able to ski off.'

I peered over the cliff. From what little I could make out in the dim light, it seemed to be a thousand feet of vertical drop, and I knew Jean's rope was only fifty yards long. 'Don't worry' – he grinned – 'you're not the first to do it.' I was not reassured.

The next twenty minutes were the most terrifying of my life. After securing the rope around my waist and between my legs, I stepped over the cliff edge.

I inched my way down in the darkness, legs trembling violently, hands soaked with sweat.

But miraculously, as he promised, I soon found myself on a snow-covered ledge, about three feet wide and six feet long. I was right at the end of the rope and there seemed no way possible off the ledge. This couldn't be the place, could it? I untied the rope, gave two sharp tugs, and Jean pulled it up and away. I was alone.

I sat on my pack and ate an apple, waiting for the sunrise as Jean had advised. He had told me that I should put on my skis and, keeping my shoulder parallel to the cliff and facing the sun, simply slide off the ledge. It was a three-yard drop to where there was deep snow and from there I could see the route down he had promised was there. 'You have to trust me,' he had insisted. Yet from where I sat, it looked suicidal.

But he was right, of course. Despite my shaking legs, my pumping heart and a relentless trickle of cold sweat into my eyes, I did as he had instructed and landed safely. I was down and off the precipice within two hours. As I sat on a rock at the bottom, listening to the high-pitched cries of black choughs soaring above me, looking back the way I had come, it looked impossible. I thought of Françoise – she would have been proud of my mountaineering feat.

I set off once more. I still had a long day's skiing ahead of me, in broad daylight, down the Miage Glacier to the town. I would be highly visible, but right then I was more concerned about the crevasses and seracs. I simply had to run the risk of being seen. The further away from the border I was, the safer I would be; the Alpini would be more suspicious of a man approaching the border from the French side. Once I reached the valley and was skirting the forest, my heart rate steadied.

I propped my skis up against a tree and strode into the village as confidently as I could, feeling acutely self-conscious. There were only old women in the streets, who stopped talking and stared as I walked past. My being here wouldn't be a secret for long. As darkness fell, I dodged into a lane behind the main street. The Maquis leader, Luigi, lived here, behind his bakery.

As his wife prepared supper I told Luigi of my route over from France. I was exhausted now, and struggling to stay awake in the cosy little kitchen, but he was keen to tell me of his plans. He had identified a key bridge to destroy and a way of diverting a river that would wash away the road. The explosives were already up there, in a hiding-place, though not yet in situ. They hoped to carry out the operation the following night, now that I had arrived. I nodded and listened.

That night, Luigi, in broken English, explained the details. 'There is a monastery at the summit, and also a major military presence. The pass is still closed to vehicles due to the snow, but I hear it might re-open early next week. The Alpini still use the road – soldiers on foot and mules for transporting supplies. Our footprints will be visible on the snowy bank above the bridge, so everything will have to happen in one night, in darkness. We can risk only a small amount of light under the bridge as the charges are laid.'

Luigi drew a detailed diagram of the bridge, which allowed me to work out where would be best to strap the explosives.

'And the river needs to be diverted at the same time,' he continued. 'It's full of snowmelt, so if we get it right there will be a torrent that should undermine the road. It's so steep there, I'm certain that, without a foundation, the road will be washed down the hillside. We do not need many men as the heavy work has been done. It will just be my brother Antonio and us.'

I used Luigi's transmitter to request an extraction. A Lysander would come to pick me up. There was a field not too far away that had been used for a landing before, in fact the one into which Françoise had been parachuted. I was advised that there was a storm coming and it would have to be in two days from now. Everything would be a rush, and I wondered if Luigi could organise a lift to the pick-up site.

As we talked late into the night, I told Luigi about the possible invasion of Switzerland and how every effort was being made to stop it. I explained that the German High Command would want the Italian army to come over the pass and into Switzerland from the Aosta Valley, to support them.

'If our work succeeds, then they won't get through the Great Saint Bernard Pass this summer,' he replied confidently.

I retired to bed, aching and exhausted. It had been so long since I had slept on a mattress. Fatigue, anxiety and my ever-present fears for Françoise were taking their toll on my mental and physical health.

The next morning I woke late and devoured a whole loaf of bread, fresh and warm from the bakery, with black-currant jam. Refreshed, I assembled a pack full of detonators from Luigi's hoard. I needed to time the explosives so they went off when we were a few hours away. At least, that was the plan.

I boiled some water on the fire and had a badly needed scrub, packed my kit and settled down with a jug of strong coffee. My mind drifted between Françoise and her ordeal and my mother and grandparents. I wondered how the winter had gone. Having enough food for the livestock, and themselves, was always the worry in March. If spring came late everyone suffered.

I dozed off, despite the coffee, thinking wistfully of my visit home almost a year ago. It seemed a world away.

*

Mother had run down the path to greet me, and later we sat on the step outside the house, enjoying the evening sun. Her two collies were at her feet and she was scratching the old one behind its ears. Mairi and my grandfather were there, too, lying on the warm grass.

I remember feeling blissfully happy. We watched the yellow-necked gannets lift on the thermal air, then fold their enormous wings back and dive like arrows into the sea to catch their prey. We saw that the sea was boiling across by Goat Island as a shoal of mackerel or herring stirred the surface and gulls swarmed above. Mother said she had seen dolphins earlier and thought it could be them agitating the fish.

A destroyer had been moored in the sea just beyond Goat Island. Over the course of the day we had seen at least a dozen craft heading up and down between us and Roshven House, as well as converted fishing boats and landing craft. There must have been a big exercise on, or perhaps SOE folk were getting loaded up and taken off on a mission.

We watched with interest from our comfortable spot in the sun, and at that moment, despite the reminders of war, I believed there could be nowhere more peaceful in the world.

One sad occasion which took place during my visit was the funeral of an old lady, a close friend of my grandmother's. We all attended the ceremony and then the graveside as she was laid to rest in Arisaig. It had been a small turnout, as is often the way with the very old – maybe twenty people at most.

Mother told us how she had been to funerals where she had been the only mourner. One such had been Maureen MacGillivary, who had lived at the back of Keppoch until she was a hundred. 'I still wonder how she got the birthday card from the king,' she mused. 'How would he have known she was a hundred?'

Grandfather had the funeral tale to top them all. Apparently, in 1933, he had attended the funeral in Beauly of Lord Lovat, his former boss in the Scouts. He told us there was likely a thousand, maybe two, lining the streets, including a hundred workers and crofters from his estate in Morar. He and Grandmother took the train together, determined to pay their respects. When they got there, they watched in awe the entire battalion of the Lovat Scouts marching ahead of the funeral procession, fifty pipers and a sea of tartan, chiefs of all the great clans, a forest of eagle feathers in their bonnets.

Chapter 7

All too soon it was time to leave. We travelled in Luigi's van to Étroubles, an hour away, leaving at dusk. Luigi's wife drove, and the three of us sat in the back, going over our plans with hushed voices. We were dropped off in a wood. By then it was nearly dark and the town was silent.

'We should go further up the road, I think,' said Luigi. 'If anyone comes we'll see their lights and can hide in time.'

I prayed he was right. With our heavy packs crammed with detonators, our skis and snow shoes, we would struggle to explain ourselves to the Alpini. We strapped on our skis, shouldered our packs and quietly swooshed away into the gloaming. I was carrying only a pistol that Claude had given me; the others had rifles. I was not prepared to rely upon the Italians' fabled reputation for mercy if I were caught.

The road up to the col had been dug into a cliff, with a thousand-foot drop on one side. I knew that if I got the blast right, it would be a huge, time-consuming job to rebuild it. We busied ourselves placing the explosives on the bridge – a short, centrally-arched construction. Apart from the dramatic location it was a standard demolition job.

But the diversion of the river would be far from standard. There was a solid rock wall keeping the torrent in a set path, and on the other side was a major gulley that veered off to the west. My job was to destroy the rock wall, creating an easier path for the water to flow, which would then pour in torrents down to where it would wash away the base of the gravel road.

I found a fissure, put in a pencil detonator set at five-and-a-half hours' delay, then packed the remaining space with plastic explosives. I had some left over, so I decided to set another explosive to go off two hours later, under a small drain on the road nearby. There was a chance this might catch any soldiers investigating the first explosion.

I was satisfied with my work. Dawn was breaking. When the explosions went off mid-morning I would be heading at full speed towards my pick-up point and Luigi would be sound asleep in his bed.

My companions were far faster skiers than me, despite their age. I kept up as best I could, but by the time we neared the village they were a good three hundred yards ahead. Suddenly I heard shouting ahead. Shots rang out. I threw myself off the path into the wood, my heart pounding. An ambush.

I took off my skis, dropped to my belly and inched forwards. Luigi and Antonio lay face-down on the ground. Four Alpini stood over them on the path, brandishing their guns, looking delighted. They would be overjoyed to have killed members of the Resistance. Later, of course, there would be astonishment that these local men had the equipment and expertise to blow up the bridge. I knew I had to get away while they were unaware of my presence. I fought the urge to shoot at them with my pistol but chose discretion over possible valour and slipped off.

My poor comrades. I crossed myself instinctively, strapped on my skis, and set off through the trees to the bottom of the snow line. I thought of Luigi's wife waiting anxiously in her van. She must have heard the shots. I prayed she would escape.

When I reached the snow line I hid my skis and snowshoes in some bushes and set off on foot. I had about twenty miles to cover and, without Luigi's help, had no liaison with Resistance or help with transport. I was going to have to go it alone. I knew I needed to find somewhere to hole up for the day and then head down the valley during the night. I had no access to a Morse transmitter, but if the weather held I ought to have enough time to cover the distance and make my pick-up point as planned. The alternative was a long walk to the safety of Switzerland and likely internment.

I found a quiet spot in a wooded area and dozed in the sun. I had a long way to go, I had barely slept the previous night, and I had no food. I felt sorry for Luigi and Jean's families. Until recently the Resistance had been fighting bravely, despite having few weapons and no military training, but infiltrators were causing havoc. These brave men and women took risks that seemed extraordinary to me.

Through the SOE I'd met some remarkable men and women, and had been promoted through the ranks at a pace that would never have happened in peacetime or in a normal regiment. Who would have thought a lad from a village of half a dozen people, miles from anywhere, would have danced with the Queen or been on good terms with

David Niven, Lord Lovat and Michael Gubbins' father? And even performed explosives demonstrations in front of Winston Churchill himself? Sometimes I found it hard to believe my own life.

*

One of the other instructors at Arisaig House had been a man called Gavin Maxwell. Despite his shyness and love of solitude, we became firm friends and would often go on expeditions together, bonding over our love of wildlife. Very few of the other staff were Highlanders, or indeed Scots, and of those, none shared the interests that my grandmother had kindled in me. Once, we climbed up to an eagle's nest above the big house and peered at the chicks. We often saw basking sharks and he told me of his plans to build a shark fishery on the island of Soay after the war.

He taught weaponry to the trainees and was an obsessive collector of foreign guns. He liked to shock the students, when wearing his kilt, by slowly stubbing his cigarette out on his bare knee – nothing compared to being tortured, he said.

His mother was the daughter of the Duke of Northumberland, though he claimed he could never envisage living in the south again, or indeed anywhere apart from the west coast of Scotland. I found him very easy to talk to, and we often discussed the aristocracy and their presence in this part of the world. Lord Lovat and the Stirling brothers, who were with me at Inverailort, owned huge tracts of Scotland, as did the French Prince Michel of Bourbon-Parma and Fitzroy Maclean – all 'toffs', as I put it to him. Not to mention many of the students and other guards officers, who accepted demotion to the ranks in order to join the SOE.

His response was illuminating. He told me that these men were taken away from their mothers aged six and despatched to boarding school, where they were bullied, beaten and told cold baths were good for them. They hunted in pouring rain for amusement, thinking it all 'jolly good fun'. I could have listened to Gavin all day, with his Cambridge drawl and his love of a good gossip.

Chapter 8

I woke with a start, freezing cold and ravenous, at sunset. I needed to reach the field to the east of Aosta by dawn and get a fire going to the north of the landing site – my signal to the pilot that it was safe to land. I stuck to back roads, jogging at a steady pace until my boots started to chafe and gave me painful blisters.

My hunger got the better of me at one point, and I crept into a henhouse, grabbed the first bird I could see, and rushed out with the farmer in pursuit, shouting and shaking his fist at me. I hurriedly stuffed the bird into my rucksack and limped off as quickly as I could.

I was worried about finding the pick-up point, but when I eventually arrived it was exactly as described; a line of poplars along a riverbank and about three hundred yards of flat field in front. I found a concealed spot in the undergrowth where I killed, plucked and cooked the chicken, skewered on a branch, over a fire. It was delicious – my first proper meal since Luigi's bread the previous morning. I thought about the brothers as I ate. Proud men, a family of bakers. They had been way past the age of retirement and had many children and grandchildren. It moved me deeply that they were prepared to sacrifice their lives for the war effort. Young Italian men had been conscripted by Mussolini and would be fighting the very people their parents were supporting. After the war there would be so many conflicts between families. And the thought of Luigi's poor widow – how she would struggle now.

To my consternation, I could sense the weather changing; there were clouds scudding over the mountain peaks and a stiff wind was picking up. I sensed snow was coming. At eleven in the morning my fire was raging. I'd heaped grass on top to create more smoke. I was anxious that my fire would alert the authorities or the plane wouldn't come now – it might have been diverted to another mission or cancelled because of the weather. But with great delight, I soon spotted the tiny Lysander, rocking in the wind, finally drift in to land.

Minutes later, we were off, although I had no idea of our destination. The baby-faced pilot told me it was Gibraltar. He chatted away about how the war was going and where he had been flying. He reckoned I was to have three days' rest in the naval mess on the island. Then I was to hitch a lift on a convoy that was stopping to refuel before heading back to Portsmouth. I would be glad of a break, though I knew my thoughts would be taken up with Françoise.

*

I hadn't been in London for months and was always delighted to visit. The buzz of the crowds, the pretty girls, the feeling that you were in the heart of things was stimulating, although it was always counterbalanced by the filthy smog and the constant apprehension that German bombing might start again. I read, just before I returned, that one hundred and seventy-three people had been crushed to death in a mass panic at Bethnal Green tube station.

But now, the leaves were just coming out, the parks were full of children and young lovers, and spring was in the air. The war was being won and people were smiling once more.

I was staying with the Gubbinses at their elegant Chelsea townhouse; they had welcomed me warmly and put me up in the most comfortable room I had ever slept in. I knew the colonel's help in getting information about Françoise would be invaluable. He put me in touch with a woman called Joan Bright at HQ, telling me that her connections would give me access to all the right departments, and so I made my way to her the morning after my arrival.

I knew that not knowing Françoise's real name would be a problem, but, to my surprise, the Canadian SOE agent gave it to me after I explained my role to him, swearing me to secrecy. *Sophie Lacroix*. I repeated the name over and over to myself. It was going to take a while for me to get used to.

The Canadian agent was also looking for her. He understood that she had been in the Italian garrison in Sallanches for a week and then transferred, perhaps to another prison or a concentration camp. It was believed that she was still being treated as a French woman, suspected of being a member of the Maquis. If this were true, I reasoned, it was most likely because she hadn't cracked under interrogation.

'We have all your details,' the agent assured me. 'I assure you that we're making strenuous efforts to find her. We'll do everything we can.'

My next stop was the Red Cross, which tracked which Allied personnel had been interred and where. But I was disappointed to discover that there was nothing in their files about Françoise. I couldn't disclose her real name, but I doubted whether that would have helped anyway.

The Red Cross clerk took pity on me. 'Well,' she said, 'it could be that she is known to them as an agent, in which case they don't ever tell us they have them. Or, if what you think is true and they believe she is French, then we won't hear either.' She leaned towards me conspiratorially. 'Tell you what, leave me an address and we'll treat you as her next of kin in the UK. The Canadians will liaise with her parents, no doubt.'

I was touched by her kindness, but the assurance brought little comfort. I knew the Red Cross organised letter and parcel deliveries to prisons, but if she was masquerading as a French woman why on earth would she receive post from England?

I had to believe Sophie was alive. Sophie. I found I couldn't use her real name, not yet. I would think of her as Françoise until I knew she was safe.

Walking back down the King's Road to the Gubbinses' house, I wondered just how much her parents knew. Were they even remotely aware that she had one of the most dangerous roles in wartime, that she may be dead, or in a concentration camp in Germany? What did the Canadian authorities do in these instances? A knock on the door and a telegram with the heartbreaking words, 'Missing in action, presumed dead'? I had to believe she was alive.

I could never reveal her terrible assignation with Kaufmann. But I was desperate to reach out to her family.

Should I write to them? And of course, if I did write, would it be as a man with a personal – perhaps romantic – interest in their daughter, or as a military colleague? It would have to be the former.

I was in a quandary about her real feelings towards me, too. Was she the delightful, chatty, seductive Françoise I had fallen for, or the hard, focused agent who wouldn't acknowledge my farewell?

I talked to the Gubbinses the next morning over breakfast and asked for their advice. The colonel, clearly sensing my anxiety, took me for a game of golf to distract me, even though I'd never played before.

As I hacked away at the manicured greens of the Wentworth Golf Club I realised that my skills with a shinty caman and ball on the beaches and pitch of Arisaig did not translate to prowess with a golf club. After a short while, I contented myself acting as the colonel's caddy as we made our way amiably around the course, talking all the time. I steered the conversation round to Françoise.

'It could take at least two months for reliable information to come back,' he told me gently. 'If I were you I should involve myself in your work and simply pray like mad. There's nothing else for it.'

That news was hard to take. 'Should I write to her parents?' I asked.

He shook his head. 'There would be no benefit, and probable harm, I'm afraid. Keep your powder dry, and let the Canadians deal with her family.'

In exchange, he pumped me for information about how I felt the SOE was going, the quality of the munitions and equipment, morale, that kind of thing. I was happy to tell him what I knew: that the early energy and spirit was no longer there and that it was now a big organisation with all the bureaucracy that you would expect. That said, I assured him that I knew the agents could never go back to a traditional army unit; they still loved the challenge and excitement of sabotage.

The colonel loved to talk about Scotland. He told me there was nothing he liked more than tramping about the lochs and hills with his fishing rod or gun. He had many landowning friends and was always cadging invitations.

We discussed a climbing course run out of Lochailort that I was desperate to go on. Having been properly shown up by Françoise in France, I wanted to improve my skills. The course was a month long and involved tackling the challenging Cuillin Ridge in Skye, as well as Glencoe. I felt that if I was going back to the Alps, it would be invaluable.

The colonel agreed, and later that day I met with my section leader at Baker Street. He said I could go on the course, but it would use up outstanding leave. I was happy to agree. Afterwards I was to take an advanced French-language course to gain more confidence, then visit both Brickendonbury Manor and Stodham Park for briefings on weaponry advances. Only after all this was completed would I return to the routine of visiting the various training centres in my role as an instructor.

I was positioning myself to go back to France. There were rumours that the Lovat Scouts were going to be trained for winter warfare so that they could be involved in the relief of Norway, and I was pleased when my section leader confirmed that I could do so. My list of tasks would include two weeks with the Norwegian Special Operations Group who had requested munitions instruction. I was greatly looking forward to helping them.

Now a well-paid sergeant, able to plan my own itinerary, do a job I relished and spend a lot of my time where I wanted to be – in the Highlands – I should have been the happiest man in the army. But thoughts of Françoise haunted me.

A week later I returned to Lochailort to discover that Major Wedderburn, the chief climbing instructor, was away on business. I grabbed the opportunity to slip back home for a couple of days. I had last spent time in Peanmeanach the best part of a year ago and I longed to see everyone.

I commandeered one of the navy canoes for the trip. It was a glorious spring day. With the tide going out, I paddled down the loch, clinging to the Ardnish shoreline so that I could report on the wildlife to my grandmother. She always quizzed me on what I had seen. I noted a pair of eider duck, a heron and a handful of seals with their adorable pups that I got within a few feet of, before they slipped into the water. I trailed a line of nylon with baited hooks behind and was certain of arriving with a haul of sea trout and mackerel. I could feel weeks of tension melting away as I powered happily homewards.

I kept my eyes out for the sheep, too. The lambing was finished and I was heartened to see a good number of twins. I had noticed in the south or abroad how ugly their lambs were compared to our pretty Blackface ones and I took great pleasure watching them gambol in the sunshine.

En route I dropped into the farmhouse at Laggan and had a wander around. Grandmother must have stayed there a fair bit during the lambing. It was just as I remembered, well-maintained and comfortable, though I noticed that some improvements could be made. I couldn't help but think it would be the ideal place to be married with a family. In fact I could think of nothing better. But the pleasure was bittersweet. My hopes for Françoise were fading.

I wandered inside the farmhouse, imagining what she might do to the place to make it a home for us. Would she even like it? I smiled, despite myself. Of course she would. Everyone loved it here; it had a special magic that was impossible to describe unless you had seen and felt it for yourself. I imagined myself leading her from room to room, telling her she could do as she pleased to make it her own. The silence, the cracks in the windowpanes and the threadbare curtains seemed to mock me as I indulged in my fantasy of Françoise and our children at home here. Sadly I headed back to the canoe on the foreshore.

As I paddled west, it was obvious why May and June were agreed to be the best time of the year in the Highlands – they were the driest months, and the midges had not yet arrived. The animals were birthing and the hills were turning green with new grass. In the old days it was when food became more plentiful after the long, hungry winter, and you no longer lay at night shivering in your damp bed.

I felt my spirits rise as I neared the beach at Peanmeanach. My mother rushed down from the house and engulfed me in an enormous hug as I clambered out of the canoe. I looked up to see my grandparents and Aunt Mairi waving from outside their houses.

'You're home,' Mother kept repeating, 'you're home, my brave boy. We've missed you so much.'

My impressive haul of fish was welcomed for dinner and my grandfather opened a bottle of Long John that he had been saving for just this sort of occasion.

'Just as well we don't get any passing visitors. I'd have been tempted to open it before now,' he said, proudly showing me the bottle.

After dinner, when I'd listened with great interest to how the lambing had gone, we had the obligatory discussion about the weather and what a cold winter it had been, how Owen was, what news there was of Father Angus, who was ailing, and who had died in the area. It was as though the whole community was there in the room.

Later, after the plates had been tidied away, the whisky came out. The opening was a ritual: the cork pulled, a sniff to savour it, then a thumbful carefully poured into Grandfather's treasured glasses with the Long John trademark on them. We each added our favoured quantity of peaty water, and raised our glasses for the toast. '*Sláinte*.'

'There must be a million men in Scotland who would kill to be drinking this tonight,' said Grandfather happily, thumping the cork back in. We'd be stringing our measure out for a couple of hours yet.

Because of our family connections, the ebbs and flows of the success of Long John Whisky were keenly watched. At their peak, the distilleries in Fort William had employed a workforce of two hundred men, working in the maltings, the cooperage, bottling, distribution and every other aspect of the trade. Prohibition had been a hard blow in the previous decade. Now, no whisky could be bought in Britain;

war measures meant almost all of it had to be sold to America because Britain needed their money. Besides, the barley was needed for food, we were told.

When Colonel Willie died at the outbreak of the war, the MacDonald family sold the distillery to a man called Hobbs. Colonel Willie's son had told me ruefully that it was making very good money indeed for the new owner. Grandfather mused that Long John himself would turn in his grave if he knew the distilleries had been sold.

As we sat happily together before the smouldering peat fire Mother began to press me for stories about what I'd been up to. So I told them what I could about my missions, trying to be truthful while protecting them from the horrors of the reality of my situation. Grandfather was all ears and loved to hear details of the weapons and explosives. Mother and Grandmother soaked in all the information about the way of life in the Alps, how the people were managing for food, how they stayed in contact with their loved ones, what the main dangers were.

There was a moment of silence.

'I was at Gaick doing a route march last summer. And heard the story of the Gaick catastrophe, do you know of it?' I said. A precious measure of Long John sat by my side and I had just waved away my mother's offer of a third piece of cake.

'Tell us, son,' she encouraged. There was nothing the family liked more than a good story, especially if it was one they hadn't heard.

'It's the tale of the Black Officer,' I began, though I was immediately interrupted by my grandfather.

'The what? Have I not heard this story?' he boomed.

'At the beginning of the last century, some men from along the Spey went off on a hunting party, beginning above Kingussie, then on to the pass over towards Blair Atholl. They were to be based at the deerwatcher's house at Gaick at the top of the glen, where they could take shelter. It was just after Christmas. They were led by Captain John Macpherson, a retired recruitment officer in the Black Watch, a man who was disliked and feared in the area. He always had problems getting men to come hunting; they would pretend to be ill or cite a sudden, pressing need to visit family. Anyway, four men were finally persuaded to go.

'Several days passed with tremendous blizzards, even on the low grounds. They didn't return when they were supposed to and their relatives were sick with worry. Now, as we all know, in times of fear or worry in those days, superstition would take over in the absence of information.

'The families were gathered together at night, all sick with worry about their men. A rescue party had been formed and was due to head into the hills as soon as the weather allowed. The fire and candles were flickering in the draught, and shawls were pulled up as the wind howled outside and snow built up against the window. Sheena Macpherson, the captain's wife, proposed they talk to their forebears, long since dead. So, sitting around the table the youngest child of one of the missing men was sat on a wooden spoon called a *gogan* and questioned.

"Will they return tonight?" he was asked.

"No."

"Tomorrow?"

"No."

"When?"

"Never!" '

Mother, Grandmother and Mairi gasped.

'So, fearing the worst, the rescue party was sent out into the atrocious conditions. Later, they were found at the deerwatcher's house where they had been sheltering. The building was completely destroyed, the heavy stone lintel lay a hundred and fifty yards away, and the bodies of the men were scattered far and wide.'

'My goodness,' said Grandfather, grudgingly impressed, 'is that a fact?'

I nodded gravely. 'They believe it happened exactly on the first of January in 1800. Captain Macpherson, the leader, was a soldier fighting for the English army. He was called the Black Officer; not because of his hair or complexion, but because he had a black heart. People in the area believed the Devil had come to claim his own.'

Grandmother sat forwards. 'What happened?'

I was keen to spin out the suspense. 'Well, it was very steep ground and there had been a major snow storm . . . What do you think had happened?'

Mother, Mairi and my grandparents set to with much heated discussion but came to no conclusion. I completed the riddle. 'It seems that they had been sheltering in the house for two or three days in the blizzard. Anyway, at night, the temperature seems to have risen and there was heavy rain, which caused an enormous avalanche. It swept away the bothy, killed the men, and spread the bodies widely. By the time the rescue party arrived the snow had melted – hence the mystery.'

A contented silence and much nodding ensued.

'It has been written that travellers through the pass on occasion hear screams and yells, entreaties for mercy, and the deep baying of dogs. To this day, none pass willingly through Gaick alone.'

'You missed the golden age of storytelling, young Donald Angus,' said Grandfather. 'Before the Great War there were storytellers, men and women, who were renowned for their collections of *sgeulachdan*. For example, before you were born, Angus Peter Gillies used to come and visit from Skye. There wouldn't have been room to stand in here so many people came, and when he was in fine form his tales could last two hours.'

'Sometimes you would hear him tell the same story five years later and it would be a little embellished,' my grandmother chimed in. 'We'd say, "Angus Peter, you know fine well you made that last bit up," and he would say, "And that's the way it was." It's how he always finished his stories.'

'He had quite a life, going from place to place, always welcome, drinking and eating the very best.' Grandfather chuckled, and we raised our glasses to his memory.

I had been brought up like this to some extent. On a November night when it was dark at four and rain was hammering down outside, my grandfather would be busy repairing a fishing net or carving a stick, Mother would be spinning her wheel making tweed to sell to the estate, and Grandmother would be busy about the house, and while they worked they would talk. It would be a titbit of news, then a story, as likely as not about our family. I could recount tales about my family going back two hundred years, in some detail. What would Françoise make of my family's escapades, I wondered. And would I ever learn of hers?

'You know the story of the grey dog from Meoble?' Grandfather asked.

'Of course we do!' we chorused, such was the tale's renown. 'But tell us again!'

Grandfather needed no further encouragement. 'Well, Dugald MacDonald, a Meoble man, left his family and his adored deerhound Elasaid and went off to fight in the Peninsular Wars. After several years away he returned home and heard from his mother that Elasaid had fully grown puppies and was with them on a wee island on Lochan Tain Mhic Dhughaill just to the north of Loch Beoraid. He was warned that the dogs had had no contact with people and barked ferociously if anyone was in sight. But Dugald decided to swim out to the island where he was torn to shreds by the young dogs. When Elasaid spied her master's body, her howls of anguish were heard in the village and people went over to the island and killed the beasts. Elasaid was said to roam the area howling until one day her body was found dead, stretched out beside Dugald's grave.'

We all knew the story well but loved hearing Grandfather's rendition of it.

'And,' he continued, 'there's a second part to the story. It's said that members of that same MacDonald of Clanranald branch see the grey dog before they die. There was an old lady who lived in a Glasgow tenement and she had told her friends she knew she was about to die because she had looked out of the window and seen a huge grey deerhound looking up at her. Sure enough, the next day she was dead. And Sheena was telling me a nun at St Francis Xavier University in Nova Scotia, also a Meoble MacDonald, saw a large grey dog just before she died.'

'These stories are precious,' I murmured.

Grandfather agreed. 'My friends, John Lorne Campbell and his American wife Margaret Fay Shaw, have been recording stories and songs from the islands for many years, and they have been out to Canada to collect material, too. They met in the Lochboisdale Hotel in 1934, and have compiled a grand collection, which they maintain at their home on Canna. These stories need to be kept alive, or else no one will remember them in a hundred years.'

Grandfather raised his glass to his lips. 'Just need to catch this last drop of *uisge beatha*, then it's bed for me,' he announced, putting out his hands so that I could pull him up.

The next day was spent with Grandmother, fixing broken gates, rounding up the tups to trim their feet (they hobbled painfully unless you did), and planting the garden with the seedlings for summer vegetables. My mother and I went out in her new boat. They wanted me to catch some fish for Grandfather to salt and smoke while the herring were in. It was a balmy evening. We rowed around Goat Island, past Priest Rock and then back in. 'Two hours and no pain in my back,' marvelled Mother. 'I do love that boat.' With a heavy load of herring, saithe and gurnard it had been a successful trip all round.

It was a good time to talk on the boat, with no one else around. She had recently received a letter from her mother, Bronwyn, who was in failing health. Reading between the lines, Mother didn't think she would survive the month. She wondered if she should go to see her again; she'd feel guilty if she didn't.

I could see she was becoming upset and didn't object when she changed the subject to my life. 'You need to have a girlfriend, Angus. You're almost twenty-seven. Don't tell me there haven't been any pretty young women turning your head when you've been away?'

Mother had been trying to marry me off for at least ten years now. Every girl on her horizon had been considered. At times it was embarrassing; once we went to a wedding in Arisaig and she had a little too much to drink. The evening was spent trying to persuade the mother of a girl called Mairi Macmaster that her daughter would be the perfect wife for me – 'for a fine young stirk I've got in the byre'.

I braced myself. 'Well, actually, there is a girl I have my eye on.'

She was delighted. 'Go on,' she said, her eyes shining.

'That's the good bit,' I admitted. 'I'm not sure if she has any interest in me, she may well be dead, and she's French-Canadian . . . not one of our own.'

Mother kept her features admirably composed in the face of the painful reality and urged me to tell her more. I told her how we had got on well and had great repartee. I described how intelligent, capable and attractive she was, with a pretty mouth that turned up at the edges, always on the verge of smiling. But of course I couldn't tell her that the last time Françoise had been seen she was being bundled into a car by the Gestapo.

'She was working in France but hasn't been heard of for weeks now,' I said. 'Neither the army nor the Red Cross can find her. And even if they did find her, I'm not entirely sure what her feelings are.'

My mother's face fell. But she leant over to hug me, nearly upsetting the boat. 'You obviously don't know girls, Donald Angus,' she said. 'I'll bet she loves you, and I'm sure she'll be all right. Don't worry too much.'

I needed to leave at lunchtime on the Sunday, so we agreed that we'd go to Mass at Polnish so that I could proceed directly to Arisaig. My heart was full of emotion as Grandfather and I got out our pipes first thing. We stood outside the house, playing a few tunes together. There was nothing more exhilarating than playing with him – my grandfather, friend and mentor. I was a bit rusty and his fingers were stiffening, but we were pretty chuffed with ourselves. Grandfather's eyes were glistening with pleasure and he could barely stop smiling as we played. We took it in turns to play the venerable Clanranald pipes. The drones were pitch-perfect; she always tuned beautifully. I knew with a stab of pride that if I never saw him again, this memory of us – facing across the loch, with the skirl being echoed by the hills and the sun shining over Roshven hill – would stay with me for ever. Later, I paddled down the loch to Arisaig, with my heart bursting with contentment.

The next day eight commandos and I passed the same church on the puffer train that was taking us towards Skye where we embarked on the most intensive training regime I had ever undergone. We went from amateur climbers to skilled mountaineers, capable of tackling extreme pitches within a week. The weather turned from glorious at the start to a downpour on the final day when we tackled the Inaccessible Pinnacle on rocks as slippery as greased glass and with visibility as far as the end of my nose. We did sea-cliff assault training from canoes, and learned how to wrap up our clothing, place our rifles on top and swim across a loch, pushing the bundle ahead of us so that the kit remained dry.

The highlight was undoubtedly submarine training, where we practised loading and unloading canoes and launching sea raids. We undertook a two-day diving course during which we learned how to attach limpet mines with timers to sea vessels and escape unseen. One day we were dropped off opposite Dunvegan Castle. We proceeded to scale the walls with grappling irons and scared the wits out of poor Flora MacLeod who lived there.

The last two weeks were spent in Glencoe: ice-climbing on the Rannoch Wall of Buachaille Etive Mòr and abseiling down Crowberry Tower in darkness. We would often repair to the Clachaig Inn at the end of the day. Over a pint of beer I told Sandy Wedderburn about my night ski across the glacier and the abseil above Courmayeur. There wasn't much he hadn't done himself, but I could tell he was pretty impressed and I enjoyed sharing my experiences with him.

By the end of the month, from a climbing perspective, I reckoned I could manage most of what the Alps could throw at me. I would now be able to hold my own climbing with Françoise, and fantasised about climbing in the Rockies with her after the war was over – God willing. Wedderburn was a Lovat Scout, and he marked my report card in such a way that I would be recognised as an expert in mountain warfare. I longed to tell Françoise.

I returned to Arisaig after the course, and was called in to see Colonel Balden.

'I have a letter for you, Sergeant Gillies,' he said, passing it over. 'You have been selected to go to Mons on the officers' course.' He reached across, smiling, and shook my hand. 'Congratulations, I believe strongly you will make an excellent officer. You leave tomorrow night on the sleeper.'

I was completely astonished and didn't utter a word. Afterwards I wondered whether Brigadier Gubbins had had a hand in my promotion. It was highly likely. His wife had told me, one evening in London, how he felt I was every bit as capable as their Michael, who was now a captain.

I knew my mother would be thrilled; my grandparents, too. I couldn't resist telling them, so I promised my superiors that I would be back at camp before nightfall even though it was a three-hour run each way.

As I ran across the rough terrain, I thought proudly of how such a big step up would surely balance things in Françoise's parents' eyes – going from being an uneducated tenant farmer to receiving a King's commission! But then a stumble on a hidden rock brought me to my senses. Why was I even considering this scenario? It was futile.

I picked myself up and ran on.

Chapter 9

Françoise

I lay on my left side, my face against the wall, in excruciating pain. I hadn't been dragged out by the guards for several days now. Maybe they had finally accepted my story? I had come so close to admitting everything. I had wanted to die. All that kept me from blurting out the truth was letting down the others, and knowing that Angus, Claude and his people would be hunted down. I thought of all the doubts expressed about women being agents; how they lacked the courage. I was the first woman in Camp X and I just could not let the side down.

My right arm had borne the brunt of the blast. I had put the grenade between Kaufmann and myself in the bed as he was dozing, then counted. I knew I had seven seconds, and I planned to throw myself to the side, but the grenade went off prematurely. The blast was horrendous. When I came to, I forced myself to look down at my arm. The skin was hanging off, and I could see bits of metal embedded in the flesh. I knew immediately that the humerus was shattered – a horrific sight – yet I felt no pain. I was numb. In shock.

Kaufmann's men were there in seconds. They dragged me downstairs, bundled me into the back of a truck and drove me to Sallanches. The men were brutal; they dragged me into the camp, ignored my wounds and immediately started to interrogate me. In our training we had been told at length about what to expect, but nothing could have prepared me. Nothing. It became clear immediately that they assumed I was a French member of the Maquis.

There was a woman in the interrogation room who sat silently taking notes, betraying no reaction to my screaming. But when she and I were alone she came over to me and wiped my forehead, complimenting me on my bravery. Her sympathy seemed genuine, and I felt she may have been on the side of the allies. I briefly contemplated asking her to get a message out that I was not talking and was alive, but I realised that could be a costly mistake. Why should I trust her?

Even in my agony I came to acknowledge that the SOE in Britain had been scrupulous in my preparation. Just before deployment I had spent a week at Tempsford, where I was measured and fitted with genuine French clothing and boots made in the Alps, made using worn fabrics and tatty leather. My purse contained French francs and the identity card of a real woman called Françoise Villeneuve, along with a pack of Gauloises cigarettes and a local bus ticket. Even the expensive Canadian fillings in my teeth, put in by a friend of my father's, had been replaced with terrible French ones. I had had a cyanide pill in the pocket of my coat, but I had been so preoccupied I had stupidly left it behind when I left Marc's house.

The Gestapo wanted the names and addresses of my accomplices: who was the leader of the Maquis in the area?

Who ordered the assassination? Did the orders come from England? Were there British in the valley? My main protagonist was a pugnacious, heavily-muscled little man. I dreaded being alone with him. He had a truncheon and my wounded arm was its target. I flinched every time he brandished the truncheon near me, and I could tell he enjoyed my fear.

Holding my head underwater in a bucket was another tactic; I came close to drowning many times. I was tied to a chair and then, his face inches from mine, he would drive the base of the truncheon down on my feet every time I said I didn't know. My toes became a bloody, broken mess. Then I would be dragged back to my cell.

After a few days, they must have realised I was not going to talk because they left me alone. They finally sent for a French prison doctor who tried to repair my injuries, but there was only so much he could do. He had no drugs to ease my pain and no food to stave off my hunger.

That same woman from the interrogation room became my saviour; she brought me morsels of cheese and bread when she could and a heavy coat which helped when I was feverish. I wondered if she could tell I wasn't French, but of course I daren't ask, and she certainly wasn't saying.

As I lay in the long hours of darkness and solitude I thought of Angus. I regretted leaving him without a glance or a kind farewell. As my mission had loomed closer it had dawned on me that it would probably be the death of me so I had to steel myself. But our time together had been so intimate it was hard to switch off my emotions. I remembered one moment in particular when I knew he was about to kiss me. I had so wanted him to.

I pictured his bewildered expression as I cut him dead. Angus was a good-looking man, there was no doubt; strong physique, nearly six foot tall, freckled, sunburnt skin and sandy-red hair, and, best of all, that ready smile. I remembered him looking at me intently that last morning – was it really just a few days ago? He must have assumed I had been executed by now. What must he be going through? I fell into a restive sleep with him on my mind.

There were few Germans in the building; almost all were Alpini. I noticed that there was no respect between the two factions; the Germans constantly bullied the Italians, barking orders and pushing them around. The Italians didn't fight back, but their resentment was clear. My saviour whispered to me that the kitchen workers often peed in the Germans' soup. It was my only smile of the week.

Without any notice, I was taken in a truck to a railway station and then endured a cramped and agonising two-day journey in a goods train full of other prisoners. There was a bucket for our waste, but with my crushed feet I couldn't get to it. I lay, utterly ashamed, soaked in my own urine. At one point, bread was passed around but I couldn't make my way through the scrum. Fortunately, an old man with kindly eyes shared half of his crust with me.

It was well below freezing at night; we huddled against each other for warmth. Two people died. I felt that all humanity had gone. At Camp X we were told that the closer one gets to permanent confinement in a prison or concentration camp the harder it is to escape and the closer you are to death. But escape was beyond me, with my crippled feet and broken arm.

We finally arrived at Fresnes Prison in Paris. It was a civilian prison, with a German commandant and French staff. It was a relief to be sent to a French prison; I had a chance of survival here, whereas in a German prison or concentration camp my chances of remaining alive would have fallen to zero. It remained vital that my true nationality was not discovered. I prayed that the Canadian military or the Red Cross wouldn't use my field name to track me down; my cover would be blown immediately. I needed to remain a French internee.

I was put in a women-only cell, mercifully. The Red Cross delivered parcels and post to some prisoners, though I, of course, received nothing.

My parents would have received the 'Missing in action, presumed dead' letter already. They would be distraught. They hadn't wanted me to join the army at all. It had been my wish alone. I was sure they would assume I had some kind of administrative role; in any event, they knew it was hush-hush and I'd told them I was based in London. They'd almost certainly never have heard of the SOE. Who had in Canada? It was a secret organisation with only a couple of hundred agents who had been told at the outset that if we were captured the Canadian government would deny any knowledge of us.

Fresnes was huge, holding thousands of prisoners. I soon discovered that the secret to survival was to lie low, not talk to others, be invisible. Food was sparse and barely edible. My only break was to be there as the weather was beginning to warm up. I was told people actually froze to death in the winter months. There were British and American prisoners, and many members of the Maquis, I was told, but I had no contact with them. The French guards were especially cruel; armed with heavy batons and moving around in groups of three or four, they took pleasure in cornering individuals and thrashing them until their bones broke. Every day people would disappear – to be executed, we could only assume. One of the women whispered to me, 'I know that guard. He's from my town, and after the war, believe me, he will die. I have him marked.'

A nervous, pale-faced lawyer named Alexandre was eventually assigned to me. After hearing my story, he exclaimed thoughtlessly how he was amazed that I hadn't been shot long before, or shipped to a concentration camp. He wondered whether one of the Italians had done me a favour in Sallanches, perhaps altering the instructions on the paperwork. He told me that the judge would decide whether I lived or died, and he was Vichy. He recommended that I plead guilty and get it over and done with, put my trust in the slim chance of the judge's leniency.

But I wanted to fight, make a case for having been blackmailed by the Resistance into killing Kaufmann, to claim that I was coerced. Privately, I feared it was a lost cause, but after having gone through so much I couldn't simply leave my fate in someone else's hands without a struggle. Perhaps my case would be delayed – in which scenario my wounds would have a chance to heal. And the tide was turning against the Axis forces . . . I was determined to hang on to hope, however weak my situation appeared to be.

I had twenty-two hours a day to lie on my wooden bench, consider my position and think of home. At my lowest ebb I found myself thinking about when I was little, when my beloved dog was caught in a trap and had to be shot by my father. As I wept in bed those many years ago my mother had wrapped her arms around me, consoled me with tender words. My distraught father had ridden to Judique overnight to get another puppy for me to greet at breakfast.

And, of course, I thought of Donald Angus, my fine Scottish gentleman. Kind and considerate. I saw how Claude and his men had respected and liked him, too. And yet, when I'd told him my father was a doctor, my mother a headmistress, and that I had been to university, I could see that he was overawed. I sensed that he felt somehow inferior – an uneducated farmer. I wished I had made it clear how thoughtful and intelligent I considered him to be and hoped he could tell I knew I wasn't superior to him.

My father took people as he found them. I knew he would appreciate Angus's qualities. Mother would take longer; although charming and outgoing, she took her time getting to know someone properly before forming an opinion of them, but once someone gained her respect, she would be a staunch ally for life.

I thought of writing a letter to Angus and sending it care of his mother through the Red Cross. It would have to be in French, though. I spent a lot of time considering what I would write. Should I be bold and tell him that I thought about him the whole time, that I wished he had kissed me when we were so close together in Claude's house? It would be strange to be so forward . . . but, as much as I longed to express my feelings, of course I knew I could not. A letter would be read before it left the prison and my cover would be doubted.

But, as the weeks passed, my fondness for Angus grew. I'd had little romance in my life, and maybe the solitude and the physical pain I was in drove me towards him as a source of distraction and comfort. Whatever it was, I needed to think that he might love me, that right at that moment he was thinking of me. I wrapped my arms around myself, imagining his embrace.

There had been a boy at St Xavier, but he had been too showy and arrogant, so I saw him off, and then there was another at Camp X, though that had been quite different. I found myself developing genuine feelings for him. He was handsome and attentive, and I enjoyed the courtship until I discovered to my horror that he was married. I was deeply hurt and furious at his deceit. Since then I had avoided close attachments.

The other women in my cell were friendly. We looked after each other. They all knew each other well by this point, and so when I arrived they bombarded me with questions: where did I live? Which school did I go to? Are you married? I used to joke with them that they were far more effective interrogators than the Germans. I suspected they knew I wasn't truly French; I occasionally slipped up and said things that I knew wouldn't have rung true. But I felt safe with them.

My toes were healing slowly. Every day I would massage them gently. After a while I could hobble to the canteen, though my right arm still dangled uselessly. The muscles were missing from my biceps but the bone was healing well. I was learning, with difficulty, to do most things with my left hand. I was glad Angus couldn't see me like this. I was emaciated, crippled, and my hair hadn't seen soap or a brush since Les Contamines.

I was informed that my trial date was fixed for the 26th of June – a whole month away.

Chapter 10

Angus, the summer of 1943

As I sat in the dining car of the sleeper rattling across Rannoch Moor I considered my promotion to officer. Until now, my rapport with men from my background was equal, but all this was about to change. I know that I would always be a Highland lad at heart. I had no pretensions and could mix with everyone, from a mess orderly to a general. I wouldn't want my friends to think I was above them in any way, and even though they might have to salute me on a parade ground in future, it would be with a smile or wink.

In London I changed trains for Aldershot.

Because I had risen through the ranks, I was excused the first two months of the officers' course and so had no need of fitness training, map reading or firearm skills. Just a month of strategy, tactics and planning, tank warfare, knowledge of the Axis forces and of our Royal Navy and Air Force. I was already competent with explosives and climbing, and I passed on some of those skills to the rest of my intake. Of over two hundred new recruits, only a dozen of us had risen through the ranks. We were considerably older than the others, typically in our mid- to late twenties compared with their late teens. We felt like their fathers as we guided these lads, fresh out of school and keen.

The course was surprisingly behind the times; we were still taught horse riding, and we seasoned men knew that in a trench the only reason officers carry a pistol is to shoot those who don't advance. A Sten gun was what was needed when faced with the enemy. Hours were spent 'dressing from the right', marching up and down in step, and presenting arms. Nothing on how to avoid trench foot, how best to stay dry, and what kit you could take that was not part of army issue, to give some semblance of comfort.

At that time I had been in the army for only three and a half years, yet the youths of seventeen treated me, at twenty-seven, like a general with a glowing campaign history. I must admit I rather enjoyed it. The Canadian Army was also based in Aldershot and we used to arrange shooting and football competitions against them. I asked a couple of officers if the SOE meant anything to them; they'd never heard of it.

The night before commissions were awarded there was a big mess night, held in the opulent Great Hall. The room glowed with a hundred candles, the light of which gleamed off the antique silver and decanters. A band of retired soldiers played on the stage as scarlet-uniformed waiters served us platters of trout and pork. The army was always good at pomp and ceremony.

After dinner, the college commandant made a rousing speech about valour, bravery and loyalty, how the Huns were on the run, and how there was talk at the top of a 'big push'. Many of the boys were accompanied by their fathers. It saddened me to think that it would in all likelihood be

the last time many of them would be together. Junior officers were cannon fodder, there was no doubt about that.
They were destined for the trenches in only a few days'
time, to be the first over the top in every offensive, poor
souls. Nonetheless I kept my expression impassive as we
raised our glasses to toast their success.

A couple of days later, I was back with the SOE, taking
receipt of a splendid, army-issue Enfield motorbike. I then
spent an engrossing three weeks, in the best of an English
summer, swotting up on arms and explosives development
in Hertford and at the Frythe Estate on the outskirts of
London. I was in my element testing silencers on Sten guns
and weighing up the best uses of limpet mines.

But the best piece of kit of all was an object that weighed
about forty pounds and was fired from the shoulder. Called
a PIAT, it was the first hand-held weapon that would
completely stop the Panzer tanks that were creating havoc in
France. It would hit a pillbox and shards of concrete would
kill everyone inside. I was convinced that this could really
turn the tide of the war. The continual research and development of arms was quite extraordinary. Hundreds of the clev-
erest people had been recruited from universities into our
factories and were churning out huge quantities to satisfy the
demand from not only our own troops but also our Allies.

From Frythe, I travelled to Baker Street to see if there
had been any news of Françoise. 'I'm afraid we must fear
the worst, sir', I was informed.

In low spirits, I met my section commander, Geordie,
who confirmed that the SOE had had a terrible two months.
Several agents had been captured in France, and the
Archdeacon circuit members had been arrested with their

codes; this had created havoc as the Germans were now using them to send false messages to the Resistance across France. There seemed to be no positive news anywhere within the SOE.

I dropped in to the church on Spanish Place in Marylebone, said ardent prayers for Françoise, and left a donation and a request for Mass to be said. It was the only thing I could think of to do.

Michael Gubbins and I met up and decided to have a night out in Piccadilly. I leapt at the chance to take my mind off my misery. First we went to the Regal Fish Shop, and then on to the White Rose pub at Charing Cross for a couple of pints. Afterwards, arriving at the Palais with its soaring domed ceilings and deep red velvet settees around the walls, we found it crammed with soldiers from all over the world, plus nurses and women from the factories, all dressed in their Sunday best.

Everyone was exhilarated by the music, the multi-coloured spotlights and the swirling dancers in their flowing skirts and feathers. The band played Glenn Miller, swing and Charleston, finishing with slow numbers for cheek-to-cheek dancing. We danced and smooched with as many pretty girls as we could, before heading outside for a breather and roaring around London on my motorcycle.

It was daylight when we staggered into bed at the Gubbinses' house. My head was spinning. Could there be any more of a difference between this high-adrenaline urban whirl and my quiet farming existence on Ardnish?

For the remainder of that summer I travelled around the various Special Training Schools, training the instructors and never spending more than a week in any one place. I managed to catch the sleeper up to Fort William and see my family for a few days when one of my courses was cancelled at short notice.

As usual, I received a warm welcome from Mother, Grandmother and Mairi, but they told me that Grandfather had a serious chest infection. The doctor had come to see him and had confined him to bed for a week, telling him to do as he was told or it could turn into pneumonia. Apparently he had sulked for a while but was trying his best to be an obedient patient. He was bored, and not being able to play his chanter frustrated him.

Grandmother was never the most sympathetic of nurses, so it was Mairi and Mother who looked after him. I sat with him for spells, listening to him coughing up phlegm and struggling to breathe. Usually he was keen to talk; now he just lay there, his complexion a dreadful waxy grey. It dawned on me that this could be the first time Grandmother had confronted the fact that Donald John might die before her.

She was in a sombre mood that night when I sat with her by the fire, but I decided to broach the subject head on.

'He's changed since my last visit,' I said gently.

She nodded, and I waited as she gathered herself to speak. 'Everything is changing,' she said. 'It's more than just old age and all that it brings with it.'

'What do you mean?' I asked.

'Well, the big change happened not long before your mother arrived here. Before the Great War, we could always find ten strong and able-bodied people to work the big field. Whenever a big storm passed through, the sea-wrack would be piled up three foot high along the shore, and we knew we had to get it onto the field before the next high tide came and took it away again. It was a struggle, right enough – long days with the wicker basket and the strap around our foreheads, carrying the stinking wet stuff up to the big field to mix with the manure from the byre – but it was so good for the soil. Then the Bochan or Mairi's husband would work the garron and plough it in.'

I smiled. 'Hard work.'

'But good work. *Productive* work. Look at it now!' She cast her arm in the direction of the big field. 'The drain is filling in, the fence always needing patches. We can't handle cattle with rushes and ragwort everywhere. Soon it will all be good for nothing. And there's nothing to be done.'

I departed the following night with a heavy heart. I hadn't realised how low spirits were at home. The winter had been hard, and with Grandfather so poorly everyone was worried. More than once, the conversation about moving to Arisaig had come up. 'We must be the last people in Lochaber in black houses,' Mother had said. 'Even on Knoydart, that dreadful Nazi supporter Lord Brocket has rebuilt the houses.'

I couldn't help but wonder, as I switched off the berth light in my sleeper compartment and settled down to sleep, whether there would be a community at Peanmeanach for me to return to.

*

My next stop was to rejoin the Lovat Scouts in Wales, where Sandy Wedderburn had been posted and had asked for me to be transferred to help train the battalion for its new role as a mountain recce regiment. I was enthusiastic, knowing that at last it was a role that the Scouts felt fitted them like a glove. The course was run by the commandos, so Sandy and I knew many of the instructors already, from Lochailort and Achnacarry. We had a fine month, climbing every mountain of merit in Wales, many of them at night. I was reunited with my old platoon commander Andrew MacDonald, now a captain. I had a lot to thank him for, because it was he who had encouraged me to join the special forces in the first place.

Andrew and I had a lot in common: three generations of being family friends. One evening, over a hard-to-find dram, I related to him tales of my father's year in Canna helping my grandmother's cousin distill the finest illegal whisky in Scotland. He was a handsome fellow with startling light-blue eyes and a ready smile, and he loved the people of the Highlands, seeming to know the history of all our men and who their fathers and wives were.

At the end of our Welsh training Sandy Wedderburn was made second-in-command of the Scouts, and it was he who petitioned for me to join the battalion in Canada, making the case that I should be made training officer as few in the British Army had the experience I had. I was delighted to be going. Andrew and I thumbed through an atlas to see where the camp in Jasper was in relation to Cape Breton, for not only did my Aunt Sheena and Françoise's parents live there but Andrew's cousins, too. I was dismayed to see that they were about three thousand miles apart. I was probably closer to Cape Breton now than I would be in the Rockies.

I wouldn't be sailing with the battalion to Canada until after Christmas. I was to spend two weeks with the Norwegian SOE at Glenmore Lodge. I had never come across a Norwegian I didn't like or who hadn't impressed me; they had quite a reputation in the SOE. Many of them had escaped from occupied Norway by way of the fishing boats that operated what was called the 'Shetland bus', taking munitions across to the Milorg, their Resistance movement, and bringing back men to fight for the UK-based Royal Norwegian Army. Their SOE unit was called the Linge Company, after their commander who had died during a mission.

There were many stories of their bravery; for example, their ascent of a supposedly unclimbable six-hundred-foot cliff and subsequent destruction of the heavy-water power plant at Vemork, needed by the Germans in their development of a nuclear reactor. This had taken place only eight months before, and had demonstrated ingenious use of timed explosives to sink the ferry carrying what remained of the heavy water. The British contingent, codenamed 'Grouse' had been cooped up for three months in the depths of the Arctic winter before the Linge men had arrived. This heady combination of skiing, climbing and blowing things up appealed to me a great deal.

I arrived at Glenmore in early December, my arrival coinciding with a visit to the Linge Company by the Norwegian King Haakon and his son Crown Prince Olav. They had arrived at Aviemore by train and spent two days at the Lodge with their men. I took Prince Olav to shoot an out-of-season stag on the Rothiemurchus estate one blustery day. Sleet was driving horizontally across the hill and we were soaked to the skin within an hour. We tramped up and down several hills, but the conditions just weren't right. However, I eventually found Prince Olav a beast in the dusk. He shot it at one hundred and seventy yards and was delighted. The stag was an old ten-pointer that we had passed on the way up the glen and I'd had him earmarked in case we had no joy further up.

The bedraggled but exhilarated prince returned to his father, with his face crimson from the stag's blood. I had blooded him in the traditional way.

They were now running late for the London sleeper from Aviemore, so I had to drive them in an old jeep at full speed to get them there on time. What the other passengers must have thought when the blood-soaked royal and his father climbed aboard I can only imagine. The prince had loved his stalking and I was impressed with him. Despite the atrocious conditions, he was keen to come out with me again and so we exchanged addresses. As we parted I promised to get the stag's head mounted on a plaque and delivered to them in London. No man would have slept more soundly on the sleeper south that night than Crown Prince Olav.

I was determined to learn as much as I could from the Norwegians. Every spare minute I had, I pestered them with questions about what they were doing: how best to wax skis, how they dug a snow hole to survive in the mountains, how to fish through ice holes, even how to manage working huskies (although, regrettably, the dogs they had brought over were shot by a local farmer for killing sheep).

With the Norwegian patrols we covered vast distances, over to Fort William to carry out a mock sabotage of the British Aluminium plant, to Falkirk to 'destroy' the Carron ironworks. They managed distances that in my opinion would be impossible to the normal soldier; I was gaining a lifelong fondness for these people.

They were serious men, not many jokes, but strong, determined and always planning for the long term. I noted that, for the rest of the SOE, civilian casualties were seen as the cost of war and inevitable whereas the Norwegians were simply not prepared to accept any. I admired their conviction and thought we could learn from it.

One night there was a dance in Grantown-on-Spey so we loaded up two truckloads of Linge men. I knew an old Lovat Scouts friend of my father who lived up behind Cluny and had an illicit still, and he generously acquiesced when I asked him to part with a dozen bottles of his notoriously rough whisky for the event.

I'll never forget the women's faces when all these tall, blond, blue-eyed, strapping young men sauntered into the hall. Soon, with the whisky going down fast and the men loosening up, there was no holding them back. There were three of us instructors who knew the dances and we soon had the soldiers and their willing partners doing the Dashing White Sergeant and Perthshire Reel. I borrowed one of the bandmember's pipes, and soon there was an Eightsome Reel in full swing. The Norwegians did their own version, much to everyone's amusement, and I later heard the talk in Strathspey was of little else for months.

One Norwegian officer, having enjoyed a dram too many, confided that he was reluctant ever to go home. He'd been spending his free time poaching deer and salmon, loved the whisky and the dancing, and had fallen for a girl in the village to boot. We touched glasses, raised them in the elaborate Norwegian way, and said skol before knocking back yet another measure.

I then had to head back to London. I was keen to go; it had been eight long months since Françoise had been captured, with no news whatsoever, and I wanted to make another visit to the SOE and Red Cross. The latter, who prided themselves on keeping track of which prisoners were at which POW camps, again told me that they had no Françoise Villeneuve or Sophie Lacroix listed. If there was a French person in a French prison they wouldn't be told anyway, so I clung to the hope that Françoise's story had borne out. Being an SOE agent in a German jail spelled death.

After all my distractions and escapades up north, my mood sank. Every night I got on my knees and prayed for her safe return, but in truth I knew I would have to face the fact that she was dead. Right now, there seemed to be no more straws to clutch.

I had been debating for a long time whether to write to her parents and now, as I threw myself despairingly onto my bed at the Gubbinses', I decided to throw caution to the winds.

17th December 1943

Dear Doctor and Mrs Lacroix,

I had the pleasure of getting to know your daughter during her time in London. I suspect you will have received the dreaded official letter; today I spoke again to the authorities here and fear that she is no longer alive.

Your daughter was a delight to me; amusing, intelligent and tender. She touched my heart in the short time

we were together, and if we had had longer I dare to
think she would have grown fond of me.

 God bless you both.
 Yours truly,
 Captain Donald Angus Gillies
 Lovat Scouts

Not long afterwards I went to Oxford University to spend Christmas brushing up my French-language skills. To my surprise I found myself enjoying it for the first time. Although I'd always been pretty quick at picking up languages, my experience in the field had highlighted my deficiencies and caused me to lose confidence in my abilities. The course was expertly taught and I knew that it would make all the difference to my ability to work with the Resistance. Clear communication was critical.

There were twenty of us on the course, ranging from female wireless operators to Foreign Office staff and a few soldiers. We had twelve hours of studying a day with native French instructors, not a word of English spoken, and there was homework at night.

A Christmas lunch was held in the dining room at Balliol College, a truly beautiful building in a lovely city. The College really went to town on our behalf with roast turkey and all the trimmings followed by Christmas pudding and, as I was informed by the professor who sat to my left, the best of their wine from their renowned cellar. It was as if rationing didn't exist. Later, my face flushed from the jolly company and wine, I sloped guiltily back to my comfortable digs, doing my best not to think about all those in the trenches with their meagre ration packs.

Chapter 11

Françoise, Fresnes Prison

As the day of my trial approached, I had become recon-
ciled to the likelihood of being transferred to a harsher
prison and then execution. Alexandre, my lawyer, was not
interested; he was merely going through the motions. I
guessed he must have been paid per trial, and a nominal
sum at that. I learned that prisoners who left to be tried for
crimes against the Germans never came back, so we had no
idea what happened next. We could only assume the worst.
Most of the inmates were there for petty civilian crimes –
theft, assault, avoiding the STO draft.

Shortly after I arrived, one inmate, who was believed to
be the head of the Maquis in Paris, heard about my exploits
and offered to meet me. I was thereafter feted by many of
the other prisoners, once word got out that I had killed a
high-ranking German officer. I met the man briefly in the
food hall and we exchanged polite greetings. My hunch
was that he was just curious.

Beatings and rapes were daily occurrences in Fresnes.
The guards would swagger about the prison administering
random beatings. My all-women cell was a haven of peace

and protection in this tense environment, and we seldom ventured out. As well as the fear of violence, hygiene was non-existent and our diet was miserable. I felt weaker every day. Some lucky prisoners had food sent in by relatives, and occasionally Red Cross parcels arrived, although they were often confiscated by the guards or the gangs. We had heard that the people of Paris were starving, with rats and squirrels being hunted for food. In addition, summer got into its stride and the heat became unbearable in our tiny cell. We didn't get outside at all. One small comfort was that, after all the massage and exercises I'd doggedly persisted with, my feet were much better. They were still disfigured, but I could walk now without too much pain.

On the day of the trial, seven of us were handcuffed, herded into an unmarked van, and locked in. The senior Maquis man was among us; he and I nodded at each other. Vichy armed guards climbed into the front and we set off.

We sat in silence for a long time as the van made its way to the courthouse, but suddenly there was an almighty crash and we were thrown to the floor by the impact. Then there was the sound of rapid gunfire. One of the prisoners screamed; he'd been hit by a bullet which had come through the van. It was pandemonium. The back door flew open to reveal Resistance fighters framed in the bright sunlight.

'Come on! Go, go, go!' they shouted.

The Maquis leader stumbled out, then disappeared around the side of the van and that was it. It was all over in seconds. The rest of us were left sitting in dazed silence. Silent Parisians watched nervously from a distance.

I saw my opportunity. I jumped out of the van, landed painfully, and hobbled as quickly as I could up an alleyway.

How long would I last before being turned in, with my hands cuffed and a prison uniform on? I had to get clear of the area now. It would soon be swarming with police and soldiers. A woman's voice called out: 'Miss! Miss! Here!'

I turned my head to see a young woman beckoning me towards her. She looked around, then pulled me into a doorway.

'Come with me,' she said, taking me by the arm. She guided me through a shop selling kitchenware, straight out the back door and then for a hundred yards along a side street into a small house. 'Wait here,' she hissed. 'I'll be right back.'

I was dripping with sweat, shaking with nerves, and my feet were throbbing. Yet somehow I felt sure that this woman was on my side. Within a few minutes she'd returned, carrying a headscarf, cardigan and skirt.

'Are you all right?' she asked. 'My name's Clementine.'

Shaking her hand, I replied, 'And I'm Françoise. Thank you so much.' I made the decision to go with my instincts and trust her.

'We need to get that uniform off you,' said Clementine as she got out her scissors, 'then we'll go to see a metal-worker near here, a good friend of mine. He can get these off you.' She tapped the cuffs. 'Don't worry, he's discreet.' She draped a light coat over my shoulders and arranged it to conceal the handcuffs.

By the end of the day, not only had I been relieved of my handcuffs and prison uniform but I'd had a good wash, my hair had been cut short, and I had clean clothes on.

'You'll have to wear a hat at all times and keep your head down,' insisted my guardian angel. 'With your looks, all the men will notice you.'

'Are you Resistance? Maquis?' I asked her as she carefully bandaged my damaged arm.

'No, no. Far too dangerous,' she replied. 'I have children to protect. Helping you today is the only thing I have done for the struggle.' She paused, looking me in the eye. 'We all know people who have been dragged off in the middle of the night and never seen again. It's about time I did something.'

I felt there was a lot more to this story, but now was not the time.

'You're very brave,' I replied, marvelling at the courage of a woman with children to do what she had just done on my behalf. She had brought me back to her own home.

'What happened to you, my dear?' she asked. 'Your feet, your arm – and you're so thin.'

I told her as much as I felt comfortable with: that I was helping the Resistance and had been caught and tortured for killing a Gestapo officer.

Clementine sat with her eyes wide in astonishment, her hand to her mouth.

Just then her two children arrived home from school. A boy and girl, aged about six and eight, they played cards and chatted, with occasional shy glances at their mother's new friend. Their mother explained that I would be staying for a few days. They shrugged and obediently completed their homework, and later, after they had eaten, took themselves off to bed.

After a nourishing supper of rabbit stew which Clementine had likely procured with great difficulty, we had a long discussion about what I should do next. I had no papers, and she knew no one in the Resistance. We were in a dilemma. Clementine confirmed that the city was very tense, that a British invasion was expected soon, and that the Vichy and the Germans in the city were conducting random stop-and-searches. She told me that her husband had been in Munich for the past three years, that he'd been taken in the original round-up and was working in an arms factory. 'The English have bombed it twice,' she said. 'He's lucky to be alive.' She had tears in her eyes. I hugged her tight. I was so euphoric about being clean and safe that my jaws hurt from smiling.

The next day my hostess told me she had to work at the shop for most of the day. Meanwhile, I slept like the dead, relishing the comfort of a mattress and sheet for the first time in months. Clementine returned with coffee and bread in the afternoon. I thought I was in heaven. We spent the evening dying my hair black. Angus would hardly recognise me now, I thought. I often found myself considering his opinion on many things. It was an entirely new feeling for me.

After a few days we agreed that I was ready to move. I was well nourished and rested. I had a canvas shoulder bag, a map of France, a sharp kitchen knife, a cigarette lighter, a thin blanket and a waterproof cape. I made a snare using wire and a peg that I planned to set each night for rabbits.

During my training much time had been spent on learning how to get back to England if one was cut off after a mission. This involved seeking the help of the Maquis and liaising with Baker Street. I could read the stars and use the sun to navigate, to some extent, but I didn't have money, a false ID, nor a pistol or contacts. To add to my worries, I was worried about how my feet would cope with the journey and whether I could manage with the use of only one arm.

There was no point in heading towards the coast. It would be swarming with troops and checkpoints, and what chance would I have of encountering a friendly fisherman prepared to take me over? Switzerland was an option, but they were interning Allied personnel rather than helping them get back to Britain. I decided to head towards Spain and, perhaps, ultimately, Gibraltar. Spain was neutral, but increasingly supportive of the Allies now that we seemed to be winning.

Clementine and I had discussed all the options. There was no chance of taking a train as all passengers were obliged to show ID cards, and neither I nor Clementine had any money for the ticket.

'Do you think you could find someone in the Resistance who could help?' I asked Clementine.

'And how would I do that!' She laughed dismissively. 'I don't know anyone. I'm so sorry.'

I had no choice. Walking south seemed to be the only way. My plan was to live like a nocturnal animal, sneaking behind roadside hedges and through woods, avoiding people at all costs, scavenging for food, sleeping in the undergrowth. There were three or four months of summer left before the temperature dropped and the rains began. Crossing the Pyrénées after mid-November would be hazardous because of snow. I had to get to Spain before then.

Before setting off I finally wrote the letter to Donald Angus that I'd been agonising over for months. I asked Clementine to send it for me.

'There's a man I treated badly,' I explained. 'I want to apologise, to let him know I cared for him. If I live or die, I need him to know what I feel. Please, would you keep it until you know it will get there? Maybe when the war is over you could post it?'

I thought about it carefully, tearing up two letters before the final one and vowing he would never know what had happened between Kaufmann and me.

June 1943, from Paris

My dear Angus,

I pray this reaches you.

I know how upset you were when I didn't say good-bye. Perhaps you will have already forgotten me, thought good riddance – I would understand that.

But I hope you realise that it was because I was upset at having to leave you so suddenly. I really was trying to protect myself and you. I wanted to come over and hug you, to reassure you, but I didn't want to break down and cry in front of the others. I believe that you had the same feelings for me as I had for you but, of course, I may never know.

As a woman I have to be <u>doubly</u> brave. I have had a difficult few months, but I am now much fitter, and with luck I'll reach safety.

God bless you, and pray for me as I do for you.

Françoise

I sealed and kissed the envelope, scribbled 'Donald Angus, Ardnish, near Fort William, Scotland' on it and prayed he would receive it one day.

The next morning, I hugged Clementine and promised to visit in peacetime. I would probably be dead if it hadn't been for her brave split-second decision to help me.

I took the Métro at its busiest time to the terminus at Châtillon–Montrouge. Clementine had assured me that tickets were seldom checked on the underground and there were rarely identity card checks. My plan was to follow the railway line on foot as far as Toulouse. There were soldiers at the station but they didn't give me a second glance as I shuffled past them in my dowdy clothes, scarf on my head, eyes cast down.

I had memorised each stage of my journey and my aim for day one was to get as far as the town of Chamarande.

There was no road parallel to the train track, which was good. I got on well at first, though by midday I was getting cramp in my toes; my feet were simply not used to the exercise. But I limped on, scanning ahead for people. Fortunately there was only an occasional woman hoeing in a field, or leading a cow on a rope; farm workers going about their work and unconcerned about me.

At nightfall I collapsed, exhausted. I kicked my shoes off. My feet were horribly swollen. I was only twenty miles into a potentially six-hundred-mile journey. I nibbled some cheese and dates which Clementine had given me, but they were supposed to be for emergencies, so I only ate a tiny amount. I had hoped to walk through the night, but my feet needed rest.

I made myself as comfortable as possible in the hollow of a tree and tried to sleep. The sky was clear, dotted with stars. The South Star would show me the way. I imagined Angus looking at them, too, and felt hot tears welling. I felt miserable, utterly alone.

When I awoke I decided to walk during daylight. This was a densely wooded area; I should be able to move fairly freely without being seen. If it turned out there were too many inquisitive people around, then I'd revert to my nocturnal plan. I cut a good strong stick to take the weight off my feet and to fend off dogs if necessary. In Camp X, Major Fairbairn had taught us many useful things one could do with a stout stick.

The railway line was a hundred yards away on my right. Now and again I would see a troop or freight train and was careful to take cover as it passed. I noted what they were carrying: fuel containers, occasionally tanks, even pigs and other livestock going to the front for food.

My need for food was now urgent. I arrived at the outskirts of Chamarande that evening, a whole day later than I had hoped, but fortunately spotted a garden full of ripe fruit and vegetables, and, seemingly, no dog to alert the owner. I waited for nightfall before climbing the fence and scooping up as much as I could carry: a lettuce, peas, tomatoes and a melon. At a safe distance, I sat down and feasted. I'd tasted no fresh fruit and vegetables since I had been back home in Canada.

I had hoped my journey would be an intrepid, stealthy trek, but the reality was a slow and agonising hobble, with opportunistic thieving from people who badly needed food themselves. It took me a week to get as far as Orléans.

One night there was a violent lightning storm and torrential rain. Terrified that the tree I was sheltering under would be struck, I cowered for hours, drenched, frozen and aching all over. I couldn't imagine anyone more miserable than I was that night.

Now and again, I would stumble across the odd farmer keen to pass the time of day, but, on seeing me close up – with my matted hair, face and hands ingrained with dirt, ragged clothes and battered shoes – they quickly moved away. Although my night-time progress was slow, it was steady. I followed the railway track, sometimes picking my way across the sleepers, ducking out of sight when trains trundled by.

I was approaching Vierzon now and the pain in my feet had been increasing. 'Run through the pain!' had been our watchword at Camp X during training, but this constant slog, day after day, was pushing me to my physical limit. I sank to my knees beside the train tracks and wept.

I had a lot of time to think as I walked. Not having company was my idea of hell; I had always needed and enjoyed the stimulation of people and conversation around me. The solitude was difficult for me, and sometimes I would sing to myself just to hear a voice. I constantly thought about what I'd do if I ever made it back to Britain. And would I ever make it home to Canada and my family?

It wasn't until Châteauroux, where I had to cross a number of major roads at first light, that I spied a long convoy of German vehicles parked by the roadside while their drivers slept. I should have crept past, but I felt a powerful urge to do something – to fight, to destroy the convoy before it got to the front line and wreaked havoc.

Everything I had been doing of late had been so cautious, so defensive, that the sight of the enemy triggered a rage in me.

There was a young, unsuspecting guard on duty, leaning against a tree, smoking, bored. I seized the moment. I drew my knife and crept up to him from behind. With one slash I cut his throat. He gurgled and spluttered quietly as I lowered him into the undergrowth. Then I crawled under the line of vehicles cutting fuel pipes until a cry finally went up. Someone had smelled the fumes. Rolling into the ditch, I slithered away. I had hoped to light the fuel and blow the convoy sky high, but at least I had caused serious disruption.

I felt energised, elated. When I was sure I wasn't being pursued, some distance away, I collapsed in a soft thicket, breathing hard, heart racing. 'Kill or be killed,' Major Fairbairn had drummed into us. The convoy would be in chaos and there would be little chance of a hunt for me. Did I feel any regret for that young boy's death? No. I wasn't just pursuing my own personal freedom, I was helping the war effort.

I should have known that my euphoria would not last long. The following day, I developed a fever, probably from drinking dirty water from a stream on the outskirts of a small town. I lay immobile for two days, semi-delirious, suffering terrible sweats and weak as a kitten. In my delirium I closed my eyes and dreamed. I was in my bed at home, the house quiet; just the rhythmic hiss of waves breaking on the shore. The door opened. I smiled. I knew it was Angus. I pulled aside the bedclothes to allow him in. His hands explored my body as we kissed. I was hungry for him, as he was for me. And then it changed. Kaufmann's face was bearing down upon me. I sat bolt upright, drenched in sweat.

Once, after I recovered from the fever, I was caught thieving by an old man. He cursed me as I made off over his garden fence, pathetically clutching a bunch of carrots. Another time I was pursued by a woman and her dog, but they fled when I turned and screamed at them, brandishing my stick. I probably looked like a madwoman.

As I trudged south, I realised that if I was going over the Pyrénées I would need to get some proper footwear. Clementine's shoes were falling apart. I was surviving on raw vegetables, berries, fruit and the occasional rabbit and chicken, but I craved bread and sugar. I knew there would be little to scavenge as autumn approached. I had been travelling for two months and was near Limoges.

I found myself in the grounds of a tumbledown château and decided to rest. I could see an old man in the grounds, picking up kindling for a fire. I observed him for a while and could tell that life was a struggle for him. My feet were raw and aching. I felt sure there would be some boots here, maybe decent food. And so, at twilight, I walked to the house, stealthily let myself in, and crept towards the sound of voices.

I turned the door handle. There was a silence as I stepped over the threshold. The old man and his wife, both in their eighties, were sitting like bookends on each side of a fire in a room that appeared to be a library.

'Pardon,' I said calmly. 'I mean no harm.'

The old man rose to his feet and, standing protectively in front of his wife, regarded me. 'Are you fighting the Boches?' he asked unexpectedly.

'Well, yes,' I affirmed. 'I'm sorry to disturb you ... I'm hungry ...'

His wife stood up, came towards me, and simply said, 'You're welcome to our home. Please, join us by the fire.'

Within minutes I was being treated like their long-lost daughter. The woman, who introduced herself as Florence, then ushered me upstairs and ran me a tepid bath. It was bliss.

Meanwhile she looked out clothes for me – her daughter's, she said sadly. I came downstairs happier than I'd been for many months. A modest dinner served on chipped eighteenth-century porcelain and delicious brandy in a crystal glass followed.

They told me they had a son who had been killed in the Great War, and a daughter whom they hadn't seen or heard of for five years.

They urged me to stay the night and I needed no persuasion. I was shown to a huge, dusty bedroom where I collapsed gratefully onto an old four-poster bed with cotton sheets full of moth-holes. There were deep cracks in the plaster on the walls, a windowpane was missing, and there was the scurrying sound of mice, but to me it was heaven. I slept more soundly than I had done in months.

I was sorry to bid them farewell. I walked off down their elegant tree-lined avenue in a stout pair of comfortable leather boots and felt a surge of gratitude.

As I approached Toulouse, the weather turned nasty. I felt a stab of anxiety. There had been days and nights of constant wind and rain, and I knew it would be falling as snow on the mountains.

That evening, I sensed movement nearby and quickly crouched down. Inching forwards, I caught sight of a dozen German soldiers, machine-guns trained down a farm track that led to a railway crossing: an ambush. I slithered back to a spot where I could not be seen. Who were they expecting?

And, suddenly, there they were. Six heavily armed local men walking towards me. I jumped out, my fingers to my lips. 'Watch out!' I hissed in French.

After explaining the situation, I took the men to the place I'd been hiding shortly before, about twenty yards away from the Germans. The Resistance leader gave the signal and all six unleashed a hail of bullets, killing the Germans instantly. There was great jubilation and patting of backs. The corpses were dragged into the dense woodland and hidden in the undergrowth, weapons appropriated, and I was led back to their village – a hero.

I told the men an edited version of my story. They were all Maquis, and I quickly realised that helping them and gaining their trust would be a major breakthrough. I spent a couple of days with them, resting, then over the next two weeks I was passed from group to group and helped on my journey south. I was looked after well and treated with respect. My reputation preceded me. Everyone had come to know of my actions and how I'd saved the Maquis' lives. Yet sometimes I felt an irrational longing to be alone again – to have control.

The Maquis had really suffered from collaborators, often with devastating consequences. The constant tales of in-fighting and betrayals was taking a toll on me. I longed to get back to Britain and, ultimately, home to Canada.

With my injuries, I felt sure I would be discharged from the army, or, at the least, reassigned to wireless or mundane secretarial duties.

However, my new comrades raised my spirits and urged me to head to Lourdes, then over the mountains to Gavarnie on the border with Spain. From there, they felt sure I would be safe; it was a well-trodden route for fugitives.

We arrived in Lourdes under cover of darkness. There I was taken to the home of a trusted couple and stayed indoors for a week. The woman started to confide in me. She told me they were Jewish and had changed their name. Most of the people in Lourdes knew their secret but protected them. She told me how the Jews there had been rounded up and disappeared. The awful rumours of death camps. Despite the protection of their townspeople, they sensed that an anti-Jewish feeling was growing and they lived in fear of their door being kicked in at night.

But on my first day there, she took me to the grotto. Showing my injuries to a priest, I was taken to bathe in the healing waters. Although I was sceptical, something about it comforted me. Donald Angus would surely have approved.

Chapter 12

Angus

I sailed out of Liverpool for Canada on the 30th of January, along with two fellow Scouts, Corporal McKay and Beaton *beag*. We were part of a convoy, with an arrival date scheduled for a week later. We felt fortunate to be on a destroyer as other convoy ships were much more vulnerable to submarines. Since the introduction of an anti-submarine depth charge called a hedgehog, which had sunk hundreds of U-boats, they were now far more reluctant to engage with a well-defended convoy like ours.

The trip across was rough. Monstrous waves slammed the boats, and everyone – experienced seamen and passengers alike – suffered terribly from seasickness. The decks were death traps, slick with deep ice that had to be chipped off daily. We were roped to the side railing and, despite our bulky sou'westers, always came off our four-hour shifts frozen to the bone.

Two-thirds of the way across, one of the merchant vessels had engine failure and had to be towed; the speed of the convoy dropped from sixteen knots to under ten. This made us even greater sitting ducks. We were only too aware of many instances, early on in the war, of entire convoys of merchant ships being sunk in similar circumstances.

The Lovat Scouts had been in the Rockies for a few weeks already and had only one more month to serve in Canada. I was delighted to be going out to join them. It was Françoise's country – albeit the Rockies were almost as far from Chéticamp as Chéticamp was from Scotland – and I longed to see her parents, to share my memories of her, and to let them know she had been loved.

On our arrival in Halifax, Nova Scotia, I realised that I was probably as close to Françoise's real life as I was ever likely to get. How far from here was Chéticamp? I quelled an urge to find a map and set off on my own to find the place.

As it turned out, we were only there for a day. We caught the Canadian Pacific Railway train that went all the way to Vancouver on the west coast. We were to get off in Jasper, where the battalion was stationed. The bunk beds were comfortable and the food was far better than anything on British trains. There was real coffee and generous portions of food, and I even enjoyed a few drams of Scotch that one of the men had bought in Halifax. The troopers spent sixteen hours each night in bed, but I spent most of the time either with my nose pressed against the glass as the train trundled through the flat, agricultural landscape of the prairies, or talking to the other passengers. An elderly Canadian couple even had the Gaelic, despite their entire family having arrived from Scotland three generations ago. They were off to see their daughter, who was married and living in Edmonton. I felt a warm sensation of connection.

We were met at Jasper station by the adjutant Geoffrey

Forrest and taken to Jasper Park Lodge, where the battalion was headquartered.

Forrest told us that the battalion was away on an exercise on a glacier and wouldn't be back until tomorrow, so we'd have time to settle in and see what's what.

I was just offering my thanks and looking forward to a relaxing start to my stay when he added ominously, 'Would you join me in my office once you have unpacked?'

Fifteen minutes later I was facing his desk.

'I'm afraid we've had a signal,' he said. 'Your grandfather has died.' He glanced down at a sheet of paper. 'On the 30th of January, in his sleep.'

'I see.'

'I'm sorry, Angus. I understand he was effectively your father, yes?'

I nodded.

'Why don't you go to the supplies department, get your kit and take a walk around?' he said. 'Clear your head, get to know your surroundings, and then join us for lunch in the mess in two hours.'

I was issued with a pair of snowshoes and other Arctic kit, and wrapped up as warmly as I could. Despite the bright sunshine, it must have been minus fifteen degrees outside. I set off at a brisk pace. I was shaken by the news and needed to push myself physically after two weeks of being cooped up.

It was good to be outside, free, in the gin-clear air. I soon settled into a fast rhythm and my mind filled with recollections of my grandfather. He had been a true Highland gentleman, and was treated as such by all who knew him. He was considerate and intelligent, only spoke when he had something useful to contribute, and had never uttered a curse. My heart ached for my grandmother; he had been her rock, and, despite her being the voluble one, she always had the utmost respect for his views. He was not only a father figure to me – as the adjutant had pointed out – he had also been my mentor.

I paused at the top of a hill to catch my breath and look out over the town of Jasper. I felt certain that Grandfather's death would spell the end for my beloved Peanmeanach. After all, with Grandmother being from Glasgow, Mother from Wales and Mairi from the island of Eriskay, they would almost certainly move to Arisaig, where there would be company and all the comforts: electricity, a dry house, a shop, the church. Peanmeanach may have been the loveliest place on earth, but the houses were decrepit and it was four miles along the track to the road – not to mention the outside privy and the constant trips to draw fresh water from the well. Who would choose to live like that these days?

The funeral would have taken place already, I realised. I could not bear that I was five thousand miles away. I hoped that Father Angus had conducted the service and piped Grandfather to his resting place.

Forlornly, I made my way back to the Lodge, contemplating what I would say in the letter I would have to write.

The battalion returned from their mission the following day as expected. The mess hall was full of my old friends and comrades, and the next couple of weeks passed in a merciful whirl of activity. All six hundred men needed explosives training – to be able to attach devices to a bridge or machinery, to handle grenades, and to plant and identify landmines. We were being trained to lead the assault to free Norway when the time came, so the men were acutely aware of the importance of skiing ability, night-time survival out in the open, and camouflage. We had been issued with impressive American clothing and equipment, but the training was brutally hard. My time with the Norwegian troops had really paid off; they were so much more advanced than us when it came to operating in severe winter conditions.

The Jasper folk had taken the battalion to their hearts. They held a dance every Saturday night, where we taught them Scottish reels and the girls taught us their modern dances. One local woman even taught the men how to ask a girl for a dance: 'You need to say, can I borrow your frame for this struggle?' We had card nights in the officers' mess and a Town versus Scouts ice hockey match. A Jasper man of Scottish descent said he had heard from his grandfather that ice hockey had originated from shinty. When the immigrants arrived, they would play their shinty on the ice and that's how the sport had developed.

Sandy Wedderburn, my old mentor, arranged a Regimental Sports Day, with slalom and cross-country skiing, and shooting. There was even an Officers versus Sergeants mass snowball fight, greatly enjoyed by all.

No two days were alike. I joined the recce troop for two days during a hundred-and-fifty-mile exercise from the icefield chalet at the foot of the Athabasca glacier to Banff and back, on skis. They took a week for the task, travelling at night and carrying all they needed for the trip. It was likely that we would be landed in the north of Norway and would have five hundred miles carrying full kit to get to the larger towns. Fitness and skiing ability were paramount.

There were several avalanches, one of which, before I arrived, killed a young corporal, Sandy Collie. This was to be our only fatality in Alberta, although others were swept away in avalanches but survived, including Major Sir Jock Brooke. He had been crossing an ice face when it started to go. No one could do anything, and as it sped up he waved goodbye, crying out 'Good luck!' He was later dug out, uninjured, a few hundred yards down below.

Following the death of my grandfather I had more sad news. Michael Gubbins had been killed on a mission in Italy. My first great friend to die. Although we had only been friends for two years, we'd had such great times together: in London partying the night away, and fishing and climbing in the Highlands. At that time I had no more information about how he died.

That night, I excused myself from dinner in the mess, went to my quarters and wrote down all the wonderful things about him and the times we shared. I didn't want to forget anything. His death cut a large hole in my life. I then wrote to his parents, celebrating their son and lamenting their loss, promising I would see them as soon as I returned. There were few parents who escaped hearing of the death of a child in this war, it seemed.

Just before the end of our tour, I went with the pipe band to Vancouver. The city was beautiful, blooming with the arrival of spring, and the band's performances were received with much enthusiasm.

On the final evening, I gave a pibroch recital to sixty men in evening dress, most of them in kilts, of the St Andrew's Society. They clapped politely; for many it must have been their first hearing of the pibroch.

Later, the pipe major told me an amusing story. On their arrival, when their train drew into Jasper, they decided to follow tradition and play a few tunes to the welcoming committee. On this occasion, hundreds of locals were waiting to greet them in the bitter cold. The pipe band lined up, and, on the word, blew air into the bags and started out on the tune. Except they didn't. All the drones had frozen so the bags merely gave out a deathly groan. He said it was the funniest thing he had ever heard.

On the day of our departure we finally received post. I had a letter from Sheena, begging me to come to Cape Breton. She'd heard I had passed through Halifax. There were also letters from Father Angus, talking mostly about Grandfather, and a long one from my mother and grandmother. Along with Mairi, they had found themselves accommodation in Arisaig where they could live together when they decided it was time to move.

It was comforting to hear the details of my grandfather's passing. He had died peacefully in the night. Father Angus had come up from Edinburgh and arranged the funeral at Our Lady of the Braes; his burial was with his kinsmen on the isle in the River Ailort alongside my father. There was a good turnout for a man in his eighties.

Father Angus wrote movingly about Grandfather's committal: 'The sun had been out, but a heavy squall suddenly hit as the coffin was being lowered into the grave.

Canon John whispered, "That's more like it," as the congregation huddled together under the lashing rain. I played "Pibroch of Donald Dhu", your grandfather's favourite, at the graveside.'

In my mind I could hear the tune reverberating across the hills.

Chapter 13

Françoise, Lourdes

I said a fond farewell to the couple who had looked after me so well and prayed they would be safe. That night I was taken by the Maquis to another safe house at the foothills of the Pyrénées, ready for a 3 a.m. departure from Lourdes. I was joined by two English pilots, Richard and Mike, who had been shot down and rescued by the Maquis. We had to wait there for three days for a guide to be organised. I learned that there was a steady flow of Allied troops being shepherded into Spain over the Pyrénées and we had no choice but to wait our turn.

I was the only one allowed to venture into the village; my clothing and fluent French were cover enough. My fellow escapees regaled me with stories of the appalling death rate amongst the Royal Air Force. Apparently very few survived even half a dozen sorties, and those who survived being shot down and made it back to England were often airborne again within the week.

Richard was passionate about his flying, saying that if he survived the war he would set up a flying school. I teased them mercilessly, dubbing them Ravishing Richard and

Mad Mike. Both had magnificent moustaches, wore their pilots' uniform with fleece jackets and smoked pipes – baby-faced caricatures of British pilots, their theory being that they didn't want to get shot as spies, but rather to be treated as prisoners of war if they were caught. I recounted some of my experiences and subsequent travels to them, which gained their respect.

We left on the day after Christmas, guided by a sixteen-year-old boy named Henri. He explained to me that we couldn't take a route through the passes, as that was where the soldiers would be, so he would take us another way. He and the two airmen set off at a tremendous clip, uphill, with me limping along painfully behind. Henri was impatient with me, and the pilots almost as much, until I explained the extent of my injuries. We all apologised to each other, and I tried my hardest to keep up.

It was only meant to be a journey of two days and a night over the mountains, with a full day's climb up eight thousand feet before our first night's rest, but the weather closed in fast and we needed to seek shelter from the gale-force winds. We were ill prepared, with no gloves or scarves and inadequate footwear, and although the men had good warm coats, I had only the flimsy one I had been given at the château. However, my months of sleeping rough and my upbringing in the vicious cold of Cape Breton winters had toughened me up. At times my British companions seemed less able to cope with the conditions.

We sheltered that night in a blizzard, huddled together in the lee of a rock. We had no skis or snowshoes, and despite making gaiters with rags, our feet were soon soaking, which was especially painful for me. Mike, in particular, seemed to be suffering from the cold. I believe that if the weather hadn't cleared up and the sun, weak though it was, hadn't come out early the next morning, he may well have succumbed to hypothermia. His temperature had begun to drop dangerously low during the night. I held him as tightly to me as I could, talking nonsense to him to keep him awake and rubbing his body to keep the circulation going. As for myself, I knew that after all I had been through, there was no way I was going to give up now.

We were relieved to get moving again in the morning, although almost immediately Henri motioned for us to crouch down as an army patrol skied past along the border, only a couple of hundred feet below us. It was a close shave, and I was impressed by the young lad's instincts.

Though hungry and tired, the remainder of our trek was incident-free. We limped slowly down the mountains, out of the snow and into Spain and safety. There was much elation. Mike had warmed up and recovered well, the scare of the previous night forgotten in our relief at having arrived.

Henri would introduce us to a member of the Spanish Resistance when we arrived, and then head on to Canfranc, where we could get a train to San Sebastian. From there, the British Consul General would arrange for a sea crossing back to Britain. This was by now the standard escape route. At Canfranc we met a hard-faced woman who was to look after us, so we said farewell to Henri. He set off back the way we had come without a backward glance.

Everything proceeded according to plan. In San Sebastian we were handed over to an efficient English couple, Albert and Margo, who were working for MI9. They put us up in a small hotel. How I loved having a hot bath. Margo trimmed my hair and gave me money to buy some decent clothing. The boys were confined to their room for their own protection, they were so obviously British.

I wandered the town on my own with my old coat and stick, my head bowed. I looked like a fifty-year-old housewife, going about her shopping. However, with my dyed hair having grown out and with some lipstick on and a fresh skirt and blouse, I felt almost presentable as we joined our hosts for some supper in one of the bedrooms. Ravishing Richard, considerably refreshed by the local wine, became a little too forward with me, so in order to fend him off, I exaggerated my relationship with Angus.

'We're engaged to be married,' I announced, relishing the words as I showed off my army-issue ring.

Margo and Albert congratulated me warmly, and I felt a little ashamed of my deceit. Margo was keen to know more about my fiancé, of course. I realised how embarrassingly little I knew, so I plied her with questions about Spain's role in the war. She explained that Spain was neutral but swung between supporting the Germans and the British. She warned me that the place was heaving with spies and assassins; we would have to be vigilant at all times.

It was towards the end of January when we were advised that the weather was right. Suddenly we were given the go-ahead to commence the final part of our journey, so we packed up in the evening and I again found myself offering profuse thanks to brave hosts. We set off in the middle of the night. There was no moon as we made our way stealthily to the harbour. Before long, in the pitch dark, we scrambled aboard a fishing boat, with another dozen escapees, all bound for Torquay.

It was to be a week-long trip across the Bay of Biscay, which was renowned for being stormy. We had to keep far out to sea to avoid the French coast and the likelihood of German sea patrols, which made the crossing pretty choppy at times. We eked out basic British Army composition rations and trailed fishing lines behind the boat. Margo had given us a sack of oranges, so we ate healthily. There were some fascinating men on board: a Cameron Highlander who had escaped from a POW camp and told me he had met Father Angus, my Angus's uncle; four pilots including my two companions; another SOE man who had finished his mission and spoke to no one; and a man named Colin, a half-Spanish British spy who had been on some unspecified business in Madrid.

At last we arrived in Torquay harbour, exhausted from the mental and physical strain of the past few months, but excited. My pilots embraced me. We'd been together for three weeks and had grown genuinely fond of one other. They were headed to Norfolk and would doubtless be flying again within days.

I was then met by a female captain in uniform who saluted me, somewhat to my surprise. My pilots, watching my departure, looked very impressed as I was whisked into a Daimler. I was told I was off to Bletchley Park for a debriefing and medical. The captain told me Brigadier Gubbins had sent her and his car especially to meet me.

As I dozed in the back of the luxurious car, I wondered why the brigadier might have done this. I knew all about him and his son from Angus, but I felt sure he wouldn't have known who I was.

When I arrived at Bletchley, my section leader gave me a warm reception. 'You're quite the hero here, Sophie. Everyone wants to shake your hand. The leader of the Maquis said you were the bravest person he had ever met. Brace yourself! We have quite an itinerary for you, I'm afraid.'

My first appointment was with the doctor at Bletchley Park who was shocked by the state of my feet. 'What happened here, young lady?' he asked. I related my story.

'And then you walked five hundred miles on them?' he asked. 'I can hardly believe it.'

I had both bare feet propped up on a chair, and he was probing them gently, with frequent glances at me. I had no toenails; two of the toes on my right foot had fallen off; and the remaining ones were grotesquely mangled. I showed him my arm. There was no muscle at all. He encircled my bicep with his finger and thumb.

'This is the end of the war for you, my dear,' he said, shaking his head regretfully.

I could have hugged him. 'I have to tell you, sir, I'm not sorry.'

'You'll need to do a full debrief and then we'll get you on a ship home. First, we'll take you up to Baker Street and sort things out with the Canadians. Generous pensions, I believe. Make sure they arrange for you to see a specialist in Harley Street before you leave.'

When I arrived at Baker Street I was astonished to be told that I was to have an interview with Brigadier Gubbins himself. I smartened myself up as best I could.

Angus had been correct. The brigadier was a delight. 'Honestly, Sophie,' he chuckled, 'we can't quite believe you're here with us. We all assumed you were dead.'

'I can barely believe it myself sometimes, sir,' I replied.

'You're the person everyone is talking about. Eliminating Kaufmann and then a four-month trek alone across France ... You've more than earned your passage back home to Cape Breton. I gather your father is a doctor. Is that correct?'

I nodded.

'Excellent. Well, first things first, the Canadian Ambassador has asked us to dine at the embassy tonight. I trust you can make that?'

That night was one I would never forget. Flickering candles lit the room, hidden from Grosvenor Square by blackout curtains. A dozen of us enjoyed sumptuous food and wine while a pianist quietly played some of my favourite old Canadian waltzes.

I was seated beside the Ambassador. Before we dined, he told the guests about my mission and then, to my utter astonishment, pinned a Military Cross on my jacket. I was heady with the excitement of the evening, my face flushed with the heat of the room and the wine.

Then, to my delight, the brigadier started talking to me about Angus. He told me he had been best friends with his son, Michael, which I already knew. I was then thrilled to hear that Angus had been pestering staff and the Red Cross for news of me since he had returned from his operation. Nervously, I asked where he was.

'He's in Canada now with the Lovat Scouts, training in the Rockies,' the brigadier replied. 'He's a fine fellow.'

I was elated to hear he was alive and well, and that he had been searching for me, though it was disappointing to learn he wasn't in London where I could see him. Nonetheless, that night I went to bed happier than I had been in many, many months.

Next day, I met with a Harley Street specialist. 'Well, my dear,' he said, 'if I were to try and make you walk properly again this is what I would do: I would break your toes again and reset them. But you could be unable to walk for two months. The alternative is to operate on each foot separately, which means you could use crutches to get around.'

Neither option was particularly attractive, since I had spent so much time in pain already. I told him that my father was a doctor in Canada and asked if he could write instructions for him, reasoning that if I had to be off my feet for months, I would prefer to be at home.

The specialist agreed, and after a few more days finalising my affairs with Baker Street and the Canadian Embassy I was off to Liverpool with a one-way ticket home. I wrote a tentative letter to Angus, care of the Lovat Scouts in Jasper, to say I was alive and heading home to recover from my injuries in Chéticamp, though for all I knew he may well have been back in Britain before it caught up with him.

After an uneventful, week-long trip across the Atlantic aboard a virtually empty ship that was due to return with armaments, I spent two days in Halifax with an old schoolfriend, Michelle. I told her about Angus.

She saw straight through me and burst out laughing. 'You've fallen in love, Sophie, it's as simple as that. Keep writing to him, then go and find him in Scotland.'

'But I treated him poorly,' I admitted. 'It's been nearly a year since I saw him last and we only knew each other for a few days. He thinks I was killed by the Germans. I know he tried to find me, but I'll bet he got over it and hasn't given me a thought for months.' I fought back tears. 'He probably has a girl in his life now . . . maybe he's married . . .'

Michelle gave me a hug. 'He'll be pining for you, my darling, I promise you that. Call your parents. Go home and get fit and well for your man.'

My hands shook as I dialled. Hearing my voice, my mother gasped. 'Sophie, is it really you? You're alive?' She shouted excitedly to my father, 'She's alive, she's alive! It's Sophie!'

'I'm coming home,' I told them. 'I'm arriving on the train at Inverness tomorrow at five o'clock.'

They were ecstatic. 'We'll be there, darling,' cried my mother. 'We can drive you home in our new car. I can't believe you are safe and sound! Everything is perfect!'

Safe and sound, I thought to myself. How would I explain my injuries? They had no idea of what I'd gone through. But I would worry about that tomorrow.

Chapter 14

Angus, Lovat Scouts, Canada

The last few days in the Rockies were spent packing. There was to be an advance party and I wanted to be with it. My friend Andrew and I had hatched a plan to visit Aunt Sheena and then for me to go on to Sophie's parents; Andrew would meet Sheena and then be introduced to the Miramichi MacDonalds, his cousins in Mull River. We marched with all the confidence we could muster into the colonel's office and asked if we could go up with the advance party to Halifax and then, during the layover waiting for the boat, take the train to Inverness.

When we were granted our chit for four days' leave, we were like excited schoolboys on holiday. After a seemingly never-ending train journey from Jasper, we arrived in Halifax and made a dash to Mulgrave for the ferry across the Canso Strait, to catch the Inverness train.

We made it with moments to spare. On the journey, Andrew and I had talked about where the battalion might be sent next. It now seemed likely to be southern Italy, not exactly the terrain for which we'd been training. Everyone

had been hoping for Norway. 'Well, at least we'll be fighting the Italians rather than the SS,' Andrew remarked.

'I gather the Italians have pretty much given up, so
Germans are more likely.' I replied. We felt that the war
was coming to a close, and survival was at the forefront of
everyone's mind.

I sent a telegram to Sheena from Mulgrave, telling her
we would be arriving by train in Mabou that afternoon.
The ice in the strait had broken up, so the ferry was running
again. If Sheena could get away, the plan was to go with
her to Mull River, then I would ride to Chéticamp if she
could get me a horse, and I would be back the next day to
rejoin her, before catching up with the battalion and sailing
from Halifax.

Later that day, Andrew and I were standing outside a
pretty white wooden house, only a few steps from the
shore. It had 'S. Gillies' on the letterbox and 'Glen Shian'
painted on the fence. There was a young woman tying up
plants in the garden. She turned to look at us. I gasped; she
was the spitting image of my grandmother and Sheena. It
took seconds for it all to sink in. She must be Sheena's
daughter. I didn't know; none of us knew. So much was
suddenly becoming clear.

'You must be Donald Angus,' she said with a radiant
smile as she walked towards me and held her hands out to
take mine. 'I know all about you. I'm Morag.'

'Morag,' I repeated. I introduced her to Andrew.

She shook his hand. 'Oh yes, Andrew, my mother often
talks about your father, Colonel Willie,' she said, before
turning back to me. 'I'm afraid Mother's away, Donald
Angus. It was me who opened your telegram, but she had

already left. She's judging a fiddle competition in Sydney and won't be back till tomorrow. She doesn't know you're coming.'

I hesitated, unsure whether it would be impolite to ask to stay, but Morag rescued me.

'You'll stay tonight, won't you? So that you can see her tomorrow? I can't wait to see her face! Please say you'll stay.'

I looked at Andrew's smiling face. And it was settled.

Andrew and I were quickly charmed by my cousin Morag. She seemed to know everything about my life, telling me she had been desperate to come and visit and still hoped to do so one day. She was married to a soldier and had a daughter of her own, Mairi, aged five, who was staying with friends. I was still taking in the fact that I had a cousin – what would my grandmother think? This was the biggest surprise to have happened in the family, ever.

That evening, after supper, we gathered around the fire and talked about Sheena.

'She's had some sad times,' Morag said. 'I can't imagine leaving home, emigrating, possibly never to return.'

'It sounds as though she has told you everything about her life before she came here, though,' I said.

'Yes,' Morag agreed, 'and of course I have her memoir.'

'Her what?' I asked.

Morag smiled. 'Mother was keen that I should know as much as possible about her old life. I think she feels guilty that she hasn't told her parents about me, so she wrote it all down one day. Would you like to see it?'

'I couldn't possibly,' I said. 'It sounds like something private between the two of you.'

'Absolutely not,' Morag insisted. 'Mother told me that she wanted me to know everything and that I was free to do as I wished with the information. Go on, Angus. I'll fetch it for you and you can read it in bed.'

Later, in bed, with some trepidation, I opened my aunt's soft leather-bound journal and began to read her memoir . . .

Sheena's memoir

The month after Colin Angus's death, fishing off Smirisary, was hell for me. I was twenty-four years old, and he and I had been close since school age, with him always around Peanmeanach. As we grew up everyone treated us like a couple about to get married anyway, and he was just preparing himself to ask my father. Father just wanted him to come over and get on with it but Colin Angus was scared he would say no.

Then the accident happened and my Colin Angus drowned. It was as if the life had been sucked out of me. I lay curled up in bed every day; my parents tried their best, always thinking of diversions for me, but I felt sick constantly – with worry, I imagined. I even went to see Father Allan about becoming a nun. He told me to give it a year, and if I was still serious we could talk again. As it turned out that was good advice.

With only a few days' notice I heard about an emigration ship leaving for Halifax from the distillery pier in Fort William. My family came with me to the dock, in tears like a hundred others, that dreich autumn day. Little did I know that it would be almost thirty years before I saw them and my dear Ardnish again. And how unbearably tragic that I never ever saw my brother, dear Donald Peter, again. He was like my doll as I grew up, eleven years younger and the perfect plaything for a teenage girl. I was told that one in six of the young men in the Highlands were killed in the Great War and it caused havoc to the continuity of the remote communities. Of the ten people of Ardnish in 1915, two of the young men were killed, and a third, Father Angus, joined the church.

On the ship across I kept myself to myself, retching and weeping alternately. An older woman from Ballachulish, in the bunk below, was my saviour, bringing me towels, basins and food. As the voyage went on, little by little she teased my story from me. It was she who told me I was pregnant; to her it was clear as day. I was filled with hope and fear simultaneously, and I remember hugging myself to sleep that night. I had a wee baby from my man.

My first job was in Mabou on the western shore of Cape Breton with the MacNeils, Iain and Dhileas. I told them about my condition and they swore not to let news of the child get back to my family. It was six months later that I gave birth to dear Morag, who shared my bed in an outbuilding. I stayed as a nanny to the MacNeils' nine children for ten years. Morag was much loved and considered one of the family. Times were hard in Nova Scotia at that time, with mining bad and fish prices low, and, although they didn't say anything, I could see the cost of having Morag and me was becoming too much for the MacNeils.

I was lucky, though. The school needed a teacher. Although English was my second language, they didn't have a lot of choice so I got the job. There was a shift happening at that time, with the older folk speaking Gaelic to each other, and the mothers to the children. But the bairns had to speak English by the time they arrived at school, and often they couldn't.

My family were all pipers, so, figuring I might have some musical ability I took up the fiddle around this time. I learnt with a boy, Buddy MacMaster, and after three years I was giving lessons myself and eventually became a judge at competitions.

My Morag was the easiest wee scrap, sweet-natured and always smiling. I don't know what I would have done without her. I never wrote to my parents to tell them of her, and as time went on it became more difficult. I am no longer sure if it was the shame of illegitimacy and fear of my parents' judgement, or if it was because I wanted to show them my daughter in the flesh so they would have to fall in love with her, as I know they would.

Morag and I had lodgings with an old widow who I became very close to, Nellie MacEachern. Her husband Ronald had died long before and had given her no children. In exchange for board I looked after the house and garden, and her, too, for five years before she passed away. I was left the house with its four bedrooms and grand view of the sea. After a while I renamed it Glen Shian, after the glen where Donald Peter is buried on his island. There is an area here in Inverness County also called Shian; it means fairy in Gaelic.

We went from surviving on other people's generosity to becoming part of the community in Mabou. We were surrounded by MacDonalds: Tearlach, Donald J. and Aoenas.

Aoenas came to my door when I first started lodging there with a present of shortbread and asked me who my people were – the inevitable question of west coast Cape Breton.

I told him I was the daughter of Donald John, son of Donald Angus, son of Donald John of Ardnish, and that was good enough for him. He knew the pipers well enough. Lineage here was pored over in detail.

And as for men, I was courted for a few years, but no one compared to my Colin Angus, even though I was aware that his attractions probably grew and his imperfections disappeared as the years went by. I looked fine for my age; my hair was glossy and the staple diet of fish kept me slim. But rarely a glance came my way. I think I became a bit too quick to judge, with too sharp a tongue for some. A spinster, a teacher, a mother, I became known as 'Sheena the fiddler'.

My parents were always asking about men in their letters. For them, marriage was the solution to the world's problems. I heard about their match-making effort long after the event, luckily. Colonel Willie came to stay with my parents before the war. They had received warning in advance and so everything was spick and span when he came; my mother would have been frantic. My father got on his pony and they would head up to Loch Doire a' Ghearrain, where Miss Astley Nicholson had a boat, and they would go fishing together. The colonel and he would spend two or three days at Peanmeanach, enjoying the blether. Most of the talk would be about the Lovat Scouts, of their children and the year my brother DP spent making whisky on Canna.

My mother wrote to say that the Long John Distillery was not going well, with prohibition in the States, high excise duties, the depression and competition – and far too many distilleries.

Apparently the colonel asked after me, and whether I'd found a man. He even suggested a *rèitach* – an arranged marriage – saying he'd heard they had a tremendous success rate. He suggested there must be many a middle-aged man in Cape Breton I hadn't met who would be delighted to meet me.

The colonel had said that some things were too important to be left to the young – I was fifty at that time – and so unbeknownst to me he wrote to some cousins in Mull River, the Miramichi MacDonalds, to try to set me up. I could just imagine Colonel Willie and my father, whisky glass in hand, cigarettes on the go, enjoying this 'solution'.

Much to my surprise, I received a letter in the post from one Big Calum of Mull River, whom I'd never heard of, asking me if I'd like to meet him at the school house dance. I was determined to say no, but after discussing it with a friend, reluctantly accepted. I had asked around and heard he worked in the family sawmill belonging to Colonel MacDonald's cousins, about seven miles upstream from the mouth of Mull River. We had a grand time together. We danced the square dances well together, knew many of the same folk, and I impressed him when the band recognised me and asked if I would play a tune or two with the fiddle.

Yet even before I met him I knew I wouldn't marry him. His wife had died, leaving him with three teenage children, and he lived with his sister. From then on I saw him from time to time at a ceilidh as a good friend. That was the way it was.

However, I became very friendly with his employers, Joe and his wife Mary Belle and Danny and Maggie MacDonald. Morag and I would often stay with them and their families at weekends to get away from school and give my dog, Ruadh, some proper exercise. I called him Ruadh, which is Gaelic for red, because he was a lovely chestnut Irish Setter, whom I adored. I became well known in Mabou for getting towed around by him.

The MacDonalds' sawmill was a fine operation. There was a big bandsaw that could slice trees four feet across. A tree went on rollers at one end and came out in planks at the other. It was driven by water from Mull River, powered by the snowmelt. Joe and Danny, the two owners, with half a dozen men, stacked roof shingles onto a wood sleigh, set the machinery, and felled and floated logs down the river to the dam. The spring and summer saw everyone at work in the fields.

Between Joe and Danny's two families, there were eleven children and Mary Belle fell pregnant with her fourth. When Morag was in her late teenage years she loved to help with the babies. Mary Belle was a lot younger than me, nearer Morag's age, but we got on very well. She soon became one of my closest friends.

One weekend Maggie and Mary Belle were having a frolic and there were eight women around the table making a blanket for the baby. As they worked they sang a song in Gaelic called 'Ho Rò Mo Nighean Donn Bhoidheach':

> *I asked her if she loved me,*
> *And she said she was above me.*
> *She opened the door and shoved me,*
> *And called me a fool.*

The post took a month between Ardnish and Mabou, so I read of Donald Angus's piping success, the gold medal win in the *Halifax Herald*, two weeks before I got a rare letter about it from my proud father.

I finally went home in 1938 for the summer, using some money from my inheritance. Ruadh had died, Morag was grown up and I didn't have ties, so it was time. The liner left Halifax in late June and a week later pulled into Port Glasgow. Mother was waiting for me on the quay. She was showing her age now; with white hair, and a bit more stooped than I remembered her, but she was very sprightly considering she was well into her seventies. We didn't stop talking for the whole five-hour train trip home. After all, we had over thirty years to catch up on.

I had one overriding ambition during the trip and that was to tell my parents of young Morag, and what was more, that she was married and expecting a baby – a great-grandchild. But as much as I longed to, it never seemed to be the right time. As my stay went on I grew more and more burdened with the secret, and willed myself to blurt it out.

I often thought that news of Morag's existence might have reached Lochaber, there were so many families with relations on each side of the Atlantic. But clearly the people of Mabou had decided it was my secret and they weren't going to reveal it.

Louise was as wonderful as I'd heard she was, and Donald Angus was handsome, helpful and kind as his father had been. Father was really quite infirm; he couldn't get on a horse without help and he was little use outside the house. Louise and Aunt Mairi's houses were in a terrible way, both desperately needing new thatch or even better a tin roof. I'm ashamed to admit I was shocked that they still drew water from the well and used an outside privy. When I mentioned it I was told that with only Aunt Mairi, Louise and my parents there, and young Donald Angus between here and Laggan farm, for the laird it was a question of 'out of sight, out of mind'. I wondered if the owner of the village, Miss Astley Nicholson, knew the state of their houses, and indeed that of the big field.

I had hoped to build some rapport with the laird during my stay. She was about my age so Mother and I rode over to the big house to make a representation about the condition of the houses. But we were intercepted by the factor. He told us he would see what he could do but reminded us that times were tough and that they received little in the way of rents and, what was more, war was coming. As if we didn't know all of this already.

My parents' house was in a much better state than those of the rest of the village. They had moved into John the Post's when the post office was shut ten years before. It had cut stone outside walls, wood panelling, a wood floor and a tin roof, instead of the blackhouses with their fieldstone walls and leaky heather thatch. Electricity, inside toilets and even telephones were common now in almost all villages, but not with us.

Mother was very active helping my nephew at Laggan, aided by her two collies. When I was with her she went with Donald Angus to gather sheep and she had a full eight hours on the hill in that Highland drizzle which soaks you to the bone in minutes, yet she came back as cheerful as if she had just been to the shed to get some coal. Her wet clothes were draped all over the furniture to dry and were still soaked the next day. I worried that she would catch pneumonia.

Louise recounted the worst moment she'd had at Ardnish. About how Donald Angus had gone down to the sea when he was about four, to throw sticks for Daffie. Louise was doing the washing in the burn and not paying close attention. Suddenly she told me that the hair on the back of her neck went up and a shudder of fear went through her body. She raced down to the shore where she had last seen the boy and there was no sign of him. Then she spotted them fifty yards out, her child holding onto Daffie's neck as the tide was carrying them out to sea.

She ran along the rocks, frantic, threw herself in and pulled Donald Angus out onto the shore. 'Imagine if I'd lost my son as well as my husband, Sheena. I would have killed myself rather than go on.' Daffie was something of a hero after that.

I saw something of Owen, whom I didn't know. He was in his thirties, living in Tarbert in a bothy with another bachelor. Mother, Louise and I went up to see him with Donald Angus. I was horrified by the squalid conditions – bits of an engine he was working on all over the main room, dirty crockery and clothing, and empty bottles of whisky. He was earning his living fishing and helping people with their engines. A man of the sea, he was happy, with no ambition to better himself or find a woman and settle down.

Father said we should let him alone. He reminded him of the Bochan, who used to live at Sloch – a man who did what he liked and didn't concern himself with what anyone else thought. I could tell Louise was a little ashamed of her brother and I couldn't help but share her sentiments, but I reminded myself that I had borne a child out of wedlock, and held my hypocrisy in check.

Louise lamented sending her brother away from Ardnish, but Father reminded her that he would have had no work here – after all, nobody knew back then that the farm would be coming our way, and at least Owen could pick up plenty of work in Tarbert – fishing, blacksmithing and mending engines.

Mother and I planned to go to Edinburgh to see Father Angus at St Mary's Cathedral. We would take the train to Glasgow, go across to Edinburgh and then back to Glasgow for my ship home. I had a farewell supper with Aunt Mairi and Donald Angus and my parents, and tried not to break down in tears.

As we set off at six the next morning, we turned from the top of the hill where we could see all before us. The big field with the curve of houses along the shore, the green of the machair contrasting with the white coral beach, then the sea sweeping across to the great house at Roshven and the mountains beyond that I knew so well. Eigg and Rum alight in the sunrise to the west. I froze the picture in my mind. I had no doubt that it would be the last time I set eyes on it.

Father rode to see us off at Lochailort and the three of us had breakfast together at the inn. I hugged him tight. Both of us knew it was our final goodbye. I cried for an hour on the train.

It was great to see Father Angus. He was fit and active and looked a decade younger than his fifty-three years. He was a monsignor now and worked directly for Archbishop MacDonald. We had tea with the archbishop, who was keen to hear of my father. Then he and my brother bemoaned falling church attendances, meagre Sunday collections and, painfully for me, children born out of wedlock. I remember my mother shaking her head with what things had come to.

They talked about Canon John MacNeil, originally from Eriskay but who had served Morar for some twenty years now. He had also been a Cameron Highlander padre with Father Angus at Passchendaele in the Great War, and famously went over the top with the men, bandaging the wounded and bringing many back to safety. His best friend, Charlie Lyon, found him badly injured from a shell in the mud several days after an engagement and carried him to safety. Canon John received a Military Cross and bar in the war. Charlie, on the other hand, was both highly decorated and court-martialled more than once for insubordination.

The next day was one I had been dreading. Waving goodbye from the railing on the liner as she pulled away from the quay, tears poured down my face as I held my handkerchief aloft. I watched from the deck until my mother was a dot.

As we passed Arran, dusk was falling and the evening chill got the better of me. I gave a final wave to my family, to Ardnish, and to the Highlands, and retired to my cabin. Disregarding the others I shared it with, I buried my face in the pillow and wept. How could I not have told them about Morag? How could I?

Chapter 15

The next morning Andrew, Morag and I were sitting on the porch drinking coffee as Sheena approached, carrying a small travel bag and her violin case. She frowned at first, peering at us all, then ran up the steps and threw herself into my arms. 'Oh, Donald Angus, Donald Angus,' she murmured as she stroked my hair.

She rushed out a couple of sentences in the old tongue, before I said, 'Andrew doesn't have the Gaelic,' and Morag interjected, 'And mine isn't as good as it should be either!'

Morag told her mother that her secret was out, though Sheena clearly knew already. I watched them look at one another, their radiant, smiling faces, saw the strong family resemblance, and wished dearly that the rest of the family could have been there.

Sheena's relief in revealing Morag's existence was immense. That evening, as the four of us sat talking after supper, Sheena suddenly dissolved into floods of tears as years of suppressed guilt and tension came to the surface. She had convinced herself that the knowledge of an illegitimate child would shock her parents and that she would be forever ostracised.

'I was already so far away from them,' she said, 'I couldn't bear to lose their love and support as well. When I was left the money in Mrs MacEachern's will, I wanted to come over to tell them. But I just couldn't . . . I couldn't. I can't forgive myself, and now Father is dead, and he never knew.'

Sheena's sobbing intensified, though it was, in truth, half in misery and half in joy. Morag was composed, even a little amused at her mother's tears. 'You think this is bad? When she arrived home five years ago after her visit to Scotland she cried for a week. If she hadn't made me swear I wouldn't, I would've written to Grandmother myself!'

Andrew was listening to all this with some bemusement.

Later, after Sheena had composed herself, she and I talked about Grandfather, and how sad we were that we hadn't been able to go to his funeral.

'But I'm so thankful I was able to go and to see them just before the war,' she said. She turned to Andrew and said kindly, 'I read about your father's funeral in the *Oban Times* when I was on Ardnish, Andrew. It sounded like he received a grand send-off.'

The next morning, we wanted to go to Mull River, but first Andrew asked to telephone the adjutant to see if the ship was sailing as planned. Morag accompanied him to show him the way to the post office and a short time later they returned wreathed in smiles.

'You'll never guess,' Andrew said. 'Two of the men have been stricken with scarlet fever and the whole regiment has been quarantined. No one's going anywhere for at least two weeks. In fact, we're forbidden to return to camp.'

What a stroke of luck! Now we could really make the most of being in Cape Breton. We began to make plans.

Morag arranged for her daughter to stay with her friend for another couple of days and Sheena suggested we all borrow a wagon and go up the Mull River the next day.

'I hope they're all there,' she said. 'Joe and his sister Anna Mae are trying to buy a hotel on the Margaree, near Chéticamp. Since Joe's wife Mary Belle died eighteen months ago, their children have been dispersed amongst several families.'

'Really?' Andrew gasped. 'How could they do such a thing?'

'Shocking, isn't it?' Sheena agreed. 'But they have no mother, money is tight, and there are so many children. I can't believe I didn't take a couple of them in myself; I feel terrible. If the hotel project doesn't work out in reuniting them, then I'll offer. Maybe I should marry Joe, he's a decent man.'

Morag was shocked. 'Mother!' she exclaimed. 'You can't say things like that!'

'It would solve so many problems,' said Sheena with a smile. 'Though he hasn't given me a second look.'

That evening we dined like kings on the lobster that was plentiful in the area, so much so that the fishermen couldn't give them away. To cap it all, Sheena produced a bottle of the Dew of Ben Nevis that she had tucked away 'for a very special occasion'.

Andrew looked as proud as punch when he saw the bottle. 'I wish the business hadn't been sold when my father died,' he lamented. 'This is truly special stuff.'

I asked Morag to tell us about her husband. 'He's a Skye man,' she replied, smiling. 'Calum Beaton from Uig. He was a miner here in Mabou, but recently the mine has been flooding and he hated it anyway. As soon as the war came along he signed up with the North Nova Scotia Highlanders. He's a sergeant now.' There was no mistaking the pride in her voice. 'I haven't seen much of him over the last five years; he's in France now. He hardly knows Mairi, and she tells me she can barely picture his face. I say the rosary for him every day. They've had a bad war, but he's been a lucky man . . . so far.' She crossed herself, and so did my aunt.

'He loves the army a bit too much, though. The routine as well as the adrenaline. When he came home on leave a year ago, he was terribly fidgety, couldn't relax. I got the feeling he couldn't wait to leave. I remember dropping a pan on the kitchen floor, and it was as if a bomb had gone off. I'm dying to have him home, but a little anxious, to be honest.'

I tried to reassure her. 'I'm afraid that's the way of it, Morag. He'll be on edge, he'll have nightmares. Remember, he'll have seen some of his best friends die in front of him. Only time will heal. All you can do is support him as best you can.'

The next day we set off with a horse and wagon, a couple of boxes of food and some moonshine. Sheena told us there were only three or four cars in Mabou; the roads were terrible and there wasn't much money around.

As we lurched down the rough track, rutted in the slush of the thaw, Sheena asked me why I was so keen to go to Chéticamp.

I pondered for a few moments. 'Well, it's a sad story and probably all top secret, mind, so you have to promise not to say a word.'

Sheena laughed. 'We're family, Angus! Of course I won't say a word.'

I smiled. 'Well, one of the agents I met was a girl from there.'

'I knew it would be a girl!' Sheena exclaimed with delight.

I could feel myself blushing. 'It wasn't like that. She called herself Françoise, but her real name is Sophie Lacroix. Her mission was to assassinate a senior German officer, which she did, but she was injured and captured. That was a year ago now, almost exactly. No one, not even the Red Cross, has heard a word about what happened to her. It's likely she was executed. I want to see her parents and tell them what a heroine she was.'

Morag, who was listening, was looking at me intensely. 'It's clear you have feelings for her, Donald Angus.'

I shook my head vigorously while Andrew said, 'Yes, he most certainly does.'

Sheena put her hand on my knee. 'You don't know anything for sure, do you? Maybe she'll be all right. We can only hope.'

It was a two-hour journey inland to the sawmill. When we arrived we found ourselves in the midst of a hive of industry. Beside a dam full of logs, two men were attaching a chain around a log, then attaching the end to a draft horse which then hauled it up the slippery wet incline, where it was levered onto rollers and into the saw.

Danny and Joe were there, Andrew's cousins, along with some of Danny's boys. Andrew and the Mull River cousins were all so pleased to see each other, saying it had been over a hundred years since the families had met up. However, the river was swollen with snowmelt, and the brothers were keen to make the most of it. There were only two or three months of the year when the river's flow was strong enough to power the saw. Work couldn't stop until the evening, so we rolled up our sleeves and helped roll logs and stack planks, while Sheena and Morag went to join the women.

The brothers were big, strong men like all the descendants from the Cranachans. They wore identical denim overalls, topped with sweat-stained fedora hats. They were both over fifty years old yet could easily take an end each of a huge log and turn it to a better place for the saw.

That evening, Andrew and I could hardly move we were so stiff and sore whereas the brothers, twice our age, acted as if they'd had the day off.

The next day was Sunday, and we were relieved to hear there would be no work.

Nine of us went off to the Big Mackinnon's bar for some Bull beer. The landlady, Big Belle, renowned on the island, was six feet tall, and poured forty-five-cent pitchers of her home brew in her parlour while her numerous children ran around the house.

When we got back to the house, there wasn't room to swing a cat. All the men were in high spirits and the long-suffering women ladled out deer stew and potatoes to soak up the alcohol we had taken. Sheena and Morag seemed to fit in like part of the family – which they almost were.

After the meal Sheena took her fiddle out, the room was cleared of furniture, and the dancing started. These huge men had the nimblest of feet as they demonstrated square dancing to us. Andrew and I copied clumsily despite the best efforts of Morag and of Maggie, Danny's wife.

'Tell everyone about the Cranachans,' encouraged Sheena. 'The children won't know, nor will Angus.' Andrew relished the subject, which had entered folklore.

'These MacDonald brothers, six of them, grew up at a farm in Glen Roy called Cranachan. They were legendary for their strength, fleetness of foot and courage. In 1849 two of them went to London and Colin won the top prizes for running and throwing the hammer. The *Times* said of him that he was "like a stag from his native hills".'

Maggie then addressed the girls. 'There is a great female Cranachan, too,' she said, 'an Australian cousin named Mother Mary Mackillop, who set up an order of nuns to teach Aborigines. She's still revered in Australia. Just imagine what courage that must have taken.

You're members of this same family, children – all remarkable people. Be proud of that.'

That night I went to sleep happier than I had been for a long time.

*

Andrew decided to stay a few days longer with his cousins to help while the river was high and Sheena, Morag and I headed back. Andrew and I agreed to meet in ten days' time at my aunt's unless I sent a telegram advising a change.

The next day we returned to Sheena's house where she insisted on cleaning and ironing my uniform, waving away my protests. 'I'm proud to be doing so,' she declared, 'and that's all there is to it.'

I was going to take the train to Inverness and from there, the man with the wagon at the general store had arranged for me to rent a horse for a few days. It was to be a three-day ride at the most.

I enjoyed the trip and was in no hurry. Crystal-clear skies, the snow had melted, and I cheerfully returned the smiles and waves I received from people as I trotted past. I was in my Scouts uniform; people had said the black-and-white checked Tam o'Shanter was not unlike that of the North Nova Scotia Highlanders.

I stayed the first night in Margaree overlooking the mouth of the river where Françoise had told me about the monster salmon she had caught. As I lay in my bed at the inn the next morning, I tried to prepare myself for the meeting with her parents. I would go into town and ask for the doctor's house. There would be tears, and an hour or two later I would be on my way. Perhaps I would return to this inn and try some fishing nearby. It would help me settle down after such an emotional visit.

I shaved and tidied myself. I wanted to look my best.

Chapter 16

Sophie

I boarded the ferry to Port Hawkesbury, then climbed into the grimy passenger carriage which was attached to the slow, empty coal train heading to Inverness.

The steam made a huge cloud as the train clickety-clacked its way through deep snow along the shoreline. At each station, there would be a long, mournful whistle as we pulled in. I enjoyed watching the comings and goings of staff and passengers and felt as excited as I had years before when we first moved to the island.

My parents were waiting at the station. I buried my face in my mother's neck, unable to hold back my tears. Mother held me at arm's length and regarded me intently. 'We were told you were dead,' she sobbed. 'We mourned for months. I was prepared to mourn for ever.'

I couldn't speak. Instead, we three hugged each other tightly.

'Why the crutches, darling?' Mother asked. 'Have you sprained your ankle?'

Mother was always the talker, the gregarious one, the optimist. I could tell my father had felt my withered arm when he hugged me, but he didn't mention it. Typically, he would wait for me to explain. We climbed into my parents' new Buick – the scent of shiny new leather was lovely – and drove home.

As we entered the house, I felt dizzy. It looked and smelled exactly as I remembered, exactly how I had visualised it in my darkest moments. I walked from the hallway into the sitting room, stroking the furniture, feeling the curtains, absorbing everything.

'Your mother didn't say earlier,' Father said, 'but we received a most sympathetic and charming letter from a fellow soldier of yours.'

I could feel the hairs stand up on the back of my neck. 'Really?' I replied as calmly as I could.

'Yes. He, too, believed you were dead and wanted to offer his sympathy. Try as we might we couldn't get any information at all about where you were. Top secret, we were told. In fact, come to think of it, another letter arrived, addressed to you this time, with French stamps on it. It arrived a couple of days ago.'

I was itching to get my hands on the letters but I forced myself to spend time with my parents, catching up on the family news.

At last, Mother handed me the letters and I went to my bedroom to read them in private. And then I read them again. And again.

My eyes filled with tears of happiness. How lovely it was to have him share my own feelings! Clutching the letters to my breast, I twirled around the room, oblivious to the pain in my feet. I was floating in mid-air, giddy. I wanted to write back immediately – but where was he? France, most likely, though by now he could have been in Scotland, London, anywhere. I rushed downstairs to tell my parents everything.

'Your face is lighting up the whole house,' said Mother. 'It's good to see you looking so well.'

The familiarity of home was such a comfort: the predictable yet delicious food, my parents looking so healthy, the endless chatter. And now this love letter. What more could a homecoming soldier want?

I should have been carried along on a tide of euphoria, yet over the following two weeks, as the pace of life slowed from frantic celebration to normal daily routines, the horrors I'd been through began to seep into my mind. I had nightmares of the torture I had endured and I would wake up screaming and thrashing around in a sweat. My mother would rush in to hold me, to try to settle me down, but the thought of falling asleep and having to face again these images terrified me. I grew more and more exhausted and emotional.

My parents were all too aware of my mental state, but I couldn't talk to them about what had happened. My father had heard from the dentist that my original fillings had been removed and replaced with poor quality ones, and what with my injured arm and smashed-up toes, they definitely knew I'd experienced something extremely untoward. They tried to question me gently, but I would just shrug and say something bland. Soon, my tone of voice made it clear I wanted no further interrogation. The misery I was going through must have been almost as distressing for them but there was nothing I could do. My parents weren't even aware of the fact that I'd been an agent in France let alone of what had been done to me in Sallanches. I vowed never to tell them.

My mother coaxed me along to social events and invited my old girlfriends around – some of whom had delightful children – but everyone could see how depressed I was and they soon gave up. My father did a remarkable job fixing my damaged feet. I wanted to be able to go for long walks as soon as spring arrived and that was now a possibility, but I knew my arm would never regain its former strength. I had written to Angus via the SOE HQ at Baker Street, but after two months hadn't heard back. It was crushing. When my mother had given me those letters on my return home I allowed myself to believe that we might have a future together, but that hope was flickering now. I stopped rushing to be the first to get to the post.

Michelle came to stay for a few days from Halifax. She was a down-to-earth, cheerful sort who worked as a reporter for the *Halifax Herald*, and I felt more relaxed with her. She and I would go for walks around the town; I could do three miles now without crutches and without too much pain. My parents were thrilled to have her there. We shared a bedroom; this was Michelle's idea to see if I would settle, and I think it helped.

'What is the name of the regiment Angus is in again?' she asked one morning, looking at me over the top of the newspaper.

'The Lovat Scouts.'

'A Scottish regiment has just arrived at the transit camp at Windsor, but it doesn't say which regiment. They're quarantined with scarlet fever, poor things . . .'

*

One day, I was sitting on the porch looking out to sea when I noticed I a man on horseback coming along the main road towards the house. It was a common enough occurrence and I went back inside, being disinclined to engage in conversation with strangers. My father was climbing into his car. Through the kitchen window I could hear them talking.

'Yes, that's me,' my father said. 'Why don't you come up to the house?'

My heart sank. I didn't care for visitors.

A few seconds later, Father entered the kitchen, the visitor in his wake. 'Look who I have here,' he said quietly.

Our eyes locked together. Neither of us moved for an age. Angus stepped towards me and pulled me into a tight hug. Not a word was said.

I eased away and recovered myself. 'Father, this is my soldier from Scotland.'

Father was late for a visit with a patient so made his excuses. Mother, who had heard the voices and come downstairs, fussed around Angus and chattered away in French. Angus and I could only glance at each other as she monopolised the conversation. My heart was pounding and my face was flushed. I slipped upstairs to calm myself down, put on some lipstick and brush my hair.

A little later I suggested that we go for a walk along the river, so we could have time to ourselves. Mother was enjoying the new guest so much that she was all set to join us, but my furious whispering persuaded her otherwise.

'Your mother's lovely,' said Angus, 'I'm so glad to have met them at last.' He turned to face me. 'I can't quite believe this. An hour ago I was expecting to be consoling two weeping parents and talking about what a gorgeous daughter they had. Instead I arrive and there's sunshine, daffodils and lambs all around!' We laughed as he repeated a favourite line of his that I'd heard before.

We talked politely about the weather, my sister in Montreal, how he had enjoyed his ride here, how the regiment was quarantined – everything, in fact, but what had happened to each of us over the last year.

I had to bring up the topic, so I took a deep breath and asked the question: 'So, tell me, Angus, what have you been doing this past year?'

'All training,' he replied. 'Going around various locations, and a wonderful couple of months in the Rockies. I didn't want to leave. If I didn't have Ardnish to go home to, I'd go and live there. Mountains, snow, sunshine, lovely people, what else could you ask for?'

'I'm glad you're safe and well,' I replied.

We settled on the riverbank and glanced awkwardly at each other.

'Françoise, it's your turn to tell all,' he encouraged.

'First of all, I'm not Françoise,' I said, squirming a bit with my subterfuge. 'That was my *nom de guerre*. My real name is Sophie Lacroix.'

'I know,' replied Angus, grinning. 'Baker Street told me. I got to know them pretty well. I was constantly pestering them about you.'

'I don't want to talk about these things, Angus. I'm sorry. Not yet.' I paused, seeing his crestfallen expression. 'But I will tell you that I was taken to Fresnes Prison. I had a lucky break when the partisans freed one of their own from a prison vehicle I was in. I took the chance and escaped in Paris. I walked the length of France, mainly at night, before meeting up with the Maquis and getting a boat back to England. Then I was shipped back here a couple of months ago.' I looked at him pleadingly. 'Please don't ask any more. Oh, and my parents know nothing so please don't call me Françoise. You'll confuse them!

We had been sitting a little apart from each other. At that moment, looking into my eyes, Angus took my hands, raised them to his lips and kissed them.

Michelle was right – I had fallen in love.

Chapter 17

Angus

That night, I tried to respond to Mrs Lacroix's many questions about my time in the army, my family, Scotland, and the peninsula that I came from as best I could in French. I brushed off questions about where Sophie and I had met as it seemed their daughter had told them little about her last year.

'I've travelled widely now and I can tell you that, even though it's lovely here, on an early summer's day, lying on the beach in front of my village, when the sun is on the hills opposite, the sea is glistening, and eagles are soaring above you, everyone would want to live there. I was blessed with the happiest childhood.'

Of course, I was exaggerating the beauty of Ardnish to try to interest Sophie in the place.

'My grandfather, Donald John, was in effect my father as I grew up, but he died at the end of January when I was in the Rockies. He was an old man and he slipped away peacefully, but it was still a shock. I'd seen him quite recently, and he'd been in fine fettle.'

Sophie touched my arm. 'I'm so sorry, Angus.'

I squeezed her hand. 'It's the end of an era for

Peanmeanach, my village. There are only three people on Ardnish now – my mother, my grandmother and her friend Mairi – and none of them were born there. When my father was growing up there were twenty-five people and three settlements, and a hundred years ago there were six communities on the peninsula.'

I took a sheet of paper and sketched Ardnish. 'This is our church, and the four-mile path down to Peanmeanach. Singing Sands is a glorious beach just half a mile beyond, and there were people living on the western point when I was young, but they are long since dead. Loch na Uamh, here, is where the ship sank that may well have French treasure on it. And there's a golden eagle that nests there, and this is where the best fishing is to be had.'

'It sounds glorious,' said Mrs Lacroix.

I turned back to my drawing. 'Laggan is the farmhouse that I'll take over – it's here. It needs some work on it now, but it's a beautiful spot.' I pointed out Roshven, Arisaig and Inverailort Houses, and where the islands of Eigg, Rum, Muck and Canna lay in relation to the village. 'The land is owned by the estate and it's not great farmland anyway. The sea provides a basic living, but it can be miserable and dangerous, especially in the winter. Aside from the farm there's little money to be made.'

I explained to them about my tenancy of the farm and how it made a good income at the moment, but that my newly widowed grandmother was in her eighties and no longer wanted to run the farm. 'The women are waiting for me to return, and then they'll move away.'

'So what are your plans?' asked Sophie.

I hesitated. 'Well, first I need to go back to the army.

There's a big push on and the end seems to be in sight . . .'
I didn't want to talk any more about the farm to Sophie
and her parents. It was far too soon. What was I thinking?
'I need to be back in Mabou in three days' time to meet
Andrew and then we go back to Halifax.'

That night as I lay in bed I suddenly heard a voice shrieking loudly in panic. I came out of my room and listened.
Sophie was being comforted by her mother, sobbing quietly
now. Perturbed, I slipped back into my room where I lay
awake imagining the worst.

The next morning, no mention was made of the incident.

'I've arranged to borrow a horse,' said Sophie, 'so we
can ride upriver and have a picnic. I know a lovely spot.'

As we rode alongside each other we chatted.

'Mother thinks you're perfect,' said Sophie. 'A handsome, gallant captain – an officer now! Riding up on your
charger. It was so kind of you to write and then to come
and visit them.'

The countryside around Chéticamp was pleasant; new
grass was sprouting through the ground that had been
covered in deep snow for six months and the river was in
full spate due to the snowmelt. We dismounted by a waterfall and tethered the horses.

'My friends from school and I always came here to
swim,' she said. 'You can jump off the rocks into the water
over there. Do you want to?'

Keen though I was to impress her, I shivered at the
thought. 'It'll be freezing!' I said. 'Let's just enjoy our picnic.'

After gorging ourselves on delicious lobster on home-
baked bread, Sophie turned to me shyly and said, 'Angus, I
need to show you something so you might understand.'

Watching for my reaction, she took off her coat and pullover, and rolled up the sleeve of her blouse.

Involuntarily, I put my hand to my mouth. 'My God, Sophie, I had no idea. What have they done to you?'

'I had a bad time in France,' she said. 'I'm damaged – and not just physically. My arm was badly broken and my feet are in a mess. I know you must have heard me screaming last night. I have nightmares that are so awful I'm scared to go to sleep. Father gives me pills to help, but if I take them they just prolong the nightmares ... Angus, I don't think we can become too close. I would make your life miserable, too.'

She started to cry. I put my arm around her and pulled her to me as her body shook. I held her face, wet with tears, in my hands and kissed it all over. 'Don't you worry, my darling, we can beat your demons together.'

'Thank you for coming, thank you for coming to me,' she said again and again as I rocked her gently.

'There are men who come back to their wives from the trenches who never talk again – broken men. But you and I will fight through it and win, I promise. I can help. I want to help.'

At last, she smiled. 'Can I ride with you to Mabou when you go?'

'I'd love it,' I replied.

That evening, as Sophie and her mother prepared supper, the doctor and I settled in the sitting room and shared a brandy.

He looked at me. 'My friend, I can see how important you are to my daughter. With you here, she is happy. Before you arrived she wouldn't see her old friends, wouldn't eat, had the worst nightmares. I'm only a general practitioner, I have no idea what to do with a patient in this psychological state. Few soldiers have returned to this area. My wife and I are glad you're taking Sophie away for a few days, though we're worried about how she'll be when you return to your battalion.'

I had been concerned that he wouldn't be happy about us going off together. After all, they had only known me for a short time. But I could tell that he was desperate to see his daughter happy again, and for that reason was prepared to overlook his religious concerns.

Our ride down the coast was glorious. Farmers were working their horses in the fields and we could see tiny fishing boats bobbing just offshore. Sophie became more animated as she told me all about Cape Breton and the way of life here.

We arrived at an inn just north of Inverness and shyly registered as Mr and Mrs Gillies. We could not look at each other as we signed the book at reception and then, giggling, took our bags up to our bedroom.

We lay side by side, gazing into each other's eyes and gently caressing each other. We had known even before we left Chéticamp that we would make love here tonight, for the first time.

But as I began to explore Sophie's body more intimately, she suddenly became distressed. Her face contorted and her body was writhing away from me.

She lay against me, sobbing gently. 'I'm so sorry, Angus. All I can see is Kaufmann. I just can't tell you what he put me through.'

I reassured her with soft words and she soon fell asleep in my arms, but my mind was racing. What had that monster done to my beautiful Sophie? To her body, mind and soul?

And yet, as shocked as I was, I knew that she was the one for me. I loved her. It was that simple.

The next morning, Sophie turned to me, squeezed my hand. 'I need to tell you what happened to me, so that you'll understand me.'

And over the next hour, she told me everything. I sat in silence until she was finished, and then embraced her gently. She was composed and self-assured again. Something dark had lifted.

*

That evening we found ourselves in Mabou. The contrast was extraordinary. It was as if we had ridden from deepest France to the Highlands of Scotland. There was a Maclean Road, a MacLennan Road and a Macdonald Lane. The letterboxes were labelled MacDonald, Rankin, MacEachern. It was impossible to see how the two communities, so close geographically, could mix. Here Gaelic was spoken and in Chéticamp it was nothing but French.

Andrew had arrived with Sheena shortly before us, full of tales of the mill. They gave a warm welcome to Sophie. 'Ah, the girl we heard so much about, and alive and well too.'

'I've never worked so hard in my life as at the mill,' said Andrew. 'Even the fifteen-year-olds were stronger than me. I loved every minute of it. Let's ring the adjutant tomorrow before we set off; there's a ceilidh at Glencoe Hall and I'd love to go to if we have time.'

Sheena had arranged for a few of the locals to come over for supper. 'They're all from the Braes,' she said to Andrew, 'so their parents and grandparents would have known your people.'

First to arrive was Donald Cameron, a stooped, elderly man with rosy cheeks and a warm smile. 'I served in the Scouts with Colonel Willie in the Boer War,' he said to Andrew, 'and I was a good friend of Donald John, too.'

A woman in her eighties told us that she'd left Bohenie, not far from Fort William, when she was a child but had known all about the Cranachans and was related to them through her mother.

Sophie couldn't believe what she was hearing.

'I'm saving the best till last,' teased Sheena. 'You'll like her – she's outrageous!'

And she wasn't wrong. A tall, striking woman and her husband arrived. 'Ah, Donald Angus,' she said, looking at me closely. 'I'm Kirsty, formerly Kirsty McAlistair from Glenuig. I knew your father *very* well.'

I was spellbound. Despite my grandparents' openness, secrets about my father were few and far between.

'The best party I ever went to was at Peanmeanach the day your uncle became a priest,' she said, to my delight. 'I danced every dance with DP; he was such a wonderful dancer. I was dying for him to kiss me but he didn't. You look just like him.' She winked at Sophie, who laughed. I felt myself reddening. 'I never saw your father again after that night, Angus. We went to Glasgow, then emigrated here after the Great War. It was tragic his dying so young.'

Kirsty went on to regale us all with tales of clipping the sheep and haymaking in the big field. She had such vivid memories of my father and Sandy and the fun they had had together. 'I can only remember sunshine, which I know is ridiculous,' she said. 'I was in awe of your grandmother; she was amazing with her collies and seemed to manage everything virtually by herself. Oh, and that vegetable garden!'

I was in my element. To hear reminiscences like this, so far from home, touched me deeply. Perhaps Sophie might be persuaded that to be a farmer's wife in the middle of nowhere wouldn't be that bad?

As we were leaving, Kirsty whispered something in Sophie's ear. I was desperate to know what she had said, but Sophie wasn't letting on.

I woke early the next morning and went into the kitchen. Sheena was preparing breakfast. 'She's for keeps, Sheena,' I told her, 'but I'm worried. Even if she accepts me, how would she manage at Ardnish? She's got a degree in engineering, for heaven's sake! And all that rain in the winter, the lack of money, the loneliness ... You know what it's like–'

'She loves you,' Sheena cut in. 'She's not the first smart woman to be lured to the glens by a man – for better or worse, for richer, for poorer, and don't you forget it!'

Later that morning, Andrew and I went to the post office to make the call. We had to be back on Tuesday first thing, the *Andes* would sail that afternoon for Liverpool and then the regiment would travel to Aberdeen to prepare to join the Eighth Army in Italy. Andrew and I cursed as we walked back; we had still been hoping for Norway.

I would have to report in to Baker Street for a briefing about my assignment and for the first time I wasn't looking forward to it. I desperately wanted the war to be over so I could be with Sophie.

As we rode together to the ceilidh that afternoon, Morag asked me for more stories about Ardnish. 'Tell us about when you were a child there, Angus. Mairi would like that,' she said, gesturing at her daughter who was sitting wide-eyed beside me in the wagon.

I didn't need persuasion. 'I was an only child, and the only pupil at the school,' I began. 'I didn't mind, though. I'd never known anything different. I had my own teacher three days a week, and he loved languages so I grew to love them. I learned French and Latin as well as being fluent in Gaelic and English.

'I would build sandcastles as high as myself, with Grandfather sitting beside me, telling stories of our family from hundreds of years ago. I trapped rabbits, and once caught a wildcat in my snare; a huge, angry beast. I ran up to the house and Grandfather came up with a sack to put over its head and we carried it over the hill, well away from Grandmother's hens, and set it free.

'And there was an old man called the Bochan when I was very young. He was rearing a golden eagle chick that had fallen out of its nest. I named it Iolair, which is Gaelic for eagle. The Bochan and I would hunt for mice and tear up scraps of meat for it, and before it was six months old we would watch it soaring above the village. I used to hope it would swoop down to me and perch on my arm. Two years later, she had chicks, on the cliffs at the north side of the peninsula. I climbed all the way down to see them, and later Grandmother told me that my father used to do the same when he was my age.'

The ceilidh was in full swing when we arrived. You could hear the fiddles, the stamp-stamp-stamp of feet and the clap-clap-clap of dancers' hands from three hundred yards away. Apart from the fiddlers, there was a pianist and people playing Jew's harps, mouth organs and even kitchen spoons. Sheena and I borrowed some instruments, and I played a few jigs on the pipes which everyone danced furiously to, and then Sheena and her fiddle joined with the band in playing Strathspeys and reels, with everyone square dancing: arms by the side and those intricate foot movements at which even the largest men seemed adept.

Morag surprised us by getting up and singing two lovely songs in Gaelic, with people joining in for the choruses.

The table was laden with food – hams, turkey, chicken and pastries – and with beer, whisky, dark rum and a local moonshine that was consumed in great quantities. My Lord, I thought, the people in Britain would be green with envy seeing a spread like this.

Sophie was new to all this. All the men wanted to dance with her, and she was like an excited young teenager all evening. I watched with a mixture of pride and envy as she whirled through the reels.

After everyone had bid farewell, we climbed into the wagon and headed in the first light to a friend of Sheena's to sleep for a few hours. Sophie confessed that her feet felt as if she'd been walking on broken glass but that it had been the best night of her life.

We rose late the next morning, knowing that there was to be a Mass at eleven o'clock. After communion Sophie whispered in my ear, 'I am praying that you'll return safe to me.'

'I will, my darling, I promise.'

That evening, Sheena, Morag and I discussed how to tell my grandmother about Morag and wee Mairi, and we all agreed that Father Angus would be the best person to break the news. I promised to take the first opportunity to see him and explain the situation.

The next morning, the early sun was shining through the window and Sophie's head was on my shoulder.

'Last night was the first night I didn't have my night-mares,' she said. 'It was because you were there beside me. I can't tell whether I'm incredibly happy that I have got you back, or completely miserable that you're leaving! But if you don't come back to me, I'll come and find you, I promise.'

I asked what she would do when I was away. She said that she hoped to teach mathematics at a school in Chéticamp, or maybe in Montreal where she could live with her sister. With conscription and the men away, there was a shortage of mathematics teachers. She said she needed to keep busy, not hang around being miserable at home. 'I'll not come to the station to see you off, though,' she said. 'I'd only weep buckets and disgrace myself. Instead I'll take the horses and head off home, try to make it in one go.'

'Don't expect to hear from me too soon, my love,' I said sadly, 'but you know I'll be thinking of you every day.'

Chapter 18

The ship was packed to the gunwales. I surveyed the scene from high up on the deck. Looking at the artillery, tanks and trucks lined up at the docks made me understood the enormous contribution the Canadians were making to help win the war. Designed to take two thousand, this ship had five times that number on board.

Training continued on board: assembling weapons, press-ups, even an officers' shooting match with pistols fired at bottles off the stern. However, the men were short of kit; there had been a fire in the stores in Jasper after Andrew and I had left.

All the talk was of Operation Overlord, the big push that we believed would win the war. As we sailed, D-Day was happening. It was the 6th of June. The officers were not that happy about going to Italy after all their recent training. Everyone wanted to go to Norway, but it was the fifth year of the war and most of the men still hadn't fired a shot in anger and wanted to do their bit. We were all painfully aware that the other Highland regiments – the Camerons, Seaforths and Gordons – had suffered huge losses while the Lovat Scouts had had it relatively easy.

After docking at Liverpool, Andrew and I said goodbye. He was desperate to do his bit for the war effort. The Scouts knew what was in store for them, but I didn't. However, I seemed to have a habit of ending up back with the battalion, so maybe I'd see them again in Italy.

I checked in at Baker Street where they registered me as fit for operations. I decided to visit the Gubbinses as I hadn't seen them since Michael had died. Over tea, Mrs Gubbins told me all she knew about her son. 'You can't imagine the sadness that the death of one's child causes until you have experienced it,' she said, as I searched hopelessly for words of comfort.

We talked late into the night about Michael and how he had loved the SOE. The colonel had been promoted to brigadier recently and had been working harder than ever since Michael's death. She hardly saw him these days; he'd not had a day off in four months.

Within a couple of days I was sent on a four-day wireless course at Belhaven Hill, just south of Edinburgh, and while there I took the opportunity to invite Father Angus to dinner at the North British Hotel.

'I have a surprise for you, Uncle Angus,' I said. 'Brace yourself.'

'Very well,' he said nervously.

'Aunt Sheena has a daughter named Morag, and Morag has a daughter of her own, named Mairi.'

My uncle was flabbergasted. 'How on earth are we only finding this out now?' he asked.

'She didn't know she was with child when Colin Angus died. She signed up for the boat to Cape Breton and was so seasick she didn't realise until she was well into the journey. She told me there hasn't been a moment since then that she hasn't longed to tell your mother.'

Father Angus scrutinised my face. 'Do you think if she didn't have a priest as a brother she would have told us before now? Did she think I would be so disapproving?'

I paused slightly too long. 'I think she felt ashamed. Maybe thirty years ago, with her so young and this sort of thing completely unacceptable . . .'

'Dear God,' he exclaimed, 'that's nothing compared to what I hear in the confessional box. I feel awful. She must have felt so lonely.'

'Might you be going up to Ardnish some time soon, Uncle Angus?' I asked. 'Sheena thinks it might help if Grandmother heard the news from you.'

I told him about Morag having been married for ten years to a Skye man called Calum Beaton, whereupon my uncle banged the table with his fist, his face lighting up.

'No! He came to see me a few months ago. We had a cup of tea and chatted about the Cranachans at Mull River and he seemed to know a lot about Sheena. He was on leave from France and was heading up to Dunvegan to see his grandparents. I wish he'd told me everything then. He mentioned he was married to a girl called Morag, but of course how would I have known? I do remember wondering why he had called on me.'

*

Back at Belhaven, I was called to the telephone. I should waste no time. I was going to Peterborough, and a car would take me to Milton Hall. I'd never heard of Milton

Hall, a huge stately home with a sea of Nissen huts. I was met by a Colonel Buckmaster.

A group of soldiers known as the Jedburghs had been selected for a new task when I was in Canada. Whereas the SOE had been clandestine and tasked with the mission of 'setting Europe ablaze', in Churchill's words, the Jedburghs (each of which comprised three men) were to be as open as possible – a highly visible support for the Resistance. We were to wear uniform on this assignment, I was told, whereas in the SOE enormous effort went into ensuring we were convincingly dressed as the locals. I wore my Lovat Scout hat and regular army fatigues. Some even wore kilts.

I was a month behind the others in my group, who were already in situ in France. I was to replace a Major Channon who had broken his leg badly when parachuting in. Because I was familiar with the Chamonix area and a fluent French speaker, I was the obvious choice for an urgent replacement. I was dropped into occupied France, along with canisters of Sten guns, Lee-Enfield rifles, Mills grenades, anti-tank weapons, as well as tons of explosives, medical supplies, clothing and food.

Claude, my old friend, was now a Maquis battalion leader. He was accompanied by a dozen men. I was with my Jedburgh team of wireless man Sergeant Bill Thomas and an operative called Leon Ball, who was attached to us from the OSS, the SOE equivalent in the USA. There was a frantic loading up of the supplies into Claude's rickety old truck before the Germans could arrive at the drop-off point and then we sped off into the relative safety of the forest above Les Contamines.

The men were living in tents in the forest and were grateful for the American ration packs. Their food had been running short and they couldn't believe their eyes when they unpacked real coffee and chocolate.

When I asked Claude how Marie was, his face clouded over and he hissed, 'She was killed last year. Driving my car. They fired at her as she approached a checkpoint. After me, of course, the bastards.'

'I am so sorry Claude,' I said, distressed by the news, but he shrugged and said nothing further.

To raise his spirits, I told him the good news about Sophie – how I'd found her in Canada only a few weeks ago and that I was intent on marrying her. 'You'll be my best man,' I declared, 'and then we'll go to Ardnish and repopulate it all by ourselves!'

Together, over the following week, we drilled Claude's three-hundred-strong outfit until it functioned like a military unit. We appointed ex-policemen and soldiers as sergeants, and started a programme of arms and explosives training and tactics for engagements with the enemy.

I relished being in the Alps that summer. The meadows were full of flowers and there were beautiful, ice-cold rivers to swim in. If we hadn't been working from dawn to dusk I would have loved to have gone climbing. I thought about Sophie all the time, how she would appreciate the scenery and the fresh air. I didn't even know if she had chosen to stay with her parents or move to Montreal.

Colonel Buckmaster had told us that a key aim was to prevent the widely dispersed German troops from moving together to build divisions or armies. Claude's superior, Henri Baud, who commanded the Chamonix battalion, had reported that the troops in Chamonix were planning to move down towards Bourg-Saint-Maurice. We agreed that the best strategy would be to trap the Germans by repeating the successful landslide of the previous year. However, because we had more men this time, we would set up an ambush so that when the Germans inevitably sent soldiers down to investigate, we would be ready for them, too.

Claude drove his truck with the explosives to Vaudagne and forty of us went over the mountain, only this time it was during the night with not a flake of snow. There was much less reconnaissance necessary since it had been done before and the explosives were in position in under twenty-four hours. I set the charges and then left Leon to push the plunger at six in the morning, by which time the rest of us would be down the mountain in readiness to carry out the ambush.

At dawn the mountain erupted, with rocks falling closer to us than we had anticipated. Two armoured cars came charging down the road. As they pulled up at the rockfall I shot them with the anti-tank launcher. Immediately the Resistance rushed forward, crowding around the vehicles, desperate to kill the Germans despite my furious yelling at them to back off. At that moment, another armoured car hurtled around the corner and a hail of bullets killed three of our men.

It was a deadly lesson in discipline for the survivors.

Leon Ball was a great character – a lover of pranks and high-risk sorties. He had discovered that a guesthouse in Les Contamines, which was used as a German outpost, was manned overnight by only half a dozen men. He crept into the guards' room, shot the man on duty with his pistol, stole the Mercedes staff car from their garage – resplendent with flag and Gestapo pass – and drove it back to the barn in Vaudagne. I couldn't help but admire his audacity and I was pleased to see how this one act of bravery inspired the others.

Every two or three days we would set ourselves goals: blowing railway tracks, pylons and bridges, as well as ambushing trucks and staff cars. The local roads soon emptied of Germans as they holed up in their camps. We controlled the roads, making sure that there was no direct confrontation with troops but harrying them, then slipping away.

Leon had a long-range rifle and positioned himself in the forest, six hundred yards away from the Hotel de la Paix where the Gestapo were based in Chamonix. He shot a German or two each day until they learned not to come out of the building. Another hotel, the Majestic, was used by the Germans for the injured and sick, mostly military, and so Leon concentrated his fire on the other building.

Then came a stalemate as we waited for the regular Allied troops on Operation Anvil to arrive. However, it didn't stop the Germans strafing us from their aircraft. They carried out a bombing raid on Les Contamines, which I suppose was unsurprising as it was now a hotbed of resistance.

Sensing the end of the war coming and that there wouldn't be many other opportunities, Claude and Henri decided we should throw a party for the battalion. It was kept a secret from the men until the day. Dead wood was dragged into a clearing to make a bonfire, a precious bullock was butchered, and I set to organising a makeshift Highland games.

While the meat was cooking we had inter-platoon competitions, tossing the caber, shot-putting, a tug-of-war and a hill race. The French loved every minute of it. I was sorry not to have my bagpipes with me to complete the event. Some wine and brandy had been liberated from a long-forgotten, dusty old cellar and inevitably everyone got drunk.

There was one ugly incident. Two Communists became a little too belligerent, and a fight nearly broke out. Claude was across in a second with his pistol, declaring he would shoot the next person who made a move or said a word on the subject.

I was surprised at Claude's heavy-handed approach and spoke with him later.

'Communism will be the biggest threat in France after the war,' he told me. 'They're recruiting already and beating up those who don't support them.'

'It's the same amongst the Italian Resistance fighters – the Garibaldi Fascists versus the Communists. At the moment they're united in fighting the Germans, but after the war, well, who knows?'

Claude said bitterly, 'Nobody will be in control. That's the problem.'

The following day I received word that the Americans were only fifty miles away. I was determined to take the surrender of the German troops in Chamonix before they arrived. We knew that the Gestapo had moved into the Majestic and armed the patients with weapons – we could see rifles poking through the shutters. Claude made contact with a hospital orderly and gave her a letter, written in English, to give to the captain, informing him that if he surrendered there would be no deaths and everyone would be treated fairly according to the Geneva Convention. If he was prepared to discuss this, he was to raise a white flag.

The hotel was surrounded. All three hundred Maquis from Les Contamines, Saint-Gervais and Chamonix were there, with only the odd shot being fired from each side. We had no idea how long they could hold out, but on the morning of the fifth day, a sheet was waved from a top-floor window.

Cautiously, we approached the hotel. We had heard that Jean Bulle, the legendary leader of another Maquis battalion in the region, had gone into Albertville with a white flag of truce to encourage the Germans to surrender. He was then made to kneel in the town square and was shot in the back of the head.

I was with Leon in his confiscated staff car, now bedecked with a makeshift Union Jack. Leon and I were in full uniform and ready for our rendezvous.

The German captain agreed to surrender and lay down arms as long as the camp was put under my control and not handed over to the partisans. A letter to this effect was signed by us. The Germans, understandably, feared that the Maquis would seek swift retribution.

Everyone who could walk was ushered out of the building, then we searched it thoroughly and took photographs. We listed those captured then did a sweep of all the other hotels that had been commandeered, collecting guns and ammunition as we went.

Within an hour or two of the surrender, the word had spread and the front of the hospital was crowded with hundreds of locals staring at the prisoners and revelling in the humiliation of the occupying force.

An assortment of cars and trucks draped with the French tricolour had arrived from Megève, hooting their horns in the places where the soldiers had surrendered. People who had been hiding in the hills for the last couple of years slowly emerged.

The celebrations went on until late that night. Everyone was kissing each other, and my hand grew weary from the constant, vigorous handshakes. My Jedburgh group were treated like heroes, having tumblers of wine and delicacies thrust into their hands. Two days later, the Americans arrived on foot and took command, having had to clamber over our rockfall at Chedde to reach the town.

It seemed on the surface that everyone in the town was celebrating, but there remained a deep resentment against locals who had turned traitor. One of the things we had not been taught in the SOE was how to handle this situation, and so we were unprepared for what came next. The Maquis had a good idea which locals had been collaborating with the Germans, and morning after morning, my team and I would see men and women lying dead in the street or hanging from balconies. The women had their hair shaved off and were then paraded in the streets to much abuse. Claude's men vigorously denied involvement, but I was certain that it was they who had been carrying out the executions. During my first visit in April 1943 there had been few Vs painted on buildings in support of the Resistance; now they were everywhere.

As Claude and I shared some wine late one night, swapping more and more unlikely stories and promising eternal friendship, I decided this was the moment to tackle him about the reprisals.

'You are a Christian, my friend. Murder is a serious sin . . .' I began. He nodded, but his eyes narrowed. '. . . and yet unarmed men and women are being murdered without a trial and in breach of the Geneva Convention.'

Claude's bonhomie vanished. 'These are the people who got my wife killed!' he spat. 'Arranged for entire families to be taken off to concentration camps!'

He was shaking with rage and I decided to drop the subject. This was an emotionally charged argument I could not win. I sensed there would be scores settled for decades across France.

The war here was over, but it continued in Italy and Belgium. We were in touch with London every day. We learned that the Americans were leaving troops in France and we Jedburghs were to be called back to London. Before we left, the Americans asked us to clear the landslide that we had caused. It took us two days of back-breaking effort, a hundred men passing stone after stone from hand to hand.

A flight was arranged for us from Chambéry at the end of August. Thereafter I would be debriefed at Baker Street.

Claude volunteered to drive us in the staff car. He was annoyed, though, because the American major had told him he had to hand back the car after we had been dropped off at the airport. I volunteered to collect Claude's truck from Vaudagne and follow Claude, Sergeant Thomas and Leon.

'Be careful, Angus,' Claude warned. 'It's a steep road with tight corners, so you'll need to make sure you use the gears to slow down.'

Chapter 19

'Angus, are you all right? Hold him up and I'll give him some water.'

I could hear voices. There were lights. And then unbearable pain hit.

'You've been unconscious for two days. Your leg's shattered and you have a head injury.'

'Angus, it's me, Leon. Claude's here, too. You've had an accident.'

'Accident?' I mumbled.

'Can you remember what happened? You crashed the truck. You missed the corner and went off the edge of the road. It must have rolled a few times, it's completely crushed. It was stopped by a tree and there was gasoline pouring out of the tank. You're lucky it didn't roll another few hundred feet and explode. A woman in Vautagne heard the noise and came and found you. We're in her house now. Here she is . . . Michelle.'

Such bright lights. Noise. A thumping pain in my head.

Claude's voice: 'Angus, my friend, we still need to get to Chambéry for the pick-up, so we'll leave tomorrow and I'll drive you. When you get back to London, Leon will get a doctor to look at you. Do you understand?'

I nodded. And then fell into a deep sleep.

The next thing I remember was being helped into a coat, propped up on the edge of a bed.

'Hey, Angus, Leon here!'

I held out my hand and tried to stand up.

'No, no! Don't move. Your leg's strapped up but you won't be able to put any weight on it. Claude's ready in the car. You're going to London, my friend. You're going to be out of action for some time.'

'Home?' I said.

'Absolutely. Let's go.'

I was helped into a huge car and made comfortable in the back seat. It felt as if I was in that car forever. I was so hot and my leg was aching.

We arrived at an airfield teeming with people.

'Who are all these people?' I asked Leon.

He turned to me. 'Most of them are SOE from all over the east of France.'

'What?'

'You trained a lot of them. They'll be getting the same flight as you so you'll be surrounded by friends.'

I scanned the faces, hoping to see someone, something familiar. I was helped from the car. People crowded round, shaking my hand, shouting my name, but I felt too woozy and disorientated to make sense of it all.

Leon called out to them: 'Please, keep back. Captain Gillies has had a serious accident. He's got a broken leg and concussion. Give him some space.'

Claude draped an arm around my shoulder. His face was kind, full of affection. Were those tears in his eyes?

'Farewell, Angus, and don't forget, I'm going to be your best man when you marry that woman of yours.' He kissed me on each cheek and gave me a tight hug, before turning to go.

Leon sat by my side on the flight. I dozed all the way. When the plane arrived at Northolt, a man came up to us and saluted.

'Brigadier,' said Leon, 'this is–'

'I know exactly who this is,' the brigadier replied, shaking my hand. 'Captain Gillies is coming with me. Don't worry, he's in safe hands.'

'There's one more thing,' Leon said. 'Our Resistance commander was adamant that a woman named Françoise should be told about Angus. But we had no idea who she was or how to get hold of her.'

The brigadier smiled at me and turned to Leon. 'Angus is a close friend of the family and I know Françoise, too. I'll look after everything, I promise. Gubbins is the name.'

'Thank you,' said Leon, saluting.

I was taken to King Edward VII Hospital for Officers in Knightsbridge where Brigadier Gubbins and his wife visited me daily. We reminisced about times we had shared and talked fondly of Michael.

The first afternoon of my hospital stay Mrs Gubbins was by the bed, reading an article in the *Express* aloud to me, when there was a noise at the door. The nurse, a fellow Scot, Catherine McColl, straightened up nervously as Matron marched in.

'Matron Jones!' Mrs Gubbins cried. 'How lovely to see you. Angus, Matron Jones is the senior nurse in this hospital and is responsible for your care.'

Matron Jones looked up from her clipboard and did a double-take. 'Donald Angus!' she exclaimed with a delighted look on her face. 'What on earth are you doing here?' She sat on the edge of my bed and looked affectionately at me. 'I'm Prissie, your godmother. You remember me, don't you? Your mother is my best friend.'

'Prissie! Of course I remember. It's lovely to see a familiar face.'

I related the story of the accident as best I could. Prissie left to do some background checks and organise some X-rays, and it was agreed that the brigadier would come to the hospital in the evening and they would decide if I could be moved.

Later, the Gubbinses and Prissie gathered around my bed. Despite heavy sedation, I did my utmost to keep up with their conversation.

Prissie, never one to withhold her opinion, took a firm stance: 'He needs to get home to recuperate as soon as possible. It's going to be six months at least for that femur to heal and I don't think this is the best environment for him. He'll need a few days post-surgery to recover, but he'll manage with crutches and plenty of painkillers. I've spoken to his American friend, Leon, and he's prepared to help Angus onto the sleeper to Fort William. He needs to go to Arisaig House in any case. When he reaches there, soldiers from Inverailort Castle will see Angus safely to Ardnish.'

'Wonderful, Matron Jones,' said Mrs Gubbins. Everyone nodded and smiled in agreement.

'Now, Angus,' the brigadier said, 'you must rest. You'll need all your strength for the operation and then the journey home.'

I was overjoyed at the thought of recovering at home.

Chapter 20

Leon helped me down from the train. Some men were waiting there to take me on to Peanmeanach.

Getting into the boat had been awkward and painful, but I enjoyed the trip, feeling more alert than I had done in days.

As the boat rounded the point, I saw the familiar semi-circle of tiny thatched cottages ranged around beautiful Peanmeanach Bay. I leant over the bow, waving with excitement. I saw a door open. A woman emerged and began running excitedly to the shore. I could just about make out her features.

She stopped in her tracks, hand at her mouth. Then she began dancing up and down, shouting, 'Angus, Angus!'

As soon as I got off the boat, helped by the soldiers, and hobbled up the beach she came to me and wrapped her arms around me. 'You're home now, Angus. Safe and sound.'

The family were shocked by my injury but I reassured them that it should be healed within a few months and that it was unlikely I'd go back to active service. This, naturally, pleased my mother.

I grew stronger by the day, and a week or so later, after a delicious supper of herring in oatmeal, we sat by the fire and basked in the warmth of each other's company. The conversation and stories flowed, like they always did.

'What do you think of my new boat, Donald Angus?' asked grandmother.

I smiled. 'She's a fine wee boat. What happened to the old one?'

'There was a tremendous storm and she was swept off the beach never to be seen again. We decided we had enough money to get a new boat, so Grandfather and I set off for Arisaig to meet Ian MacMillan, a man who had a reputation as a good boat-builder. And here she is! Thirteen foot, pointed at each end, a foureen, so either two or four can row her. Larch planks, an ash frame and oak stanches for the oars to pull against. We chose the colours, too – the red trim and blue band across the top.

'It was a great occasion, and we all wanted to be involved in her return, so Peter Blackburn, Morag, Mairi and I headed up a few weeks later to collect her. We named her after the boat owned by John MacEachan of Roshven, who traded arms and brandy along the west coast a hundred and fifty years ago. As we rowed her home, Peter told us the story of the original *Little Katie*. Do you want to hear it?'

'Of course,' I replied.

'Well, MacEachan was a smuggler who lived in Clanranald's original house at Roshven. *Little Katie* had a crew of three and they would "obtain" whatever people wanted, up and down the west coast, from the French. The goods were kept hidden behind a small island near Ardnish, out of sight from anywhere apart from Laggan itself. After the Rebellion times were hard. The English troops raided constantly, and the bagpipes and tartan were banned. MacEachan was said to have been a charming man with a huge character and wit – it was said that he had a woman in every port up and down the coast.'

'A proper rogue!' I laughed.

'If Clanranald or any of the lairds wanted some good French burgundy, then MacEachan was the man to provide it. He would meet Locheil's man at Loch Nevis and they would load up a couple of horses with cases of wine and take it over to Achnacarry, or they would be guests of Macleod at Dunvegan, having dinner and staying the night in the castle. Macleod said that he loved having MacEachan around but he always made sure his daughters were locked up before he extended an invitation.

'MacEachan was said to have been the man who got his hands on the French king's lost gold and that is why he was so rich, but your grandfather insisted that this was not so; it was still to be found.

'King Louis of France apparently sent gold across to help pay for the Rebellion, but it arrived late and was said to have been buried on an island on Loch Eilt. Those islands are deep in heather and have tall Scots pine trees on them, and what's more, it could be buried on any one of three or four islands. There are other rumours that it's actually on Goat Island. But your father swore that the French frigate that sank in Loch na Uamh had the treasure on it.

'There was one man in Arisaig whom MacEachan had angered. He was said to have told the English garrison at Fort William about the French privateers who would sail up to meet MacEachan and unload brandy, guns and other contraband. The man from Arisaig died in his bed one night, killed by a sword. Soldiers were sent to Roshven to arrest MacEachan for the crime, but he'd had word they were coming and fled to the isle of Eriskay, where he boarded a ship bound for Canada. He settled there and had a family. Ironically, MacEachan himself was murdered in Canada, although I don't know the details.'

'Probably caught with someone's wife,' I said, grinning.

Mother laughed. 'Anyhow, that's the history behind *Little Katie* for you. We were so proud when we brought her home. It was a four-hour journey. Your grandfather had cut some roundwood and we collected a pile of seaweed so we could pull her ashore with so little manpower. I had cleaned out an old noost in the machair and we hauled her into it. It makes a great shelter against the storms.'

'Noost,' I repeated. 'I love the word.'

'It sounds like a cross between nest and roost. Quite appropriate, really.'

*

One day I reached under my bed and pulled out the box that contained my belongings. My shabby working clothes and Sunday best and, wrapped in tissue a beautiful tweed kilt jacket. I tried it on; it was a perfect fit.

'Miss Charlotte's thank-you gift, she came by with it.' Mother had slipped into my room unnoticed.

Mother smiled and sat down beside me. 'You did an amazing thing. Arisaig House burning down and you one of the men who ran to help. It was only she and her sister in the house at the time apart from two servants who didn't survive the blaze. They were on the fourth floor and had no way out. But when you got there you were able to save Miss Charlotte's dog who had been locked in a room, and you helped to move out a lot of the furniture and paintings. It was a brave thing you did, Angus.

'Miss Charlotte never got over it. She'd had a rough time of it already – her parents dead, her oldest brother mentally afflicted and her two other brothers killed in the Great War. But this jacket was her way of saying thank you. I suggested that I spin some tweed in her estate colours and she could get it turned into a jacket at MacLellans in the Fort. And there you have it.'

'It means a lot to me,' I said, taking off the jacket and replacing it carefully in the box. I wondered at what occasion I could possibly wear such a special garment.

Mother left me to sleep. I could hear the murmur of the women's voices next door.

'When you and I move to Arisaig, he'll be all alone, Morag.' My mother sounded distraught. 'How can we do that to him? How will he ever find a wife?'

I could hear scraping noises. Someone was riddling the fire for the night.

'We'll just have to stay here for a bit longer so we can help him out, won't we, Louise?'

I felt incredibly touched at my family's support as I turned, smiling, with my face to the wall. I knew I needed to keep the farm and live here on Ardnish. It wasn't just me that had to make a success of the place, Mother, Grandmother and Mairi needed me to. I could feel my father and grandfather willing me on. Hundreds of years of family history depended on me for its continuity.

The next morning, I tucked my bagpipes under my arm and went down to the beach. The sea sparkled in the sunshine and a lone seagull banked on the light breeze. I turned to face my home, Peanmeanach.

Raising the mouthpiece to my lips, I blew into the bag. Despite the awkward crutches, my fingers instinctively flew to their place on the chanter and, closing my eyes, I began to play my father's favourite air: 'Pibroch of Donald Dhu'. I really was on the mend.

Chapter 21

Sophie

It had been five months since I'd said goodbye to Donald Angus. I knew my part-time teaching job at Chéticamp wasn't what I truly wanted to do. Although I still had occasional nightmares, my mobility was much improved. My mind constantly turned to my Scottish soldier. Where was he? What was he doing? What was he thinking?

I had been astounded when my father told me about the call. Brigadier Gubbins had telephoned my father and told him that Angus was home on extended leave in Ardnish after a terrible leg injury. I knew at that moment I had to be with him.

My parents were aghast for a while at the prospect of my travelling across the Atlantic – they felt I was not yet strong enough, physically or mentally – but they conceded that I fared so much better when I was in Angus's company.

And so, when the brigadier spoke to me the following day it was not a matter of if I would go; it was a matter of when. There was a boat, the brigadier had said, leaving in a few days from Halifax, travelling via Boston, and I could get on it if I wished.

I had no doubt in my mind: I would be on that boat.

My parents drove me to Inverness to get the train. Sheena and Morag were at the station, very excited, to wave farewell and give me a package to carry to Ardnish. There was such a lot of kissing, hugging and waving out of the window as the train moved off. My tears were a bitter-sweet mixture of joy and trepidation.

My father had booked me on the ship, steerage. My fellow passengers seemed to be men keen to see what business could be done in Britain now that the war was coming to an end. I had little to say to them, and simply revelled in the comfort and in my own company.

Mrs Gubbins was waiting for me as the liner disembarked, and that night she and the brigadier took me to supper in Soho before waving me off on the sleeper headed to Fort William.

'I hope the shock of your arrival doesn't kill him!' the brigadier quipped, kissing my cheek. 'He's one lucky man.'

'My dear,' said Mrs Gubbins, 'if you find that things aren't right, and I know you know what I mean – it's fine to say so, to come away. Relationships comprise two people and you have no responsibility towards a man you don't truly love – or who doesn't truly love you. But having said that, I wish you all the luck and love in the world. Godspeed.'

I woke after a comfortable night on the sleeper and had breakfast in the lounge car, rather enjoying the crisp white tablecloth and terrible food. The train was chugging at walking pace, it seemed, across a bleak, wild landscape that the guard informed me was Rannoch Moor. However, the early morning sun shone on the mountains and glistened tantalisingly off the lochs. I spied two shaggy ponies, saddled, waiting to be led across the line, and deer galloping away from the track as we passed.

I changed trains in Fort William and got talking to a lady who pointed out the sights as we made our way to my final stop at Lochailort. Her incessant chatter calmed my growing nerves.

'Go first to the inn,' she advised. 'They'll keep your suitcases and show you the path to Peanmeanach. It's a breathtaking walk.'

I did as she said. As I walked I could hear Angus's voice saying to me, 'On the right is our beautiful church but it's no longer in use. And remember to look out for the eagles that nest on the cliffs to the north.' Sure enough, I saw two eagles soaring high above the most beautiful loch, which must be the one that he had promised me was full of fat brown trout. I vowed I would be back soon to cast a line.

Birds were flitting ahead of me in the heather as I stepped carefully along the roughly paved path. A hot autumn sun blazed overhead and there wasn't a sound apart from my footsteps, the murmur of waves, and birdsong.

The path took me along to a knoll and there, below, was a big field and a crescent of houses along the beach, overlooked by the mountains beyond. I had to sit on a rock and compose myself. My heart was pounding. It was just as I had dreamed it would be.

Two figures in the distance saw me and waved. A woman. And a man – Angus? Was it? I caught my breath and waved back, then headed down to Ardnish and home.

Also available by Angus MacDonald
Ardnish Was Home

Gallipoli, 1915. Donald Peter ('DP') Gillies, a young Lovat
Scout soldier, lies in a field hospital, blinded by the Turks.
There he falls in love with his Queen Alexandra Corps
nurse, Louise, and she with him. As they talk in the quiet
hours he tells her of life in the west Highlands of Scotland,
where he grew up, and she in turn tells her own story of a
harsh and unforgiving upbringing in the Welsh valleys.

Cut off from Allied troops Donald and Louise decide to
make a perilous escape to freedom through Turkey, Greece
and on to Malta – the first stage on their journey to a new
life together in Donald's beloved Ardnish.

ISBN 978 1 78027 426 3
£8.99